SCHOOL OF HARD KNOX

Stories That Break Father Ronald Knox's Ten Commandments For Crime Fiction

EDITED BY

Donna Andrews, Greg Herren, and Art Taylor

Photo of Marcia Talley and Kate Charles
at the Church of St. Andrew, Mells
Photo credit to Rory Chase

SCHOOL OF HARD KNOX

Stories That Break Father Ronald Knox's
Ten Commandments For Crime Fiction

EDITED BY

Donna Andrews, Greg Herren, and Art Taylor

CRIPPEN & LANDRU PUBLISHERS
Cincinnati, Ohio
2023

For information contact:

Crippen & Landru, Publishers

P. O. Box 532057

Cincinnati, OH 45253 USA

Web: www.crippenlandru.com

E-mail: Orders@crippenlandru.com

ISBN (softcover): 978-1-936363-78-0

ISBN (clothbound): 978-1-936363-79-7

First Edition: September 2023
10 9 8 7 6 5 4 3 2 1

CONTENTS

Introduction - Jeffrey Marks   7

Not Another Secret Passage Story - Donna Andrews   13
A Matter of Trust - Frankie Y Bailey   17
The Dinner Party - Nikki Dolson   33
The Intruder- Martin Edwards   57
The Ditch - Greg Herren   73
Dichondra - Naomi Hirahara   87
Baby Trap - Toni LP Kelner   99
The Stolen Tent - Richie Narvaez   113
The Rose City Vampire: An Accidental Alchemist
Short Story - Gigi Pandian   133
Chin Yong Yun Goes to Church - SJ Rozan   143
The Forlorn Penguin- Daniel Stashower   155
The Island Boy Detective Agency - Marcia Talley   163
Ordeals - Art Taylor   171

Knox Vomica - Peter Lovesey   183

Contributors   `191

Introduction
By Jeffrey Marks

Two priests were prominent in the early twentieth century, Father Brown and Monsignor Ronald Knox. The former was a fictional sleuth developed by G. K. Chesterton. The latter was a very real priest and mystery author.

Ronald Arbuthnott Knox, born in 1888, was a Renaissance man of the mystery world. After attending Eton and Balliol College, Oxford (where Lord Peter Wimsey supposedly matriculated), he became a fellow of Trinity College, Oxford. Two years later, he was ordained as a priest in the Church of England and was assigned to be the chaplain at Trinity College.

However, after World War I, he resigned from the Anglican Church to become a Roman Catholic priest. His family was so aghast that his father disinherited Knox, cutting him from the will.

As a chaplain at Oxford, he enjoyed puzzles, writing his own *A Book of Acrostics* in 1924. In the same year, Knox wrote a non-mysterious work entitled *Sanctions: A Frivolity,* where a character, loosely based on Knox's brother, has created a framework for fair play detective stories.

Knox began to write Golden Age detective stories, starting with The Viaduct Murder in 1926. He wrote six novels and three short stories during his priestly tenure. ("The Adventure of the First Class Carriage," a Sherlock Holmes pastiche, is included in our clothbound edition of this book.)

The rules appeared again as an introduction to *The Best English Detective Stories* of 1928. When the article was reprinted in 1946, it became known as "The Detective Story Decalogue" and later "The Ten Commandments for Detective Novelists."

While many mystery authors had previously broken these commandments, he still wanted to formally declare his "fair play" rules. The Detection Club went so far as to adopt them as the oath of initiation into the organization.

At the end of World War II, Knox published his translation of the Latin Vulgate Bible. Published in three volumes, the New Testament portion appeared in 1945.

Knox died in 1957. Evelyn Waugh completed his biography of Knox two years later.

Not to be outdone, S. S. Van Dine doubled the number of American rules. Van Dine's reflected the differences between detective fiction in the U.S. and the U.K. These rules included the exclusion of the Mafia in the solution to the story, no "the butler did it" denouements, and an insistence that detective fiction has a detective.

We've asked some of the best American and British authors in the mystery short fiction field to take a stab, so to speak, at breaking one or more of these rules. It's not as easy as it might seem, but these authors are up to the task.

Knox's Ten Commandments are included here for reference since it's been nearly a century since the rules were first published. Each entry includes historical context.

1. The criminal must be someone mentioned in the early part of the story, but must not be anyone whose thoughts the reader has been allowed to follow.

Of course, it's unfair not to mention a character till the end of the story, attributing motive, means, and opportunity to the killer only in the last pages. The reader should have the chance to meet the character and determine if he has a sufficient motive, etc.

For the case of the point of view character who is the killer, this rule is the epitome of the fair play structure. The reader must be able to trust the main character's internal monologue. In reality, it's impossible to edit one's thoughts to the point where a particular event would never cross the mind. Pretending that the character has these powers pushes the reader beyond the suspension of disbelief. Four years after the first appearance of this rule, a particular mystery author would use a journal, thinking that the printed word could be edited – and cause a furor in the mystery world.

2. All supernatural or preternatural agencies are ruled out as a matter of course.

The inclusion of the supernatural is always a double-edged sword. If the author uses actual supernatural elements in the work, the story crosses into the fantasy or horror genres. Certainly, means and opportunity are irrelevant if Casper could walk through walls and kill the victim. However, John Dickson Carr has written wonderful books where the supernatural is front and center.

On the other hand, the use of supernatural elements came to be ignored. The savvy reader knew the rule and that they could be ignored.

The killer uses coincidence or creates those elements to supply a red herring for the detectives.

3. Not more than one secret room or passage is allowable.

Like Rule 10 about twins and the rules about multiple people fulfilling one role, the idea of numerous passages or secret rooms can overwhelm the reader. A single secret room can allow the sleuth to see where a person might have been hiding for security or malfeasance. A secret passage could let a character get from Point A to Point B. Multiple passages would allow all the characters to traverse the building without fear, meaning that alibis and opportunity would be worthless to the reader.

4. No hitherto undiscovered poisons may be used, nor any appliance which will need a long scientific explanation at the end.

This is a rather specific swipe at the character Dr. Thorndyke, who spent a significant amount of time at the end of the story explaining the devious nature in which the victim was killed. Author R. Austin Freeman had his own laboratory to test each of his unique solutions. While his accuracy was unimpeachable, the plots tended to slow to a crawl to explain what had happened.

5. No Chinaman must figure in the story.

While this looks horrendously racist at first glance, the truth is that in the 1920s, including an Asian almost always meant that character was guilty of the crime. This was the era of Fu Manchu and the Yellow Peril. Knox thought that this bias led to an easily solved plot.

Fortunately, these plots grew less acceptable by the decade's end, with authors like Erle Stanley Gardner and Earl Derr Biggers refusing to participate in such stereotypes.

6. No accident must ever help the detective, nor must he ever have an unaccountable intuition that proves to be right.

This rule has vexed me. Perhaps I have overthought the word "unaccountable" here. So many times in a mystery novel, Watson will be nattering away about some topic, only to have the sleuth's eyes widen as he gets a hunch that solves the case. Is this unaccountable intuition? Perhaps, but frequently the detective will explain later why the name "William" solved the murder, or the lack of dusting in the home was the solution to the case.

Of course, deus ex machina is never allowed. The answer cannot be found by overhearing the killer's confession or learning of the killer's journal, which was never mentioned in the story.

7. The detective must not himself commit the crime.

Beware of this ploy if the book is the last in a series or a standalone. The detective has not killed anyone in book ten of a twenty-book series. The detective would either be found out and jailed or escape without punishment. Still, the sleuth would no longer be an instrument of justice.

Some books skate this line by allowing the killer to escape justice—so the evildoer can commit suicide. The moral rectitude of allowing someone to kill him or herself is suicide by detective; however, this trope is still often used.

8. The detective must not light on any clues which are not instantly produced for the inspection of the reader.

Nothing is worse than the detective picking up a vital clue, palming it, and saying, "Aha, now I know everything."

However, this can be used in a way. In some stories, the sleuth will pick up something and say, "This is what I need to bring the perpetrator to justice" (i.e., they can now convict the scoundrel in court.) In this case, the detective knew what to look for and where to look for it. This is just a substantiation of the solution, which the detective should uncover while sharing the details with the reader.

9. The stupid friend of the detective, the Watson, must not conceal any thoughts which pass through his mind; his intelligence must be slightly, but very slightly, below that of the average reader.

Watson was Sherlock Holmes's sidekick who analyzed a walking stick using the methods of his friend —except he was entirely wrong. Hastings, the assistant to Hercule Poirot, spent more time looking at women with auburn hair than looking for clues. Christie sent him to South America after a few adventures.

The Watson character is often the narrator of the mystery, giving the author a buffer between the sleuth and the reader. The result would not be fair play if the narrator hid facts and deductions. However, the author may use the Watson character to incorrectly interpret the clue's meaning. Hence, Watson may see a diamond on the floor as a gem robbery. In contrast, Holmes deduces it as a lost diamond from an engagement ring.

Blessed be Father Knox for removing the too-stupid-to-live Watson. That Watson, who has never heard of World War II or doesn't inform the sleuth that he will meet the murderer alone, has no place in a fair play mystery. The character should be on the level with the reader and not just a method of making the reader feel superior, even if the reader doesn't make the correct deductions in the end.

10. Twin brothers, and doubles generally, must not appear unless we have been duly prepared for them.

Of course, we're not talking about the Bobbsey Twins here. Since Knox was outlining the rules for fair play, a body double or a twin violates those rules. Look-alikes mean that alibis are worthless. If Twin One is at the bar, he can't be at the country home killing off his wealthy wife—but Twin Two can be.

To prepare the reader for the notion of twins, clues that suggest a character is not a single birth must be given: Two sets of wardrobes with two unique styles, two very different behaviors to the same person or experience, or suggestions that the twin was simultaneously seen in both the bar and the country home.

While I'm confident Knox's wording merely reflected the masculine-oriented words of the time, his words only mention brothers —not sisters.

You will notice that the number of stories exceeds the Ten Commandments provided by Father Knox. There's a reason for that. As a retired teacher, I had to use tests where the student had to match a word from Column One with another vocabulary word from Column Two.

Invariably, my students only had to marry seven or possibly eight items. After that, finishing the test was a matter of guessing since the student had two or three things left to match. I decided to make it more difficult, knowing the above-average intellect of Crippen & Landru readers.

Part of the book's fun is guessing which story goes with which rule, though a story can match more than one rule. We hope you will play along and provide us (**orders@crippenlandru.com**) with your titles and rules. Prizes will go to the first correct entries in subscribers, website orders, first time purchasers, trade paperbacks, and clothbound editions.

So, there are fourteen stories and ten rules. I wish you all the best of luck in solving the matching-up here – and no guessing!

Not *Another* Secret Passage Story
By *Donna Andrews*

I felt something thumping against the bottom of my desk—lightly at first, then harder. I closed my eyes, took a deep breath, and summoned all my patience. Then I leaned down until my mouth was close to the floor.

"Use the main library door, please," I shouted. "This trap door is not presently in service."

Mr. Ernest Throgmorton didn't use the main door, of course. I heard a ghastly scraping noise, and a section of the bookshelves to my right swung out, revealing the cobweb-draped form of my employer.

"The secret passage from the dining room needs cleaning," he said, as he dusted himself off, shedding not only cobwebs but also plaster dust and mouse droppings.

"I've already informed Mrs. Ainsley," I said. "Unfortunately, the housekeeping staff is a little backed up." I stifled the urge to point out that supervising the household staff was not normally part of a librarian's job.

Ernest grunted absentmindedly. He was staring up at the ceiling. It always made me a little nervous when he stared too long at any portion of Throgmorton Hall. It usually meant that he thought he'd detected yet another trap door, secret passage, or hidden room. So far, in the six months since he'd inherited the house from his grandfather, he'd discovered fourteen trap doors, three hidden rooms, and twelve secret passages. I'd lost count of the number of secret compartments, hidden spy holes, and other architectural oddities he'd found along the way.

I'd also lost count of the number of perfectly harmless bits of floor, wall, and ceiling he'd tapped, probed, sampled, taken apart, or simply ripped out altogether, just because there might have been something hidden in, under, or behind them.

If only Jonas Throgmorton hadn't added those fateful words to his will.

"The clue to the whereabouts of the family treasure may be found in one of the secret passages," his will stated. "And the treasure shall belong to him who finds it."

Did he envision that his descendants would still be hunting for the treasure more than two centuries later?

Of course, most of the Throgmortons had long ago concluded that the family treasure was no more. If there ever had been a treasure in the first place. They assumed some rakehell Regency dandy had dug it up and used it to pay off his gambling debts. Or some late Victorian wastrel. Or an early twentieth-century heir who had to cope with crippling death duties. I'd never known Ernest's grandfather to behave in this ridiculous fashion, tearing down his own house about his ears. Of course, he'd only hired me to curate Jonas Throgmorton's justly famous library three years before his death. Perhaps at Ernest's age he'd been just as ridiculous.

Behind Ernest another figure emerged from the secret passage and sneezed vigorously several times. I recognized his nephew, Justin Throgmorton.

"Damn it, Uncle Ernie," Justin said. "This place is a health hazard. Don't your staff ever do any cleaning around here?"

"It's hard for them to keep up." Ernest scowled in annoyance. "The place is so big. And no, I can't afford to hire more staff. Not until I find the treasure."

"Maybe if you got rid of some of this junk you could make do with the staff you've got." Justin glanced around as if surveying a garbage midden rather than a valuable and well-organized library.

"I'm not selling off the family history," Ernest said. "You can do what you like when the place is yours. I hope by the time that happens you've developed a greater appreciation for tradition. But until then the junk, as you call it, stays."

He tugged at the worn copy of the *Aeneid* that opened yet another secret passage—this one leading out to the gazebo in the middle of the garden—and left.

I stifled a sigh of annoyance and put down the ledger I was updating. I did wish Mr. Ernest would take the trouble to close the secret doors behind him.

Justin was gazing around with an expression that was almost thoughtful.

"No offense," he said. "But if Uncle Ernie ever kicks the bucket and I get the house, I'm going to toss out all this junk and turn this into a media room. A big high-def TV there." He pointed toward a case of rare manuscripts. "A couple of leather recliners there. I could replace a lot of those shelves with cabinets for the stuff I still have on physical media, and store my action figures on the rest."

I managed not to shudder at the vision he called up. Granted, the Throgmortons hadn't exactly paid much attention to the library over the past two centuries. Old Jonas had been quite the scholar, but I doubted that any of his descendants had ever opened a single volume. Still, they had all been proud of the library—as a status symbol if nothing else.

"Of course, Uncle Ernie will probably live forever, like Great-grand-dad," Justin said. "Still, a guy can dream, can't he?"

Something occurred to me.

"Mr. Ernest's health has always been excellent," I said. "But should you find yourself suddenly in possession of the house and its contents, I would advise against merely tossing the books."

"I should maybe take them to a used book store?"

I reached over to the upper right side of my desk, which was topped by a carved wooden unicorn. A quick twist of its horn popped open a small secret drawer by my left elbow. I took out a business card.

"I would recommend taking them to a rare book dealer." I handed him the card. "This one in particular would offer top dollar and take the entire collection instead of trying to cherry-pick the most valuable ones and leaving you wondering what to do with the rest."

Justin pocketed the card and nodded his thanks. He strode over to the main library door and stood in front of it, studying the frame and the carved expanse of the door.

"Okay, I give up," he said. "How do I open this one?"

"With the knob," I said gently. "It's just an ordinary door."

"Didn't know they were allowed around here." He grasped the knob rather timidly—clearly he'd encountered some of the booby-trapped ones elsewhere in the house—and departed.

I went back to my desk in a thoughtful mood.

I didn't like Justin any more than Ernest. But Ernest had so far resisted all the blandishments of the various rare book dealers who'd inspected the library—including the several I'd recruited to act as a front for me. I was determined to make the contents of the Throgmorton library my own, but after more than two years of watching my emissaries negotiate, I'd finally accepted that Ernest would never sell.

Justin, on the other hand . . . I could work with Justin.

But could I afford to wait until Justin inherited? Ernest was only forty-five, in perfect health, and from a family whose members were noted for their longevity. He could easily outlive me—unless he managed to do himself in with his own carelessness. I shuddered, remembering the incident two months ago, when he'd been careless with a blowtorch during one of his demolitions and nearly set fire to the east wing. Next time we might not be so lucky.

I had long ago decided on the best way to do away with my employer should the need arise. After uncle and visiting nephew had both retired for the night, I used a convenient secret passage to bypass the locked door of the north tower. I ascended to the top floor and pulled aside the rug just outside Ernest's bedroom door. The trap door was still there— one of the first he'd found, long since proven to hold no secrets, and thus long since forgotten.

Originally, opening the trap door had revealed a hidden stairway that led all the way to the cellars, but during his searches Ernest had removed so many boards from the stairs that the whole thing had collapsed, leaving behind a sheer five-story drop onto a huge pile of bricks and lumber.

I removed the pegs that held the trap door together and dropped the pieces onto the rubble below. I carefully replaced the rug. It sagged a bit in the center, but in the dimly lit corridor Ernest wouldn't notice that. Then I crept back to my tiny room in the servants' wing and went to sleep.

When the police knocked at my door to inform me of my employer's sad fate, I provided a convincing display of distress—all the more convincing since I managed to convey that my distress arose largely from the prospect of being unemployed. After learning from Mrs. Ainsley that only Ernest owned a key to the tower door and hearing her strident diatribe about how the house was falling apart around her ears, the police ruled Ernest's death accidental.

I took Justin up on his invitation to stay on long enough to pack up the books he was selling to the dealer I'd recommended. I had to work to disguise my delight as I carefully packed up box after box of books. My books now. All mine. Many of them rare, valuable, and beautiful— but more importantly, once I had them all to myself, I was sure I could solve the puzzle in Jonas Throgmorton's will. I'd already found enough hints to convince me that I was on the right track. All I needed was enough uninterrupted time with Jonas's books.

Amusing to think how generations of Throgmortons had wasted their time tearing the house apart. Jonas had been a reader. A scholar. A lover of books. Not surprising that it took a librarian to realize that the secret passage mentioned in Jonas's will was not a physical passage but a literary one. A passage in one of his books.

Correction: one of *my* books.

I returned to my packing with renewed vigor.

Matter of Trust

By Frankie Bailey

Eudora, New York
Tuesday, November 23, 1948

Annie Gibson brushed away the snow melting on her windshield and plucked the folded sheet of paper from beneath the wiper. "Just a minute, sweetie," she said to her eight-month-old son who was watching her from the front seat.

She got into the car and smiled at the baby in his booster seat. "Isn't the snow pretty, Johnny-kins? See the big, fluffy flakes? But we need to hurry and finish our errands. We want to be snug at home before the streets get slippery. First, just let Mommy see who left her a note."

The paper was a page torn from the kind of ruled composition book children used. The message was in sprawling print.

Ask him what he did.

No signature. Just that one sentence.

Ask him what he did.

Annie stared at the note, then dropped it on the car seat. It slipped under Johnny's booster. She would have to remember not to leave it there.

She started the car, heard the *whoosh* of the heater, switched on the windshield wipers.

The village was busy for a Tuesday afternoon. Thanksgiving was only two days away. Everyone was trying to get errands done before the snow came.

Annie waved as she passed Miss Henderson, the librarian. She needed to pick up another knitting book.

The baby gurgled, and she reached over to touch his arm. "I'm sorry I had to bring you along with me on my errands, sweetie. Do you miss Grandma? She'll be home in time for Christmas."

Warm air was coming from the heater now, but she couldn't stop shivering.

Who would leave such a horrible note? Who would walk up and put that under someone's windshield wiper, making the person who received it wonder what it was about?

* * *

The meat loaf was ready to come out of the oven and she was mashing the potatoes when Jack came in from the garage. He stopped, foot raised, at the kitchen door.

"Oops!" he said. "Wet shoes."

She laughed as he made a show of drawing back his foot. "Thank you, darling."

He came back wearing the leather slippers she had left by the bench.

Annie said, "And tonight, husband, we're having apple turnovers."

"My turn to say 'thank you,'" he said. He kissed her on the cheek she turned toward him. "You smell nice."

"Cinnamon and allspice. Makes both cook and house smell nice."

"Do I have time to change before dinner?"

"Ten minutes. Will that do?"

"Be back in five."

"Try not to wake Johnny," she said.

"I'll be as quiet as a whisper."

Annie smiled. He always made her smile.

She brushed her bangs back from her forehead with the back of her hand. If she couldn't get into the beauty parlor soon, she'd have to take the scissors to them.

She could hear Jack whistling softly. But that was all right. Johnny sometimes fell asleep to his daddy's whistling.

She was not going to hurt her husband by showing him a silly note. The person who'd left it had probably put it on the wrong car. Or had been playing a joke that wasn't funny.

* * *

They were listening to "The Bing Crosby Show" when the telephone rang.

"I'll get it," Jack told her. "I know you don't want to miss Bing."

She tried not to listen any more than she usually did.

When she heard him say "looking for a contractor" and that he would give him the information tomorrow at the office, she knew he was talking to Travis. The two men, best friends, had come to Eudora from Buffalo after the war. They had been looking for a place to strike out on their own. Jack, the real estate agent, and Travis, the contractor. They had gone in together to rent, then buy, an office building on Main Street.

Jack had met and married Annie, a Eudora girl. Travis was still a carefree—and sometimes careless—bachelor. A danger to the hearts of the women who fell for a handsome war hero.

Jack had gone to war, too. But he was ready to settle down after it was over.

Except for his weekly night out with the boys. He and Travis were on the same bowling team. Beer and bowling every Thursday night.

Jack was finishing his call on the hall phone.

Annie turned her attention back to the radio and her knitting,

* * *

Friday, November 26, 1948

Annie was paying the delivery boy from the cleaners when she remembered the note.

She had put it in her purse when she got home on Tuesday afternoon. Put it there, first, not sure if she would show it to Jack. Then, reluctant to throw it away when she didn't know who had left it or why. Put it there in her purse and been so scatterbrained this morning she had forgotten it was there.

Jack had asked if she had the checkbook. She had been making his breakfast and listening to the morning news. She had called back, "Look in my purse."

Now the inner pocket of her purse where she'd put the note was unzipped.

"Thank you," she said, accepting Jack's shirts and suit from the delivery boy.

"Have a good day, Mrs. Gibson."

She carried Jack's dry cleaning into their bedroom and hung the shirts in their place and the suit with the others.

Then she went back into the living room and looked again at the unzipped inner pocket. The note was still where she had put it. Still folded.

If Jack had seen the folded piece of paper, he had probably thought it was a grocery list. There was no reason why he would have taken it out and read it.

Except last night, he had asked if something was wrong. They had been listening to the radio, and he had reached for his coffee cup and her attention had been caught by his hands. Hands that looked as if they should belong to a concert pianist.

She had blurted that out soon after they started dating; he had laughed and said he was tone-deaf.

Last night, he had turned his head and caught her staring at his hands. He had asked what was wrong. She had said she was woolgathering. Thinking about her post-Thanksgiving errands. All the things she needed to get done tomorrow.

Maybe this morning, he had thought of that and been curious about what she planned to do today. Maybe he had taken the note out and read it.

Ask him what he did.

If he had read that ugly message, what had he thought? Why hadn't he asked her about it?

* * *

Annie had promised to work at the church bazaar that afternoon. She wanted to get Johnny dressed and ready before the sitter came. This was a new woman and she wanted to start off well. She would need the woman's help until her mother got back from visiting her brother and his family in California.

After the sitter arrived, she had a few minutes to herself. She decided to bring Jack his lunch. A turkey sandwich and some pumpkin pie. He loved Thanksgiving leftovers even more than the first day.

She was parking down the street when she saw Jack coming out of his office. She was getting out of the car, ready to call out to him, when Travis came out of his door.

She glanced at her watch. Only a little after eleven. Early to be going out to lunch. Maybe they were going to look at property. Jack had told her they wanted to buy another building as an investment.

They started to walk away. Jack, talking and gesturing. Travis, leaning on the cane he used when the leg he had been shot in during the war was acting up. He had told her, laughing, that women never minded his bum leg. They wanted to soothe his pain.

He had a crew that did the work he lined up. So, the leg wasn't as much of a hindrance as it might have been.

They got into Jack's car. Annie watched them drive away. And wondered why she hadn't called out or waved to attract her husband's attention.

There was a trash can on the corner. She dropped the brown paper bag with his lunch into it.

* * *

SUNDAY, NOVEMBER 28, 1948

The phone rang as Jo Radcliffe was wondering if God or anyone else would notice if she missed church. No one had told her when she agreed to serve as the temporary public health nurse how often she would be called out in the evening. Last night, it was a woman who had gone into labor while she was scrubbing the floor. Having delivered four children without a problem, she had decided to have this one at home. That might have been fine if her doctor hadn't been busy at the hospital and baby number five hadn't decided to present himself feet first. But they had managed.

And the phone was still ringing. Jo tumbled out of bed and grabbed her robe. She ran down the stairs, bare feet on hardwood floor, regretting she hadn't stopped for slippers.

She grabbed the receiver from the hook. Whoever it was, was determined.

"Hello," she said.

"Jo, Eli Gordon here. Sorry to bother you early on a Sunday morning."

"Oh, Chief Gordon. That's okay, I was awake. What can I do for you?"

"Would you mind coming over to the station?" He paused. "I could sure use your help with something."

"I gather this is serious." Dempsey, her Aunt Meg's Maine Coon cat, paused at the top of the stairs to sit down and lick his paw. "An emergency?"

"We have it under control. But the sooner you can get here, the better."

"Okay, I'll be there in about forty-five minutes."

"Thank you, Jo. I appreciate it."

Jo hung up the receiver. The chief had obviously not wanted to share whatever it was with any curious listeners who happened to be on her party line. Whatever it was couldn't be good.

Dempsey strolled past her, plumed tail in the air, ignoring her presence.

He was still sleeping on Meg's bed. And resisting any effort by Jo to offer him comfort.

She followed the cat down the hall. Even if she wasn't going to have time for a leisurely Sunday breakfast, he expected his.

* * *

"One of my men found him sitting in his car," Chief Gordon said as he handed Jo a mug of black coffee. "The car was in the middle of the street, and he was sitting there behind the steering wheel."

"Was he already dead?"

"Dying," Chief Gordon said. He settled his bulk into his chair. "Dead by the time the ambulance got there."

Jo took a long sip of coffee strong enough to use as an oar. "What does she say about why she shot him?"

"Nothing. She's not talking."

"But you're sure she did it?"

"The two witnesses who heard the shot and looked out of their bedroom window said it came from the bar. Then they saw him come staggering out the door and get into his car. He didn't get more than four or five blocks down the street before he slammed into the curb."

"And they called the police?"

"They called. So did three other concerned citizens. Except for that bar, it's a quiet neighborhood over there."

"And no one else was in the bar? The owner?"

"Got a call from his wife who wanted him to come home. She had the flu and was throwing up. He left as soon as he'd gotten the last customer out the door. He asked the girl to lock up. When my officer went in, she was back in the office, sitting at her boss's desk. The gun was right there on the desk."

"Her gun?"

"Her boss's. He kept it in the desk drawer."

Jo took another sip of her coffee. "If you think she should have a medical evaluation, a doctor—"

"Got one if we need him. I'm hoping you can help me with her sister."

"Her sister?"

"Different last names. Different fathers. The sister is a Rossi."

"Christina Rossi?" Jo said, remembering a slender, dark-eyed teenager.

Chief Gordon nodded. "That's her. Said she met you when the library asked you to talk about having been an Army nurse."

"She came up and asked me about nursing school."

"She's here. She got someone to give her a ride as soon as she heard what had happened. Lila doesn't want to talk to her, but she won't go home. Anyway, she's just a kid—"

"Fourteen. She said she was starting high school this year."

"And they live in a trailer park out near Mulholland Road. I don't feel easy about sending her back out there by herself."

"Child welfare—"

"When I asked her if there was anybody she wanted me to call, she said you."

"She asked you to call me? We had one conversation that lasted all of ten minutes."

"Seems like you made an impression on her." Chief Gordon gave her one of his slow, thoughtful looks. "She could use somebody to help her get through this. Doesn't look good for her sister." He paused. "I hate to see her go into foster care. It's her sister that's done the crime."

"You don't expect me to—"

"I thought you might just keep her for a few days."

"What good will that do? If her sister isn't released, she'll still—"

"You never know what might happen."

Jo set her half-empty mug down on his desk. "You said Lila Tate shot a man. Are you saying it might have been self-defense?"

"I don't know what it is. She's not talking. I just think it's kind of odd, don't you?"

"Maybe they were involved with each other. A lover's quarrel."

"That's possible. With a girl from her background, it might even be likely that she'd have a male friend who would help her out now and then." Chief Gordon leaned forward. "Except her boss was surprised, couldn't believe it when I told him what happened. Now her boss, Bill Pope, is a careful man. He likes to keep his head down. That's how he's managed to keep that bar open for almost fifteen years. He wouldn't hire a girl who was likely to cause him trouble. Wouldn't leave her alone with his money or his gun. So, I'm thinking Lila might have a story to tell. In a few days, she might be willing to talk. But in the meantime, we've got the problem of her little sister, sitting there all alone in our meeting room, crying because Lila won't see her."

It was a long speech. Jo stared at him, knowing that he knew he had her. She almost cursed out loud.

"All right. A few days. She can stay with me a few days— if we can get approval."

Chief Gordon smiled. "Just to save some time, I've already put in a call. The lady I talked to was happy to give us her approval. We just have to do a little paperwork."

"Did you ask Christina if she knows anything?"

"I couldn't get my tongue around that. I hate questioning kids about grown-up stuff." He paused. "Maybe you can ask a few questions when she's with you."

"I set myself up for that one, didn't I?"

* * *

"Should I call you Christina, or Tina?" Jo asked, glancing over at her silent passenger.

Aside from thanking Jo for coming and saying yes, she would like to stay with her, she had said almost nothing. She was almost as silent as her half-sister in her jail cell.

The two sisters had only a passing physical resemblance. Lila Tate was short and curvy, with bleached blond hair and a cynical curve to her mouth. She'd reached for another cigarette and mumbled, "Thanks" when Jo told her Christina would be with her.

"'Tina,'" the girl beside her said. "Lila calls me 'Tina.'"

She was still staring out of the window, but Jo heard the tears in her voice.

"Tina, it is," Jo said. "Why don't we go out to your place and pick up some of your things."

"Okay."

"You'll have to give me directions."

Tina directed her to six or seven trailers on a scrawny plot of land at the end of a dead-end road. There was a ranch house down the road that might belong to the person who owned the trailer park.

"How do you get to school from out here?" Jo asked. "You go to school in Eudora, right?"

Tina nodded. "A couple of other kids and I walk down to the fork of the road. The bus picks us up there. Sometimes Lila drops me off when she has to go in early for her other job."

"Her other job?"

"She works part-time at the diner on Main Street."

"I don't remember ever seeing her there."

"She works in the kitchen." Hand on the car door handle. "Do you want to come in?"

Jo wasn't sure what she should say. She wanted a look inside, but she didn't want to embarrass her. "Would you rather I wait here?"

"It's okay if you come in. Lila made me help clean up before she went to work yesterday."

The interior of the trailer was what she had expected. Cramped, with cheap fixtures. But everything was in its place. Tidy was the word that came to mind. Stale cigarette smoke balanced by two lush green plants on the counter.

"Someone has a green thumb," Jo said. "Those are beautiful plants."

"Lila," Tina said. "She's always wanted a real garden. I'll go get my things, so we can go." She looked back over her shoulder. "How long do you think I'll be gone?"

"At least a few days. If you need more, we'll come back."

"That was Mrs. Ingram who was looking out her window when we drove up. I should ask her to keep an eye on the trailer while Lila and I are gone."

"That's a good idea."

* * *

Jack was on the telephone when Annie came back from putting the baby down.

"His brother's coming in from Buffalo," he told her when he hung up the phone a few minutes later. "He says the police told him they can't release the body until there's been an autopsy."

Annie shook her head. "I can't believe this."

Jack said, an edge to his voice, "You never thought Travis's wild side would catch up to him?"

"I always hoped you would be a good influence on him."

"Well, at least, none of them would have shot him." Annie wrapped her arms around her waist. "I liked Travis. He could be funny and charming, and he deserved respect as a war hero. And, he was Johnny's godfather."

"And his dog liked him?" Jack said.

"Yes, he did. Do you think his brother will take Max?"

"If he doesn't, we will. Travis would have liked Johnny to have his dog."

"And a collie isn't so big," Annie said. "I'm going to go check on the pot roast."

"I don't have too much of an appetite."

"Do you think you might be coming down with something?"

His laughter startled her. "Annie, my best friend was shot last night. He's dead. That—"

"I only meant . . . I know how upset you are." She brushed at her bangs. "Sandwiches and coffee. How's that?"

"Fine," he said. "I'm sorry I snapped at you."

"Don't be. It was a stupid question."

"I'm going to my study for a little while."

"I'll call you when everything's ready."

She watched him leave. Then she sank down on the sofa.

* * *

Monday, November 29, 1948

On Monday evening, Jo came home to find Tina—who had been allowed to stay home from school— sitting on the sofa reading a book. She was reading aloud the book to Dempsey, who was curled up close against her, his paws on her leg.

Dempsey spared Jo a glance out of his golden eyes. His tail twitched, but he returned his attention to Tina.

Tina glanced at Jo, smiled, and went on with her lively rendition of *The Wind in the Willows*.

Fascinated, Jo sat down in an armchair and kicked off her shoes. Tucking her feet under her, she settled back to listen to the story, too. It was a long time since she had visited with Toad and company.

She would never have expected shy, retiring Tina would be such a mimic.

Perhaps it was the rhythm of the book that was holding Dempsey enthralled. Or, maybe it was the arm Tina had curled around him as she read.

Jo's eyes drifted shut. She woke with a start when she heard Tina laugh. "We'll finish the rest of it tomorrow," she told the cat.

Jo yawned and stretched. "What shall we have for dinner?"

"I can make it," Tina said. "I make dinner for Lila when she's tired."

"Why don't we do it together? How about hamburgers? I've even got frozen French fries."

"I've never had those. But I love hamburgers."

Dempsey followed them into the kitchen. He curled up on the cushion in the bay window.

"You seem to have won Dempsey over," Jo said.

"I like him. He kept me company today."

Jo took the ground beef out of the refrigerator. "I heard from Chief Wilson that Lila was arraigned today. That means she had her first appearance in court. She has an attorney now, and he had her enter a plea of not guilty."

"But if she shot the man—"

"Her lawyer says it's still better to plead 'not guilty' for now. That will give them a chance to work on her defense—to figure out the best way to present Lila's case and explain what she did."

"Do you think if she tells them what happened, they might not send her to prison?"

"That depends on what happened. Since Lila won't talk about it—"

"But maybe she'll tell her lawyer."

"Maybe," Jo said. She broke an egg and beat it. Added it to the ground beef. "Did Lila ever mention Travis Boyd to you?"

"No."

Jo reached for a knife. "Do you like onions on your hamburger?"

"Not really. I'd rather have pickles and catsup." Tina glanced over at Dempsey. "He looks funny with one leg up in the air like that while he licks himself."

"He would rather call it 'grooming' himself. In case you haven't noticed, Dempsey is a very dignified cat."

Tina giggled. "I wanted a kitten or a puppy, but Lila said we might have to move and we might not be able to take it along."

"When did she say that?"

"A long time ago. When I was eight or nine. We were living in an apartment then. After that we moved out to the trailer park."

"Do you like it out there?"

"It's okay. Do you want me to set the table?"

"Please. Then would you feed Dempsey while I'm getting the burgers on?"

Dempsey had eaten and settled in for a nap, and they were having dinner when Tina put down her hamburger. "I think something happened. Something with Lila."

Jo picked up a French fry and took a bite. She didn't want to spook her by questioning her too closely. "Want to tell me about it?'

Tina nodded. "One night, she . . . her car broke down. Someone brought her home. I think there were two men. But it was dark, and I only saw the shape of the one who got out. She was sitting in back, and he opened the car door. I ducked down so they wouldn't see me. Then I heard Lila coming in, and the car drove away. I got up, but she told me to go back to bed. It was a long time before she came to bed." Tina paused. "I could hear the water running in the bathroom. And then when she came to bed, she was just lying there."

"Did you ask her if anything was wrong?"

"I tried to, but she told me to go to sleep."

"When did this happen?"

"In October."

"Early October? Late?"

"Early. The first week in October. I know it was Thursday because I'd been listening to 'Charade Quiz' on the radio."

"Did she say anything the next morning about what had happened?"

"She said the car wouldn't start and she got a ride home. She got a ride with Mr. Ingram back into town that day. She had to get the transmission fixed in the car, but her boss at the bar loaned her the money."

"But…" Jo said, choosing her words, and reminding herself she was talking to a fourteen-year-old girl. "You think Lila was upset about something when she came in that night? Maybe she was worried about paying for repairs. Could it have been that?"

Tina shook her head. "She worries about money all the time. This was different. She was . . . that morning, it was like she was dazed, and she had this bruise on her wrist." Tina looked away. "I think those men hurt her."

Jo said, "Do you think . . . if that was what happened . . . is there someone she might have told?"

Tina poked at the half-eaten hamburger on her plate. "Lila wouldn't want people to know if something like that had happened. She wouldn't want them to think . . . you know what they think about how it's the woman's fault."

"Yes. But it isn't."

"But they already think . . . when you don't have a lot of money . . ."

Jo nodded. "People have all kinds of wrong ideas. But sometimes keeping a secret can be worse than dealing with what they might think."

Tina's head came up. "How do you know that? You live here in this big house and you're a nurse and you were in the Army. How do you know how it is for Lila and me?"

"I don't. But believe it or not, I might have a secret or two."

"You do? Is it something bad?"

"Something that people might find surprising."

"What?"

"Maybe I'll tell you one day. Right now, we need to think about how to help your sister. If something did happen that night, maybe Travis Boyd was involved. That might be something that Lila's lawyer could use in her defense."

"You think so?"

"I think we should let her lawyer and Chief Gordon know so they can investigate."

Tina sighed. "Lila isn't going to like it that I told."

"She might feel humiliated and embarrassed, but she'll know that you're only trying to help."

* * *

FRIDAY, DECEMBER 3, 1948

That Friday afternoon, Jo was back in Chief Gordon's office.

He said, "We know now Travis Boyd was at the bar that evening with his bowling buddies. Pope, Lisa's boss, remembers Boyd was loud and happy. Still there for last call."

"So, it's possible he was still around when Lila went out to her car and discovered it wouldn't start," Jo said. "Do you think her lawyer will be able to get her to talk? Maybe she'll talk to me now."

"That's the other reason I called you to come in. She does want to talk to you. About her little sister."

"I wish she'd see Tina."

"Well, she's willing to see you. That's a start."

Lila came out wearing the plain blue dress that was standard issue for the few women who passed through the jail. She sat down on the other side of the table and lit a cigarette.

"Hello," Jo said. "It's good to see you again."

"Forgive me for not making nice, but I'd just as soon not be seeing you again," Lila said. "I'd rather not be in this jam."

"I can understand that. You probably didn't intend to kill Travis Boyd."

"I didn't think about it one way or the other. I wanted to keep his hands off me. I pointed the gun at him and shot him." Lila took another puff of her cigarette. "I want to talk to you about Tina. How long are you going to let her stay with you?"

"It was supposed to be only a few days," Jo said. "I'm not equipped to be a foster mother to a teenage girl. So, I think you'd better work with your lawyer."

"Nothing I say is likely to get me out of this mess."

"If Travis Boyd was one of the men who gave you a ride the night your car broke down—"

Lila glared at her. "What do you know about that?"

"Tina told me something happened. If Travis Boyd did rape you—"

Lila laughed. "My sister's a kid. What's your excuse? Didn't anyone ever tell you that girls like me don't get raped? We either sell it or give it away."

Jo nodded her head. "And living in a trailer doesn't do much for your credibility either. But if there was another man . . . if you told them who—"

"And he denied it happened. Who do you think they'd believe?"

"Don't you think you owe it to your sister to at least try?"

Lila stubbed out her cigarette. "I killed him. They aren't going to let me just walk out scot-free."

"Did he come to the bar to attack you again?"

"He came to tell me to leave his best buddy alone."

"The man who was with him?"

"And who went for a walk in the woods while Travis bent me over the hood of his car." Her eyes flared. "And then his buddy, Jack, had the nerve to play the gentleman and help me out of the car when they dropped me off. He asked me if I was all right."

"What did you do to make Travis warn you?"

"I left her a note—Jack's wife. I was driving by and there he was walking her out of his office. His pretty, smug little wife pushing their baby in a stroller. He kissed her— that was how I knew who she must be. And then just before Thanksgiving I was leaving my job at the diner, and I saw her getting out of her car with the baby. And . . ." Lila smiled. "I left her a note."

"What did it say?"

"Just, to ask him what he'd done."

"Did she?"

"Nope. Afraid of what he might say, I guess. But she kept the note. He found it in her purse. Then they saw her outside his office." Lila smiled. "Travis wanted to make sure I hadn't done more than send her a note. That I hadn't spoken to her directly."

"What did you tell him?"

"Nothing I could repeat to a lady like yourself," Lila said, her smile mocking. "But he didn't care for what I said. He put his hands on me again. This time I was ready. A knee in his family jewels. He screamed and cursed and staggered about on his bad leg until he fell. That made him mad. He looked like he wanted to kill me. When he got up and started toward me, I grabbed the gun out of the drawer and told him to stay away. He kept coming. And I shot him."

Lila picked up a matchbook and put another cigarette in her mouth. Her hands were shaking.

Jo reached across the table and took the matchbook. She struck one and held it out.

"Thanks," Lila said.

Jo said, "You have to tell your lawyer what you've just told me."

"I'll think about it. About Tina. . . are you going to—"

"She can stay with me until after your hearing."

* * *

MONDAY, JANUARY 24, 1949

Jack Gibson was not what Jo had been expecting. He had moved to the village after she left, and she hadn't crossed paths with him and his wife since she returned.

She had expected to see some indication in his appearance, in his expression, that he was the kind of a man who was capable of walking away and leaving a woman to be raped.

But he sat upright, looking pale but composed as Lila told her story.

When he was called to the stand, he glanced at his wife, who had come in with him and sat beside him. He raised his hand and swore to tell the truth.

The courtroom was quiet, tense as everyone waited to hear what he would say.

Lila's lawyer, young and earnest, opened by asking Jack Gibson about his occupation, his family, his friendship with Travis Boyd.

"Your good friend?"

"My best friend since high school."

"And you both moved here to Eudora from Buffalo. Is that correct?"

"Yes, we both thought there were business opportunities here."

"No other reason?"

Gibson shook his head. "I had no other reason."

"What about your friend, Travis Boyd. Did he have any other reason for leaving Buffalo?"

"He was working with his brother. Travis wanted to strike out on his own."

"And in three years, you both became respected members of the Eudora business community. Involved in civic and charitable activities."

"Yes."

"And joined a bowling league."

"Yes."

"On the evening of Thursday, October 7, 1948, did you participate in a bowling tournament?"

"Yes."

"You both did?"

"Yes."

"And your team won?"

"Yes."

"And you went to the Seafarer's Bar to celebrate."

"Yes."

"How long were you there?"

"Until closing."

"Both you and Mr. Boyd."

"Yes, I was riding with him."

"And were you riding with him when he was chivalrous enough to offer Miss Tate a ride home when her car wouldn't start?"

Jack Gibson looked at his wife. Everyone in the courtroom waited. Jo wondered for a moment if he was going to refuse to answer. He hadn't been charged with anything, but still . . .

"Yes, I rode with him." He cleared his throat. "I was there when he . . . when the incident involving Miss Tate occurred."

"The incident? You mean when he raped her."

"Yes." His voice was hoarse now. "When he raped her."

"And you let it happen?"

Jack Gibson looked down, around, blurted out, "He said she liked it rough. He said . . . I thought he had . . . they had before . . ."

"And even though he offered you a turn, you were courteous enough to walk away."

"Yes, I didn't want to watch."

"Because Miss Tate had screamed, because she was struggling and trying to escape?"

"I didn't know what he was going to do. I asked him to stop the car because I needed to take..." Color rushed into his face. "I had been drinking a lot of beer. I needed to . . . I went further into the woods and I got turned around finding my way back . . ."

"But then you heard Miss Tate scream and you ran to see what was happening?"

"Yes, I thought something was wrong. I—"

"You didn't think anything was wrong with what you saw happening?"

"I didn't know what to do! I didn't think he would . . . if she didn't really want to—"

Annie Gibson stood up. She said, "Excuse me" to no one in particular.

The courtroom was silent as she walked out. On the stand, Jack Gibson bowed his head.

Jo heard a small sound between a sigh and laughter. She looked at Lila. Lila smiled back. An odd twist of her lips as tears ran down her cheeks.

The Dinner Party
By Nikki Dolson

Teresa paced in her mother's living room practicing what she would say to a stranger:

"Hi, I'm Teresa. I'm here to collect the debt you owe." Or:

"Hello, Adamson sent me. Time to pay up." She laughed at herself. Since she'd started doing this job, she still hadn't quite figured out her script. She sounded like a character from the old sixties Batman show that her daughter, Violet, watched reruns of sometimes. If she was a character from that show she wouldn't be Batman or any of the supposed good guys. Teresa considered this as she put her shoes on. Working for Nick Adamson, she was fully in that morally gray area. She didn't hurt people but she knew she was breaking the law, collecting debt for him. The local newspaper once called him a crime boss. If he was that, then what was she? A henchwoman?

A car honked outside pulling her from her thoughts. That would be Clayton, always five minutes early. *If I'm late, assume I'm dead,* he told her once.

She left a note on the bathroom mirror for her mother, who was still sleeping off a night spent dancing with her gentleman friend, and another on the fridge reminding her mother to pick up Violet from her friend's house later. By the time she made it outside, Clayton was out of the car and holding the back door for her to slide in.

"I can't sit up front?" She pouted. She enjoyed teasing him.

"This is work. It'll look better with you in the back. You look nice, by the way," he said.

She wore a navy silk dress and matching shoes. A gold bracelet at each wrist and a circle of gold at her neck. "You always say that to me."

"You always look nice. Should I not mention it?"

"You'd stop if asked?"

"Of course." He winked at her.

She rolled her eyes and got in, her skirt trailing across the leather seat. Clayton flipped the end of it up and out of the way of the closing door. Teresa sighed as she relaxed into the seat. The car was a new black 1988 Cadillac. She was there the day Clayton had driven it off the lot and it had the most comfortable upholstered seats she had ever had the pleasure of sitting on. The ride was so smooth, Teresa barely noticed when Clayton executed a U-turn on her residential street and flung them out into traffic.

"You're coming in with me still?" she asked.

"Definitely. I'll be your shadow in there. I'll blend in."

Teresa laughed. Clayton was a six-foot-five white man in a gray suit accompanying a black woman to a party no one invited them to attend. He wasn't going to blend in and neither was she. She was just going to have to make the best of the circumstances.

Yesterday afternoon she'd been called in to see her employer, Nick Adamson, in his suite of rooms on the eighth floor of his hotel. He sat behind his large desk with his back to the windows daring his enemies to take their shot. A decade into his power and no one had. Teresa had sat in the chair in front of his desk fidgeting and trying to stop. Adamson took off the sunglasses that hid his damaged eyes. Very few knew that cataracts had destroyed the vision in his right eye. Surgery had mostly saved the left.

"I have a collection for you. I was going to send Clayton and one of the others, but my wife reminded me that you could do it and make smaller ripples. It's worth five thousand to you."

"I'll do it." The words were out of her mouth before she had a chance to really consider it. Usually, she made an extra couple hundred a week. Enough that her mother's carefully budgeted pension was never spent on her or Violet. Enough to help cover the vig on a debt she carried because of her ex. With five thousand dollars she would be that much closer to paying it off. That much closer to being back in her own home and out of her mother's place.

Adamson nodded and slowly wrote down something on a square of paper. He tilted his head, so his good left eye was a little closer to his task. He folded the paper and held it out to her. She reached for it.

"You're sure?" he asked.

"Yes. Wait, do I have to hurt anyone?" She drew her hand back.

"No. Just talk them into paying you what they owe me." He put his glasses back on. "Next time don't wear the competition's uniform when you come to see me."

She smoothed a hand over her Showboat Hotel & Casino uniform blouse. "My apologies."

"Everyone gets a second chance in this organization. Just don't disappoint me."

So now Teresa sat in the leather backseat practicing what she would say to a stranger and hoping she wouldn't disappoint Nick Adamson.

* * *

Clayton moved them easily through traffic then onto the long straight-away toward the mountains. The house they were headed towards was technically in Las Vegas but it was well outside the city proper. The dinner was at the home of some well-to-do snowbird and this would be the last chance to corner Harvey Worley before he left town. Once Harvey did that, Adamson would send some people to break his legs or likely worse. It might be Clayton who went. She looked at Clayton's hands gripping the steering wheel. She'd seen those knuckles bloodied on more than one occasion.

"We're almost there. Relax," he said.

She saw him looking at her in the rearview mirror. "I'm fine. You just watch the road. We need to get there in one piece." He chuckled and pressed the gas pedal. The desert scenery blurred, and she closed her eyes to enjoy this last moment of peace before work began.

Metal posts appeared, tipped with white reflective paint. The car slowed then turned left. In the distance, Teresa saw the house rising from the desert. It was built upon some small nub of mountain; its plateau was forty feet or so above the desert floor. The road they were on was obviously maintained but there's only so much you can do with gravel for a surface. The homeowners must spend thousands on upkeep alone, Teresa thought as they bounced along. Oh, to be this wealthy. She thought of her own house. Her fairytale cottage she called it. Built in the fifties, it had a turret like a castle. Three tiny bedrooms. As her ex-husband Victor advanced at the bank, they made improvements. Ripped up the carpet and put in hardwood floors. Redid the kitchen with top-of-the-line appliances and marble counters even though they ate out every night. Her beautiful house that someone else was renting now, living out her life. Their clothes in the walk-in closet she'd made from the fourth, smallest bedroom.

She was jostled from her thoughts as the car turned again. Ahead was a steep incline. As the car rose, her view of the desert expanded. In the distance were dark clouds. The car crested the top and there was the house. It was long and low, ranch-style, with windows along the entire front but a second floor was offset with a matching wall of windows. Its white painted brick exterior and teal front doors made Teresa think of Palm Springs and the banking convention she'd attended with Victor. She and the other wives had toured the town and homes within it guessing which homes had once housed Hollywood actors they loved.

Clayton stopped the car at the front door. "Think these doors are big enough?" she said as he helped her out. He didn't answer. She looked up at him but he was looking behind her. She turned to see the storm clouds moving fast. "That's not good," she said.

He said, "I think this needs to be a quick trip or we may be stuck here. Flash flood warnings are going to be issued. All this desert between us and the city, we might not have a way back for hours."

"Definitely." Teresa took a breath and rang the doorbell. Clayton parked the car behind the other cars that lined the driveway. He was just walking back when the door opened and a white woman with long blond hair wearing a yellow sundress that showed off her legs stood looking at Teresa and slouched against the doorframe.

"Well, hello there. Tell me, Queen, do the men just fall at your feet?"

Teresa slipped on a smile. "Yes. I'm quite good at stepping over them."

The woman let out a short sharp bark of laughter. "Who are you?"

Teresa lifted her chin. "Teresa Graham."

"And who are you?" Clayton had just arrived at Teresa's side. The woman looked Clayton up and down with a wry smile on her face.

"Clayton."

"You're a big one. Are you together?"

"We're friends," Teresa said extending a hand. The woman pulled Teresa in and looped her arm around Teresa's. "I'm Evelyn. Let me give you the tour." Teresa looked back to see Clayton staring at her. She mouthed "come on" at him and turned back to Evelyn.

"Welcome to the Winter House. This is the formal living room and over there the informal living room. We'll get there." She gestured right at the expanse of room facing the endless row of floor-to-ceiling windows. There was a fireplace, a bar against a few feet of wall without a window, and two leather chairs on either side of a central fireplace, an oversized ottoman off to one side. Across the room in what Teresa supposed was the informal living room, she saw a full-sized piano, a couch, and the other people she'd soon be having dinner with. Behind the fireplace was a staircase which led to bedrooms and more bathrooms and more space. Beyond the staircase, a hallway that led to a bathroom and at least one other room but the door was closed and Evelyn didn't say what else was down there.

Teresa's entire house was smaller than the first floor of this place. Toward the back of the house were more windows that faced out onto a pool and a deck that was the length of the house. Here were the dining room and galley-style kitchen with a counter that separated the rooms. The dining table was set for eight. The house was beautiful, but it felt oddly empty to Teresa. She realized there were no curtains. Just the expanses of windows, then white walls and more glass. Nowhere to hide except their bedrooms or bathrooms. She inwardly recoiled at the thought. Sometimes you've got to be able to shut out the world even if you are alone in the middle of the desert.

Another right toward the front of the house and they arrived at the party. The guests in attendance had their wineglasses aloft.

Evelyn handed her a glass of white wine. "To get you started. Will your friend be drinking?"

"If he wants."

Clayton waved her off. Evelyn shrugged and addressed the other people in the room. "Everyone! This is Teresa. She eats men like air."

With that introduction Teresa wasn't surprised at how they stared at her. She summoned her best smile as she saw them trying to classify her as animal, insect, or unknown. They looked at Clayton, who was again just behind her, a faithful shadow who did not smile at all.

Evelyn, above it all by general disposition or drug enhancement, said, "This is Garrett and James, art dealer and artist. Together a decade now and still just babies."

The men were handsome and fit. Good tans and smiles. One balding; one bald. They were casually dressed in shorts and loafers, their identical button-down striped shirts untucked.

Evelyn pointed at the man next to the piano. "This fine fellow is Harvey, professional boyfriend."

Harvey Worley, Teresa's target tonight, was a tall man with slightly too long hair slicked back. He was dressed in white shirt and trousers and a tweedy suit jacket. He nodded at her and sat down at the piano.

"And of course, this is our hostess, Amy." Amy, the woman refilling wineglasses, gave her a tight smile.

Evelyn sat down on the arm of a chair, wineglass in hand. Her body language said she was done and now she was drinking so someone else could carry the conversation.

"Amy, the house looks great," Garrett said, and everyone resumed their conversations.

Teresa sat on an ottoman, the leather smooth and cool under her body. Clayton leaned against the wall not far from her. Conversations drifted from talk of New York to how they had shut down their east coast homes. Teresa mentioned the dark line of clouds that loomed over the left side of the house. A storm was inevitable. She wondered aloud if the roads would flood. She glanced at Clayton. He nodded slightly.

"I wouldn't worry about it. It's never been a problem for us before," Amy said.

"Didn't you say this is the earliest you've ever come to the Winter House?" asked Harvey.

"Well yes, but it's Las Vegas, the weather is pretty constant here, like Los Angeles."

"It is consistent, but September or October is when the rain comes."

"Do you live here full-time?" Amy asked Teresa.

"Are you from here?" asked James

"No, I'm not, but I've lived here for fifteen years."

"Seems like she would know better than you about October weather, Amy," Harvey said.

"Let's hope the storm is brief then." Amy's smile didn't reach her eyes as she turned her back on Teresa and changed the discussion to how happy she was to have missed the early snowstorm that was burying the New York area. Everyone agreed until Evelyn said she loved new snowfall and how there was nothing quite like New York in the very early morning. "The snow like a blanket of silence and then the cars come and mess up the bed," she mused, more to the bottom of her wineglass than to anyone in the room. There was a murmur of agreement, then there was talk of going home right after Christmas. The New Year's parties were grand after all. Harvey hung back from the group. Teresa moved in during Amy's telling of an epic story of misery involving the help. Teresa tapped him on the shoulder. He turned around and looked down at her. "Well, hello. You're pretty. Let me guess, you're a singer?"

Teresa grimaced. "I can't hold a tune."

"How terrible," Harvey said.

"No, it's good to admit your foibles. "

He lifted his wineglass and they clinked glasses. "To foibles."

"And large financial debts."

The white man went whiter still. "Who are you again?"

"I work for Nick."

He grabbed her elbow in a painful grip and spoke through clenched teeth. "Not here." He downed his drink and made excuses as he cut through the room. Teresa circled the back of the gathered guests and was a step behind him when he opened the nearest closed door and entered the room. It was the office. She closed the door behind her and he was in her face leaning over her.

"What are you doing here?"

Teresa spoke more to his chest, suddenly sure he'd hit her if she made eye contact. "Mr. Worley, you know why I'm here."

He stepped away and paced at the end of the room. She leaned back on the wide wooden desk and waited. "I might be able to give you something. I need to speak to my wife's manager." He glanced over at her.

She kept her voice calm. "Think of me as your grace period. Give me something and I'll keep Mr. Adamson off your back a little longer. Don't, and he'll have someone else come to talk to you."

He glared at her, nodded, and bolted from the room. Teresa counted to ten and then left, heading not back to the room of guests but to the bathroom located deeper in the middle of the house. Once in the bathroom she locked the door and exhaled a long breath. She kept waiting to get better at the confrontations, but it wasn't getting easier. These men, so far it had only been men Adamson had sent her to collect from, were always a little afraid and expressed this fear with anger or sarcasm. She rubbed her arm. She could still feel Worley's fingers on her skin. She counted to ten, then to ten again, until she was calm and ready to pretend she belonged. She managed to take a wrong turn out of the bathroom, heading right instead of left, ending up around the corner from the kitchen. She heard voices pitched low. It was James and Garrett standing at the windows that overlooked the pool.

"I wonder why she's playing at a casino? I heard she turned down July Fourth at the Hollywood Bowl," James said.

"I think she has money problems," Garrett said.

"Didn't everyone lose when the market stumbled, but it's been a year. She must've recouped what she lost."

"All I know is that I read an interview with her in Town & Country where she talked about her investments, and I think she sunk a bundle into the stock market and lost a lot."

"I hadn't considered that."

Thunder clapped and startled everyone. Teresa made a noise. James and Garrett looked around at her. Teresa gave them a half wave and made her way back to the safety of the ottoman. The natural light dimmed dramatically, and the rain began to fall. Table lamps were turned on. Harvey was at Evelyn's side. Amy was making her way around the room, jumping in and out of the conversation and refilling glasses as she went. When she arrived at Teresa and her empty wineglass, she sat down next to her.

"I thought the Adamsons were coming," Amy had popped up without Teresa noticing.

"They couldn't attend but didn't want to leave you with a lopsided dinner so we're here." Teresa smiled at her like they were old friends. Someone hit the keys on the piano and Amy walked away saying, "Is Harvey going to play?" There was a reshuffling of people around the piano.

"Can I talk to you?" Evelyn asked then lead Teresa down the hallway, back to the office again.

"So Adamson sent you? Harvey said I'm to give you this." She held out her wrist with a bracelet on it. Teresa touched the gems.

"I'm here to collect money not jewelry. How do I even know those are real?"

"They're real. The bracelet was a gift from Harvey to Caroline. She lets me wear it sometimes."

"Who is Caroline?"

"Oh, Caro is his wife. She's upstairs resting."

"You're her manager? Who is she that she needs a manager?"

"Caroline St. Clair. The singer?" Her voice carried an incredulous note.

Teresa knew the name. She once sang backup for Elvis, James Brown, and other greats before finally breaking out on her own. Almost as good as Nina Simone, the critics said, which was good enough to win her deals and get her voice on movie soundtracks. Teresa owned a couple of her albums. Her voice was legendary, then she retired after an illness. She went to rest after a major tour and never came back.

"Harvey is her boyfriend."

"Yes. Though we both try to manage her. Will you take the bracelet?"

"Maybe. Does Caroline know about the debt?"

Evelyn leaned against the desk and fumbled with the clasp on the bracelet. "She might know. She might not care about any of it."

Teresa stepped over to her and took over releasing the bracelet from her wrist. "Any of it?"

"Harvey and I," she began but stopped.

"An affair," Teresa said. Evelyn nodded. "Did he tell you about all the money he owes, and is he gambling or is it something else?"

"It's not really my job to ask."

The bracelet, a fiddly thing with a clasp and screw mechanism that made sure it never left a wrist without permission, finally opened and swung free. Teresa closed her hand around it and slipped both hands into her pockets.

"Are you in love with him?"

Evelyn looked surprised. "I've never let myself think it before this moment but yes. For me, at least."

"You might try to pull back on those feelings. He's maybe a little shiftier than you think."

"What do you mean?"

"The money problems. An affair with you. You don't have to squint very hard to see that maybe he's using you to cover things," Teresa said gently.

"No. He wouldn't use me like that." Evelyn stepped away. "You should go out first."

* * *

When the women returned to the living room, everyone was clustered together talking. The conversation broke up and the group opened up to include Evelyn again. Clayton was leaning on the bar. Teresa sidled up to Clayton and whispered, "What did I miss?"

"Not much. They tried to figure out who I am and what our relationship is. Then Garrett mentioned being owed money, which started this huddle."

"I heard something about that too. Where's Harvey?"

"He headed upstairs."

"Will Adamson take jewelry?"

"He has before but he doesn't like to do it. That's what he offered? What did Evelyn want with you?"

Teresa explained all that had happened.

"Let's get out of here then," he said.

A redheaded white woman announced dinner and everyone moved into the dining room.

"We can't be rude. Can't make waves, right?" She turned to follow the group and heard him sigh. He shouldn't complain, she thought. He was getting dinner out of it. Then they'd be gone. There were worst ways to spend an evening.

At the table each place setting had a name placard in front of the plate. Teresa and Clayton sat across from each other at the spots for the Adamsons, After Clayton was James and an assigned spot for Harvey, with their backs to the windows and the pool. Evelyn and Garrett were next to Teresa down the other side with their backs to the wall. Amy sat at the head of the table and at the other end was a spot for Caroline. An awkward silence descended, then came another woman's voice from the kitchen. Evidently Jennifer and Edward were falling behind according to her. Two servers appeared with plates of salad to set before them all. One was a tall willowy black woman and the other was an older white man who looked so weary Teresa thought he should be the one sitting down. They must be Jennifer and Edward.

* * *

Upstairs, Caroline upended Harvey's bag on their bed. She ran her hand along the inside of the bag. She shook out each piece of clothing and then folded it and placed it back in the bag. Once she was sure she had checked every inch of it she tossed the bag back in the closet. She sat down on the end of the bed.

Damn damn damn, she thought. He must've thrown her little bag of pills away when she was asleep. Her hands shook. She pressed them together between her thighs, willing the tremors to settle. The bathroom, she said aloud to the room, and quickly tiptoed from her room down the hallway to Amy's bedroom. She slipped into the en-suite bathroom and opened the medicine cabinet. She was greeted by a line of prescription bottles.

"Oh yes," she breathed. Amy had a bottle full of ten-milligram Benzedrine pills. Caroline wanted to scream in happiness. Instead, she counted out eight pills. . . no ten. Ten was a good number, she told herself. The bottle went back on the shelf and she scampered back down the hallway to her own room where she took two and waited to feel like Caro again. A happy Caro. That's who Harvey found when he opened the bedroom and saw her checking her makeup in the dresser mirror.

"Hello, darling," she said.

"Dinner time."

"Oh good, I'm starving."

"You okay?" He reached out to touch her face. She leaned into him.

"Of course, I am. Now let's go eat." She took his hand and led him from the room.

* * *

Teresa turned to see Harvey and a tall blond woman enter the room. He was attempting to guide her to her seat, his hand on her lower back and his body all but blocking the other diners from her view but she stopped next to Teresa.

"Hello, I'm Caroline."

"Caro, this is Teresa and her friend," Harvey said.

"Nice to meet you," Teresa said extending her hand. The women shook hands.

"Caro before you sit, can I talk to you, please? Just for a moment," Amy said, rising from her seat.

"But dinner?" Caroline glanced at all the faces looking back at her.

"Five minutes, then the main course."

Teresa watched the women leave. She caught Clayton's eye. He shook his head just once as if to say, we aren't here for the drama. Harvey took his seat. Evelyn began stroking Clayton's arm. He turned to her, smiling. Harvey didn't seem to care what Evelyn was doing. He engaged Garrett in conversation and James turned to Teresa inquiring how she liked living in Las Vegas and the desert. From down the hallway Amy and Caroline's angry murmurs drifted to the gathered diners. Then Amy was back. "Edward," she said as she swept into the room, "please bring the wine for everyone now."

The main course was served. There was fish for the non–red meat lovers and filet mignon for the rest. More wine was poured. Then there was only the pleasant clink of silverware on porcelain and murmurs of appreciation to the hostess. Amy smiled as if she had cooked it all herself. Teresa thought of the parties she had thrown for the businessmen Victor occasionally brought home. This was a level of wealth well beyond what she had had.

Caroline didn't join them right away. Nearly everyone was done when she took her seat at the table and apologized for joining late. It was clear she'd been crying: her red eyes were apparent to everyone. Teresa said the steak and roasted potatoes were excellent, possibly the best she could ever remember having. James reminded Garrett of the dinner they'd had at his club in New York. Evelyn joined in. Teresa saw how they were covering for Caroline so she could eat without it seeming like everyone was waiting on her. It was sweet, how they took care of her.

Conversation was a pleasant mix of memories of the last time they were all together— "Do you remember being so drunk you fell in the pool, Caro?"— and art, with James discussing his new show and Garrett regaling the table with the story about one particular art collector who would not shut up about the Cindy Sherman photographs he had missed out on: "He said, 'Everyone has a Sherman and I need one now.' I said, 'I don't know what you want me to do about it. Cindy Sherman has her own dealer and it's not me.' Then he called me an old queen and stomped out."

"They dated in the sixties," James stage-whispered. Several people said "of course" and began laughing while Garrett pretended to be scandalized.

"We didn't date in the sixties. We skulked around," Garrett said.

"Then you met me." James gazed fondly at Garrett.

"And you saw a handsome man with a bit of money."

"You had a great ass."

"Had? Ugh! Well, here's to love." Garrett raised his glass high.

"To love," they all said. Teresa saw Harvey gazing at Caroline like she was the only woman in the room. Caroline was clearly still upset but she joined the toast. Evelyn's glass lifted but her eyes were on Harvey and Caroline.

* * *

Before dessert could be served, Caroline excused herself. She went down the hallway and slammed a door.

"Why don't we have a little break before dessert? I don't think Caroline is feeling very well," Amy said.

Evelyn sighed loudly and stood up, but Harvey said, "Don't, Ev. I'll go." Harvey patted her shoulder as he went by.

The diners left the room in groups of two. Amy and James led the group. Clayton and Evelyn walked arm in arm. Teresa, then Garrett right behind her.

"I hate when they fight. The rest of us always end up suffering," Garrett said to Teresa.

"Does it happen often?"

"No but there's a reason we haven't been together in a while. Come on." He led her to the bar where he poured whiskey into glasses. James was at the stereo. Amy was sitting on the opposite end of the couch from Clayton, who had a lapful of Evelyn and he didn't seem to mind that at all. James put on a Tina Turner album. The sound was kept low and the music acted like a buffer for all of the conversations taking place.

Teresa and Garrett were huddled close on either side of the bar.

He said, "We used to get together twice a year. Once in the Hamptons at Caroline's house, then here in the winter or sometimes Palm Springs. Two years ago, they had a big falling- out, and the next get-together Caroline didn't show up. The next summer, no one got invited to the Hamptons house. Without Caro, Harvey, and Evelyn attending there was room at our place for Amy and her beau of the moment. But it was always less fun without Caro and Ev. Though we could all do with a little less Harv." He chuckled.

"Did he do something?"

"Well, it's always been clear he was just there for the money. Everyone knows he's been cheating on her. No one wanted to tell her though. Once she stopped touring and singing, he did seem to correct that behavior. He really stepped up to take care of her. But maybe that had more to do with the conservatorship."

"Conservatorship?"

"When Caro was at her worst, the drugs and the parties that went on for days, her parents conspired with Evelyn to take control of her finances. So now Caroline gets a monthly allowance and Evelyn pays her bills. Even that didn't stop her. Her parents dying did though. Car accident."

Garrett leaned closer to her over the bar and dropped his voice lower. "They died and she tried to die too." He touched his wrist.

Teresa shook her head. "That is very personal. I don't need to know about that."

"Well, don't bring it up and she'll never know. She never talks about it anyway. That's why she's in long sleeves year-round."

Teresa wanted to move on from this discussion topic. "Do you think she's ready for the stage?"

He shrugged. "Whether she's ready or not, she probably just needs the money. I heard they sold all her jewelry. Everything she wears now is costume."

"Everything?"

Garrett nodded. "High-quality fakes. Would fool most everyone except those with an eye for it." Teresa drank her whiskey down and silently fumed. Harvey was trying to send her off with fake jewels. She'd never live it down if she brought back fakes. What if Adamson dropped her and demanded full payment? She'd never get her house back.

James returned to his partner's side, kissed his cheek, and swung an arm across his shoulders. "So what've you two been whispering about?"

"Nothing good yet," Garrett said and winked at Teresa.

"Is he trying to get you to buy a painting? He can be so pushy when he wants to be."

"Not at all."

"I'm not pushy. I'm a salesman."

"I know, baby. Business will pick up." James kissed him on the cheek. "Do you know what they're fighting about?" James asked.

"Today? What's worth fighting about between old friends? Money or men. Or both." Garrett took a sip of his drink.

"Always fraught territory," Teresa agreed.

"Exactly. The second I heard that Amy had reached out to Caro and she was coming, my bags were packed. I had hoped we wouldn't see a repeat of the drama but here we are."

Teresa looked over to where Amy sat alone. She seemed to have given up being the attentive hostess. Evelyn giggled loudly and gave Clayton's broad chest a pat.

"They need me. Harvey will never be able to talk her down without me." Evelyn winked at Teresa. "Don't let anyone else throw a tantrum until I get back." Then she too disappeared down the hallway.

"Amy, do you want a drink?" Garrett called to her.

"I'll take it to her," Teresa said.

She crossed the room to the couch where Amy sat. "Thank you for having me," Teresa said as she handed Amy the drink. "Are you okay?"

Amy took a moment to sip from the glass. "When are you leaving?

You've had enough time to do what you need to do here. I didn't promise Adamson access to my friends all night." She seemed very upset, but Teresa didn't think it had anything to do with her.

Before Teresa could respond, Garrett sat on the arm of the couch. "What did you say to Caroline to make her so upset?"

"Why does everyone assume it's me who did something wrong? You all coddle her too much. She isn't famous anymore. She's a has-been. She's playing Vegas, for God's sake." Amy stomped out of the living room and upstairs, presumably to her bedroom.

A few minutes had passed, then they all heard a knock on a door and Evelyn's voice floated down to the hallway to them. "Caro, honey. You okay?" In the silence between songs a door opened and closed.

Teresa sat down next to Clayton. He was slightly disheveled from Evelyn's fingers in his hair. She'd undone a couple of buttons on his shirt too. Teresa could see chest hair peeking out.

"I see you've made a friend," she said.

"I see you haven't," he grumbled.

Teresa gestured at him. "You might want to fix your hair." He ran his fingers through his hair and it all fell back into place. He looked at her for confirmation. She nodded but then pointed at her chest and he looked down at his and swore under his breath while doing up the buttons and fixing his tie.

Minutes later, Harvey walked into the room, then stopped midstride. Everyone was looking at him. "Caro's fine. No need to worry."

"Who's worried? Come have a drink," Garrett said.

Edward appeared on the other side of the room and announced dessert was ready. The group all filed into the dining room once again. Teresa and Clayton trailing behind.

"The jewelry is fake," Teresa said. She relayed her conversation with Garrett. "Guess it's good we didn't leave straight away."

Clayton swore softly. "We should go now. Clearly he doesn't have anything."

"Adamson is going to be angry."

He shrugged. "He will be but not with you."

Teresa shook her head. Clayton stood in front of her blocking the others' view of her. "Hey, it's all right."

"I just need the money," she whispered.

"There will be other collections."

"Not this big. I can't keep doing this job. I can't keep living with my mother." She blinked back tears.

"This won't be forever. He likes you. You have time."

"Sir, ma'am? Would you take your seats?" Edward's wrinkled face was unsmiling. Teresa got the distinct impression he was very tired of waiting on people. He led them to their seats. Three chairs sat empty.

Down the hallway, Caroline or Evelyn said, "I'm going to have a cigarette outside," but Teresa couldn't tell which woman said it. Then Caroline joined everyone at the table, bypassing her seat to sit next to Clayton. She took a big swig of someone else's wine.

"Caro, your sleeves," Garrett said.

Teresa saw her shirtsleeve was rolled up, revealing thin white lines running down her forearm.

"Forgive me. I didn't mean to stare."

Caroline shrugged. "I stare sometimes too. Part of me can't believe I tried it. Another part of me is terrified I'll do it again."

"You won't. You're past that part now," Harvey said from farther down that table.

"Will the other guests be joining us?" Jennifer asked. Edward stood just behind her in the doorway. Teresa wondered where the redheaded server had gone. Thunder sounded directly overhead. Everyone was startled, and then the lights went out.

"No one panic. It's not that dark." Clayton said and he was right. Everyone's eyes adjusted. The sky outside was dark gray.

"Are there any candles?" Teresa said. She pushed her chair back and went into the kitchen with the staff.

"There should be some in a lower cabinet," Garrett said. The stove was gas and candles were lit quickly from a burner. Simple silver candleholders were found, and the table was quickly transformed by candlelight.

"I better go find Evelyn. She probably looks like a drowned rat by now," Harvey said. He took one of the candles and went down the hall.

Minutes ticked by. Lightning lit up the dark skies.

James said, "Has anyone checked on Amy?"

"I'll go," Teresa said.

On the upstairs landing Teresa saw several closed doors but she could clearly hear a voice coming from the door nearest to her. Teresa pushed open the door and saw Amy in the meager light coming through her bedroom window with the phone to her ear.

Teresa said sorry and began to close the door but Amy told her to come in and gestured at the corner of the bed. Teresa sat and within a minute Amy said good-bye and hung up the phone.

"Evidently, we aren't the only ones in the dark. I have friends further east. The roads are impassable right now. Everyone is stranded. I guess you'll be staying longer."

Teresa stood. "I'm sorry you can't kick me out quite yet. Dessert is being served."

Downstairs, someone screamed. The women rushed from the bedroom and down the stairs. Everyone crowded the hallway between the kitchen and bathroom. Clayton was in front of them all, telling them to get back, to give her some room. Amy pressed forward through the throng of people, Teresa right behind her, until they emerged to see the circle of light on the floor and bloody footprints that led to the office. Jennifer was crying, huddled into Edward's arms just outside the door. He was patting her back, whispering softly to her. Clayton held the flashlight. "It's Evelyn," he said to her. A bleak finality in his tone. Caroline screamed, then fainted.

* * *

Teresa was the one holding the flashlight now. She was in the bathroom because she wasn't ready to see Evelyn yet. The bloody footsteps had led from this room to the study. Here was a large amount of blood smeared across the tile floor and the broken pieces of a milk glass bowl. A pretty thing that had shattered when it was knocked off the shelf. Small pieces of it crunched under her heels and three large, curved pieces lay on the floor splattered with blood and on a couple pieces she saw a waxy residue. Amy must have used it to burn candles in the bathroom. Eyeing them all, she surmised a piece was still missing. Teresa wondered if the record playing had hidden the noise of it breaking; could it have masked the sound of Evelyn's murder?

Teresa went to the study and played the flashlight's beam up Evelyn's prone body. Teresa had seen a dead body before but never like this. Never outside of a coffin. The dead had always been cleaned up and made to look like the person was only sleeping, only moments away from waking up and going on with their life. Evelyn was clearly not sleeping. The beam of the flashlight illuminated her bloody feet. Then her yellow sundress, drenched in dark blood. Teresa moved around the body and played the light over her head. The long blond hair, free of blood, was half covering Evelyn's face. Her blue eye gazed unseeing up at the flashlight's beam through the strands of hair.

Teresa went to her knees just outside the pool of blood. She set the flashlight down, shining on the body's torso. With both hands she heaved up, lifting one side of the torso from the floor. The flashlight illuminated the white, blood-slicked glass sticking out of the body. There was so much blood. Teresa suddenly felt lightheaded and fell back against the desk. The body rocked back to the floor. She tilted her face toward the ceiling and counted her breaths to keep panic from setting in.

She focused again and there was Clayton filling up the doorway, his arms folded over his chest. She slowly rose from the floor and continued to look. A candle still in its holder was snuffed out in the blood. It seemed Jennifer had walked into the room and slipped in the blood before seeing the body. The evidence was clear where her first step on the hardwood floor of the room met the pool of blood then slipped right as her balance teetered. She stepped backward but it was too late to keep from falling. Then realizing what she had slipped in, Jennifer screamed, bringing them into the hallway. It was too dark to see who had been missing, or who they hadn't noticed had been gone the entire time.

"How's Caroline and Jennifer?" she asked Clayton.

"Caroline is pacing and crying. Jennifer is getting drunk with everyone else," he said.

"I'm going to need a drink too."

"I'll buy you a drink at the hotel. We need to leave now." His voice had that sharpness he used when he wanted her to listen. Usually, it was to get her out of the room so he could brutally beat a man. Clayton was her driver, but mainly he was her muscle. He kept her safe.

"Road is washed out," she said.

"Says who?"

"Amy. She called her neighbors down the road when the power went out. We're stuck."

"I can get us through."

Teresa sighed. "We have to find out who killed Evelyn,"

"Look T, I know you hate to fail but there is a dead body. We are the ones who don't belong here. Any minute those people are going to remember that."

"And what's to stop them from blaming us when we leave? No. We need to figure out who did it."

"Adamson will keep the cops off us. Or is this about the money still?"

Teresa sighed. "Yes it's about money. Everything is about money. My house was being foreclosed on so I borrowed money, then that guy sold my debt to Adamson. The only way to keep my house is to work off this debt. So now I do this job, with you, and if I finish this job, I get five thousand dollars and that much comes off what I owe him."

"There'll be other opportunities."

"You don't understand. I am not supposed to be here. This isn't my world. My world is in that house. So you don't have to help me, but don't you get in my way either."

Teresa shoved the flashlight into his hand and pushed past him. Clayton watched her go. The stiffness in her back. The way her hair bounced with each step. Only five feet three inches tall and she could probably tear the house down with her bare hands. He shook his head and went to back her up.

"What's your plan?"

"For now, be all menacing and help me keep them here and under control." He looked at her and she smiled. "I know it's a stretch but try your best."

Clayton walked out into the living room, clapped his hands, and the overlapping conversations ended. "We are all stuck here. Once the storm passes and it's safe maybe we can all go."

"We need to leave now," Garrett said. He had James's hand gripped tightly in his own.

"The police will want to talk to you. To all of us," Amy said. Her voice had a panicky edge to it.

"Is that strictly necessary?" Garrett asked. He was frowning.

"Evelyn is dead," James said. He yanked his hand away from Garrett and went to make himself another drink.

"We should call them." Amy sat down with a drink.

"If you try to leave now, you'll end up upside down in a ditch and drowning in flood waters," Clayton said. Everyone looked at him. Then the group began to shout at each other about what they should do.

Quietly Teresa told Clayton she was going to ask the staff some questions and maybe look around. Before she went to the kitchen, she laid a hand on James's back. He whipped around, clearly startled.

"You nearly made me spill my drink." He gulped some of it and then leaned back against the bar.

"I can't imagine what you must be feeling." Teresa rubbed his arm.

"It's just so awful," he said.

"When did you see Evelyn last?"

"Why are you asking me? I didn't kill her."

"I'm asking everyone. Take a breath."

"I don't know." James threw his hands up. "She went to help Harvey with Caroline."

"You don't think Harvey did this, do you?" Garrett said from behind her. He moved next to his partner.

"I'm only asking questions."

"But Harvey?" Garrett whispered.

"He was cheating with her. Maybe it ended?" James whispered right back. The men continued whispering, rehashing the things that Garrett had told her earlier. Teresa left them and continued toward the back of the house. She paused at the hallway that led to the bedrooms and bathrooms and the office. The busy, busy office. Where she had met with both Harvey and Evelyn.

* * *

In the kitchen, the staff sat at the breakfast bar. Teresa smiled at them. "It's good to meet you all. You were doing a fantastic job tonight. Do you mind if I ask you some questions? Where is the woman with the red hair?"

Edward said, "That's Rebecca. She said she wasn't feeling well. I think she went to lie down in the back of one of the vans."

"I'm sorry, what's your name and did you believe her?"

The chef, who was short and had her hair braided then twisted into a bun on top of her head, said her name was Tanya. "I didn't believe her but we were behind. If she didn't want to work, then she was just in our way."

"How long have you worked with her?"

"A year or so. She's a cocktail waitress at the Frontier. That's where we met. We pick up catering shifts a couple times a month," Jennifer said.

"Did she seem all right today? No problem doing her job?"

"She was fine. Excited to see Caroline St. Clair," Jennifer said.

"She knew who was going to be at the dinner tonight?"

"I did too. It's why they brought me in and paid me double to cook tonight," Tanya said.

"Double?" the servers said in unison. The chef just shrugged.

"You two knew also?"

"It was the way they got us all to work tonight. The promise of good tips," Edward said.

* * *

Teresa found Clayton watching over the group in the living room. She touched his arm and he followed her to the sliding glass door at the end of the room and together they stepped out onto the pool deck. The rain pelted the awning covering the patio. Teresa shivered. Clayton took off his suit jacket and draped it across her shoulders.

"They knew Caroline was going to be here and that red-haired server, Rebecca, is missing. They think she's lying down in the back of their van."

"You think maybe one of them did it? That Rebecca did it?"

"I don't know but if she's not in one of the vans then she definitely looks guilty. Did you find out anything?"

"They're pretty tightlipped. The only talking going on is 'Hand me that bottle of liquor.'"

"Understandable. Power's off. Their friend and loved one is dead.

And one of us did it," she said. He looked down at her, but she was staring at the pool. Focused. Maybe thinking about her house.

"Well, I didn't do it."

"I believe you. Will you check on Rebecca?"

"Sure. It's only a little rain."

"I'll keep your jacket dry."

He stepped out into the rain and jogged down to the side of the house and out of sight.

Back inside she hung his jacket on the back of a dining room chair to dry. Looking at it something occurred to her. She went to the living room to make sure she was right. There was Harvey sans jacket. Had he given it to Evelyn when she'd gone to have a cigarette? Teresa went down the hallway beyond the hall bathroom and the study and found a laundry room with a door to the outside. The tweed jacket was on a hanger, slightly damp at the shoulders. She brought the fabric to her nose but smelled nothing but cologne and wet wool. She tried the door. It was unlocked. She stepped out onto pavers and to her right was a gravel drive and a white van with the logo for Black Tie Catering on its side. The rain was subsiding now. She ran through it to the back of the van.

There, Clayton was inspecting the red-haired server's scalp as she sat in the back of the van under the interior roof light. The woman's face looked red and swollen.

"What happened?" Teresa caught her breath.

"Harvey happened," Clayton all but growled. Rebecca refused to come back into the house. Teresa ran inside and quietly asked Jennifer and Edward out to sit with her and they obliged.

* * *

Teresa stood before the group of old friends with Clayton at her back and said, "Someone attacked Rebecca."

"Who's Rebecca?" James asked.

"One of the servers." The power returned just then. The lights winked back on and Tina Turner's "Proud Mary" was turned into an awful dirge as the stereo slowly spun itself back up to speed. Teresa was already moving to turn it off when Harvey beat her to it, turning it off with a vicious twist of the knob. "Sorry. I just couldn't take it." Tears stood in his eyes.

"I understand. You liked her," Teresa said.

"I did. She was good fun."

"And she covered for you."

He glanced at the others, then said, "I didn't need cover."

"So Caroline knew about you and Evelyn?"

Harvey marched over and pulled Caroline up from the couch to hold her at his side. "I love Caroline. Everything else was…"

"And it's because you love Caroline that you attacked the server?"

"I didn't," Harvey protested.

Clayton stepped around Teresa and grabbed Harvey by his shirt front. "I saw what you did to that woman. You're saying she's lying?" Clayton shook him. Teresa took a step forward, not to stop him but see Harvey's face and then Caroline's. She was looking at her feet.

"Let me go." Harvey squirmed in the big man's grip.

"Teresa, he killed Evelyn," Clayton said.

Harvey went wide-eyed. "Okay, I did hurt the girl. She was selling Caro drugs. I just wanted to keep her safe. But I wouldn't have hurt Evelyn like that. Never."

"Bullshit," Clayton pulled back his fist. Garrett and James each grabbed an arm and pulled him away. Harvey sank to the floor like a spineless doll. Amy rushed to his side.

"When I came back inside Caro was in the hallway. She knows I didn't do it. Didn't you see me?" Harvey was pleading now.

"I…I don't remember," Caroline said backing away.

"You were right there in the hallway." Harvey looked confused.

"Harv?" Garrett said. Clayton yanked himself free of their grip. Amy slid away from Harvey. Teresa saw deep confusion on his face and betrayal.

"You were in the hallway?" Teresa turned to look at Caroline.

"I don't think so," she said. "Harvey, did you kill her?"

"You know I didn't," Harvey said. He was pleading with her.

"She was there for me all of these years. Now she's gone. I won't have anyone now."

"That's not true. We're your friends," Garrett said.

"You all just want things from me. My fame at your parties."

"Oh please," Amy muttered.

Caroline's gaze locked onto her. "And my money."

"No, Caro. I gave Harvey a loan to keep you afloat. It was only after Black Monday I asked for payments on that loan. It's not my fault you're broke and now you have to play Vegas. You're a lounge act. A has-been," Amy said.

"Liar!" Caroline rushed across the living room and slapped her. Amy stumbled backwards. Clayton went immediately between the two women and pushed them apart.

Teresa pulled Caroline down into one of the leather chairs. "Did you argue with Evelyn? What happened in the bathroom?"

"Nothing. I was upset with Amy. That's it."

"Harvey, what were you two talking about?" Clayton asked. He was looming over the man on the floor.

"Caro wanted to know if I was jealous of the attention Evelyn was giving you. I told her Evelyn was nothing to me. A moment later there was the knock at the door. I left and Evelyn went in. Then I went outside to confront that server. She said she'd go to the tabloids and tell them that Caroline St. Clair was an addict. Things got out of hand. I...I got out of hand. I'm sorry."

"Stop talking, Harvey," Caroline said.

"What did Evelyn say to you in the bathroom?" Teresa blocked her view of Harvey. Caroline looked up at her, then she was on her feet.

"She was going to leave me. She said that if I wanted to spend all of my money on drugs and never make another album that was my choice, but she wouldn't stay to watch it happen. She said I was cruel. That Harvey and I had manipulated her to get more money." Caroline's hands twisted against each other. Her gaze flitted from face to face.

"Evelyn never went outside to have that cigarette, did she? That was you pretending to be her." Teresa's voice was gentle now.

"No." Caroline paced back and forth.

"How did she die?"

"I didn't mean to do it. We argued and that bowl broke. I was picking up the pieces and she tried to leave. Before I realized what I'd done she was on the floor and that piece of bowl was sticking out of her. She grabbed me and I shoved her away. She didn't move anymore. I thought she was dead."

Teresa slowly reached for her left arm and unrolled the sleeve, covering up the scar and revealing a wrinkled but clean blue sleeve. Teresa did the same for the other arm. Caroline began to shake as the sleeve unrolled. With every fold undone she shook more until the smear of dark red blood appeared and she burst into tears.

"Oh, Caro," Amy said.

"None of you took care of me. The one person who did was going to leave. What was I supposed to do?"

"Honey, we all took care of you. We gave you money. All the money you needed," Garrett said.

"No, you gave Harvey money and he gambled it away. Didn't you, Harvey? There wasn't enough for me."

Harvey went to her and embraced her. "I took care of you or I tried anyway." She pushed him away and collapsed into the leather chair. He sat in the other chair and put his head in his hands. All of the friends moved to surround them. To offer what little comfort could be had. Teresa called the police.

It was agreed that everyone would explain to the police when they arrived exactly what happened but not who Teresa and Clayton were. Amy did most of the talking. Fortunately, Caroline admitted to what she'd done without much prompting by the officers. It was nearly midnight by the time Teresa and Clayton drove down the long drive and back into the city.

Into the quiet of the night, the wind rushing past the open windows, Clayton said, "I'm sorry you didn't get the money. I know you were counting on it."

She reached out across the seat and patted his arm. "I don't think I was supposed to."

Clayton frowned. "Why do you say that?"

She shrugged. "I don't know. It's just that everyone there needed money. Garrett isn't selling much art these days. We know Amy needed the loan paid back." Teresa replayed the events of the night. Teresa overhearing the conversation about Caroline being broke. Amy being irritated that she was there but not insisting they leave. Evelyn flirting with Clayton, maybe to keep him busy while Garrett told Teresa stories about Caroline and the friends group? "What if the wrong person died tonight? Maybe Nick Adamson knew something was up." Teresa looked at him. He said nothing. "Would Nick Adamson send us in as his sacrificial proxies?"

"Don't get yourself worked up about it. It went sideways tonight. It happens. There will be other collections." He turned on the radio and a pop song played a bouncy tune about love.

It was a moonless night and the desert under the night sky was formidable, but the air was clean and cool and they drove with the windows down all the way back home.

The Intruder
By Martin Edwards

Peering through the trees, Gough watched his wife ring another man's doorbell. The darkness was relieved by a crescent moon and although Laura was fifty yards away, he didn't need his field glasses to be sure of her identity as she approached the house. That floral-patterned headscarf didn't quite hide her long blond hair; besides, he'd know the sway of her hips anywhere. His night vision was excellent, a huge asset in his job. Now it was confirming his worst fears.

The front door opened to reveal a man with dark floppy hair. Yes, that was Jake Vaughan, no question. Peter had never met the man, but he'd looked him up in old newspapers in the Central Library and seen plenty of photographs.

The couple embraced and then Vaughan whispered something which caused Laura to squeal with laughter.

'You are awful!'

Her voice carried through the evening air. When she pulled off the headscarf, her hair rippled in the autumnal breeze. Jake Vaughan laughed too. Within moments they'd abandoned any attempt at discretion. Not that they were taking much of a risk. This was the far end of Mereside Lane, where the track, unmade and pot-holed, petered out close to the brook. During daylight hours you saw a few dog walkers, but at this time there was never anybody around. Nobody except the local park ranger, who was now grinding his teeth so hard that it was a miracle they didn't break.

The couple went inside. Vaughan banged the door shut behind them. Peter Gough swore savagely and an unseen owl hooted in reproach.

A light behind the lined curtains of a ground floor room was suddenly extinguished. Moments later, an upstairs window was illuminated. They'd wasted no time in heading for the bedroom.

A shiny burglar alarm was fixed just below the eaves of the house. Its red light winked at Gough, as if mocking his impotent fury.

Gough's temples thudded. If he hadn't had such a sickening emptiness in his stomach, he'd surely have thrown up.

He blundered back through Mere Woods. Reaching his hut, he took a swig of brandy from his flask. Until this evening he'd hoped against hope, but in his heart he'd already realised that he'd lost her. All the signs were there. A smarter man would have spotted them sooner, he supposed. But love is blind, and he still loved Laura as much as on the day they'd first met, when she'd brought a pack of young Cub Scouts to do some pond-dipping at the Mere with the local ranger.

He switched on his little transistor radio. It was tuned to the local station and Christopher Cross was singing 'Arthur's Theme'. Gough remembered taking Laura to see the film earlier in the year. She was a huge fan of Dudley Moore and he liked Liza Minnelli, but they hadn't been to the cinema since then. At one time, they went to the Regal every other week, but they'd simply got out of the habit. He worked long hours in all weathers and she was so busy with a hundred and one activities.

His heart sank as the disc jockey introduced 'Your True Troubadour', describing it as 'the greatest hit from our very own pop star'. Actually, Gough knew it was Jake Vaughan's *only* song ever to reach the charts. A snatch of the mawkish chorus – 'I want you so much/I want your touch' – was more than Gough could bear. He turned the dial with such fury that it broke.

A pity, but what did a cheap broken radio matter, compared to a broken marriage, a broken heart?

Gough closed his eyes and counted to ten. He mustn't give up on Laura. He wouldn't, couldn't do it. He'd fight to the end.

Nobody had given Britain much of a chance a few months ago, he reminded himself. Not when Argentina invaded the Falklands. The islands were eight thousand miles away from here. And yet we'd done it, we'd sailed out there and taken back what was rightfully ours. General Galtieri was vanquished and everyone said his complete downfall was only a question of time.

How much easier to rescue one woman from the clutches of a single rapacious has-been.

* * *

By the time Laura got back to the cottage, Gough had sunk into the depths of his favourite armchair, leafing through *Life on Earth*. The telly was on in the background. *Newsnight*, with Peter Snow. He was paying no attention to either of them.

'Good meeting?' he asked.

She sighed. 'Not bad. It did drag on a bit.'

He glanced at the clock. 'You're telling me.'

'We're planning activities for the run-up to Christmas. There's so much going on at this time of year.'

'Uh-huh.' She looked tired but happy, and he knew exactly why. 'I put the dustbin out.'

'I'll do the ironing tomorrow.'

Ah, those domestic rituals, the fabric of married life. The bin, the ironing, paying the milkman. Was it so deadly dull that the only escape was with another man?

As if by way of answer, she gave an extravagant yawn. 'That's it, I'd better get off to bed before I fall asleep right here. Night, night.'

She dropped a kiss on his head and was gone before he could protest or suggest a nightcap. He remained where he was for another half hour, wondering where he'd gone wrong. He found himself humming that tune from *Arthur*. Catchy melody, and its message struck a chord. *Once in your life you will find her...*

After Laura agreed to marry him, he had a stupid grin stuck on his face for weeks. Thirty-four and set in his ways, he simply couldn't believe his sheer good fortune. She was ten years younger, a happy-go-lucky soul blessed with beauty and a caring nature.

Later he'd found out that Laura was on the rebound when she accepted his proposal. She'd fallen head over heels for some corporal in the army, but on a tour of duty in Ireland he'd met some colleen, got her pregnant, and decided to marry her. Gough couldn't imagine how anyone could possibly dump someone as lovely as Laura, but for him it was a gift.

Besides working as a mobile hairdresser, she helped out in the local school. She adored kids and it was a bitter blow for her when the doctors said she'd never be able to have a child of her own. She suffered from occasional migraines and for a while she sank into a depression, though Gough did his best to urge her to snap out of it.

They'd discussed adoption, but Gough wasn't keen. He wouldn't have minded becoming a father, but he was happy enough for it to be just the two of them. He had everything he wanted and for a while he believed Laura was equally content. She admired his love of the natural world. The birds and animals which lived around the Mere and in the woodland made his work such a joy. Truth was, he preferred the company of those creatures to most of his fellow human beings. In company, he found himself tongue-tied, but Laura was so chatty and gregarious, it was inevitable that she'd find her own amusements. She was forever getting involved with community groups, whether it was the Cubs and Scouts or volunteering to help out with Meals on Wheels. His wife was kind and considerate and he worshipped her for it.

When had he first realised that something wasn't right? Weeks ago. At first he'd put it down to the time of the month or the strange way that women behaved sometimes. He was a simple soul; he didn't pretend to understand the way their minds worked.

She'd begun to evade his attentions in bed and he'd also noticed a hint of distance when they were together in the evenings. They didn't have a blazing row. Hardly ever was a cross word spoken, except when he forgot to take off his boots at the door and left a trail of muddy footprints all over the carpet. Somehow she just seemed less interested in him and his doings. Dreamy. In a world of her own. At first he found this quietness restful, until it dawned on him that when a talkative woman falls silent, it's seldom a good sign.

He brooded over the change in her, trying to figure out what he'd done wrong, hoping to pinpoint the time when it began. In his line of work, you needed to be meticulous and he did have a good eye for detail. He was sure he hadn't missed a significant birthday or anniversary, but he noticed that she was dressing more smartly, wearing lipstick and other cosmetics when she went out. When he mentioned it, she was a picture of innocence.

'You want me to look nice, don't you?'

A worm of suspicion nibbled away at his innards. What was going on - surely she wasn't seeing someone else? The instant the question crossed his mind, he banished it. Laura was loyal and trustworthy. She'd never look at anyone else.

But with every day that passed, he became more convinced that she was up to something. She worked irregular hours and both of them came and went as they pleased. This gave her every opportunity to keep things from him. Twice he caught her out in a lie about her whereabouts, after making it his business to bump into friends of hers, accidentally-on-purpose. Usually his distaste for small talk caused him to steer clear, but they were perfectly happy to chat. Through artful, seemingly casual enquiries, he managed to confirm that Laura had not been with them when she'd claimed to be.

He wanted to give her the benefit of the doubt. What if she was cooking up some delightful surprise for him and keeping it a secret? What if she had a health problem that she didn't want to worry him about, and was seeking medical advice on the quiet? But he told himself not to be naïve. There's none so blind as those who will not see. Her repeated deceits were deliberate and it was stupid to pretend that the obvious explanation was untrue.

The worm of suspicion grew within him, until it became like that monster in *Alien*, ready to burst out. He racked his brains, desperate to identify possible rivals. Surely it wasn't the village librarian, whose camp manner amused her so much? Nor the head teacher at the local school, a bald fellow in his fifties with a short temper?

He was baffled until he recalled an occasion she'd mentioned a while back. There had been a spate of burglaries in the county and she'd always worried about security. Not that they had much to steal. Shortly after they'd moved into the cottage, she'd asked the local crime prevention officer to come round. On his advice, they'd had new locks fitted to all the doors and windows.

Someone told her about a handyman called Essie who lived in the town and was willing to supply and fit dummy alarm boxes to people's houses. They didn't cost much and they were supposed to deter opportunistic villains. Gough told her that no burglar would bother with them; their poky cottage would offer thin pickings. But she'd got a bee in her bonnet. Since they couldn't afford a high quality system, a dummy box on their front wall would give her peace of mind. In the end, Gough let her have her way, and when she'd called on the handyman, she'd bumped into someone she recognised.

'I could hardly believe my eyes! I mean, you'll never guess!'

He shrugged. Gossip didn't interest him.

Her eyes shone. 'Jake Vaughan! Isn't it incredible?'

The name meant nothing to him.

'Don't gawp like that! Surely you remember? The singer! He got to number seven in the Top Ten, back in 1969!'

Gough had never paid much attention to the charts. The sounds he loved came from the natural world. Birdsong in the morning, the skitterings of unseen creatures in the brambles and long grass, the soft swish made by the swans cruising around the Mere. Laura, on the other hand, was a devotee. Her crushes had included Paul McCartney, Cat Stevens, Uncle Tom Jones and all.

Jake Vaughan, she explained, had just bought a big house in the village, at the far end of Mereside Lane. He'd come up from London after splitting with his girlfriend. Now he was performing on the northern club circuit as well as guesting on cruise ships from time to time. Gough was rash enough to say it sounded like the man's career was washed-up.

The colour rose in Laura's cheeks. 'At least he's made something of his life! And he's seen the world!'

She stormed out of the room without another word. Gough went for a walk in the woods and when he got home, no further mention was made of Jake Vaughan.

In hindsight, the change within Laura dated from that conversation. He'd tried to tell himself not to be a jealous fool. There was no chance she'd ever get mixed up with some superannuated pop star. He was letting his imagination run riot. Laura was a thoroughly decent woman, and the truth was she was far too good for him.

While researching Jake Vaughan, he'd discovered that the man was a regular Casanova, with two marriages and innumerable relationships under his belt. In his hey-day he'd been a gossip columnist's dream. Now his career had waned and Gough enjoyed a dismissive newspaper reference to him as a 'one-hit wonder'. He was good-looking in a raffish way, lean and hook-nosed, with that trademark floppy hair. Gough could imagine Laura finding him irresistibly attractive. She was easily impressed. A seasoned philanderer with a gift of the gab would find her easy prey.

This evening, when she announced she was going out to a specially convened Women's Institute meeting, her excitement was palpable. Gough could tell that she was star-struck. You didn't get all dolled up for an evening of jam and 'Jerusalem'. That was why he'd decided to keep watch on Mereside House. The scene he'd witnessed proved he was right.

He'd allowed himself to hope that she might be paying a professional visit. She was a women's hairdresser, not unisex, but a long-haired pop star might have unusual tastes. Even so, you didn't greet your hairdresser like that and then take her upstairs.

Was there an innocent explanation for that sickening embrace? Might she be carrying out some kind of good works on behalf of the community that involved the singer? Suppose they were simply Just Good Friends…

No, no, he was clutching at straws. Laura was having an affair with Jake Vaughan and he needed to do something about it. He couldn't bear the prospect of losing her – far better to lose his own life. But the reality of the situation was inescapable. How could a simple ranger compete with a sexy celebrity, the man who had taken a banal ditty to number seven in the hit parade?

Again he cast his mind back to the Task Force, sailing to the other end of the world to save the Falklands from the invaders against all odds. If you had the right attitude of mind, you could accomplish anything.

* * *

Across the borough, the Corporation employed half a dozen rangers, but Gough had always been based at Mereside. Because he'd been born within a couple of miles of the Mere, he knew the area like the back of his hand. He was diligent and reliable and his supervisor was content to leave him to his own devices; he passed on the occasional diktat from Corporation House but turned a blind eye if Gough chose not to follow instructions to the letter. The Mere and its surrounds was a beauty spot and outsiders who came to visit, as well as local dog-walkers and ramblers, were agreed that Ranger Gough was a treasure.

He loved his job. No two days were ever the same. Rangers needed to have organisational ability and a broad spread of skills, everything from habitat management to talking to parties of school children and educating them in the arts of pond-dipping and basket weaving. He worked long hours and when darkness fell and everyone went home, he had Mere Woods to himself. His own private kingdom.

Every day he had to inspect his patch for any litter and hazards and make sure they were removed. In spring and summer he spent a lot of time cutting grass as well as monitoring and recording the wild life. Now it was autumn, it was time to thin out the woodland. He had his hands full, but that was his choice. Who wanted an assistant, some wet-behind-the-ears kid, making a nuisance of himself? Far better to keep himself to himself. And do it his way, like Old Blue Eyes. Now there was a *real* singer.

As he walked through the trees on his daily patrol, he mulled over Laura's betrayal. He couldn't find it in his heart to blame her. Yes, she'd fallen into temptation, but it was Jake Vaughan's fault. If Vaughan had never existed, their marriage would still be as perfect as ever.

By the time he reached the reed-fringed edge of the Mere, his mind was made up.

There was nothing he could do to persuade Laura to see sense. She was besotted with Vaughan, no question. Whatever Gough said, she'd take her lover's part. He might easily provoke her into leaving him for good. Impossible to take that risk.

No, as someone once said: There is No Alternative.

Jake Vaughan must be taken out of the picture permanently. And that meant he had to die.

* * *

It is one thing to decide to kill someone, quite another to conceive an effective plan of action which can be executed with minimum risk of failure and maximum likelihood of success. The act of murder itself didn't hold any particular terrors for Gough. In the course of his work, he'd gained ample experience of putting creatures out of their misery. A cygnet with a broken neck, a squirrel ripped to pieces by a cat. The difference was, those dead animals were innocent. Jake Vaughan had brought his fate upon himself. He should have kept his filthy hands off Laura. Really, Gough was ridding the world of a pest. It was no worse than trapping a badger or digging a sett. There was nothing soft about Mother Nature.

The challenge was to devise a plan to remove Vaughan without getting caught. He was weighing up the possibilities over breakfast when Laura announced that she'd changed her mind about giving a few hours to the Girl Guides. There was a meeting tonight and although she'd previously said she had too much on her plate, she was going to show her face after all. Her manner was casual, but in trying to make it sound like a throwaway remark, he felt she'd given the game away. Another assignation with her lover was on the cards, he was convinced of it.

In the hut that afternoon, he caught a snatch of the local news. There had been another burglary, twenty-five miles away. The burglars had broken into a mansion and coshed the owner. They'd made away with 'a large quantity of valuables', leaving their victim in intensive care.

How about faking a burglary at Mereside House and using that as a cover to murder Vaughan? The criminals were becoming more violent and the police obviously didn't have a clue about how to stop them.

It wouldn't be easy. One of the potential snags was that shiny burglar alarm. Gough remembered Mereside House coming on to the market. A big detached with large grounds in a desirable rural spot, it carried a hefty price tag despite being badly in need of renovation. Vaughan must have a few bob. He'd probably acquired plenty of valuables over the years. No dummy alarm for him. He wanted to protect his property, so he'd opted for the real thing. Damn him.

And then there was the question of timing. How to be sure that Laura was safely out of the way when he killed Vaughan?

Of course, you couldn't eliminate every risk, but Gough was uneasily aware that he'd only have one chance to get it right. He wrestled with the problem throughout the day and hadn't come to any firm conclusion before returning to the cottage for his tea.

Laura had popped into The Codfather on her way home and she presented him with a large plate of battered cod and chips.

'I'm in a bit of a rush,' she explained. 'Busy evening.'

Gough grunted. She wasn't quite able to suppress her excitement, he thought. She had hardly anything to eat herself before rushing upstairs to get ready. When she came down again, she looked quite beautiful.

'Is that a new frock?' he asked.

She raised her eyebrows. He seldom commented on what she wore. In fact, he hardly ever noticed it.

'Yes, as it happens. I...treated myself. I've been so busy lately, I felt I deserved a pick-me-up.'

Gough knew nothing about women's clothes, but he was prepared to bet that the frock – which revealed rather more of his wife's splendid bust than he felt appropriate for a Girl Guides meeting – was an expensive present from her lover. And as for a pick-me-up, he was grimly aware that Vaughan was likely to spend the evening giving her just that.

'Must dash,' she said.

She put on a coat which also looked suspiciously unfamiliar, but didn't give him time to study it before rushing for the door.

'Bye!'

He gave her a couple of minutes to walk down the road and then went out himself. His destination was, he felt sure, the same as Laura's. The difference was that she would never walk through the woods at night. She'd go the long way round, past the shops and the post office, before turning up towards Mereside Lane. The high heels would slow her down, and by taking one of the short cuts he knew so well, he was sure to be a good ten minutes ahead of her.

Once again he stationed himself behind the trees. The air smelled of autumn leaves and damp earth. In any other circumstances, he'd close his eyes and inhale the aroma of the countryside. But now he had to keep alert.

This was just like the other night. A ground floor light was on and the red eye of the burglar alarm winked at him, as if in contempt.

Eventually Laura came trotting down the track. She was carrying a pocket torch to help her dodge the pot-holes and went through the gates before delving into her coat pocket.

Gough watched as she brought out some keys and opened the door, pulling it behind her as she went inside. For a few seconds, the alarm light's winking paused before resuming.

He felt as if Vaughan had kicked him in the stomach. The bastard had only given Laura the key to his house....

Tears stung his eyes. They were serious about each other. Any time now, she'd move in with him. Breathing hard, Gough clenched his fists.

No time to lose. It was do or die.

* * *

Gough arrived back at the cottage a full two hours before his wife. She came skipping through the door, unashamedly elated. It was, he thought, only a matter of time before she confessed her affair and broke the news that she was leaving.

'Good meeting?'

Laura giggled. He'd have guessed that she and Vaughan had been drinking even without smelling the alcohol on her breath.

'Oh yes. Still a lot to do, mind. Anyway, I'm worn out. Better get to bed. Night, night.'

When she was safely ensconced in the bathroom, he checked her coat pockets and found a key ring decorated with a heart. There was a mortice key and a smaller key which bore a name he recognised. Sentinelco was a leading manufacturer of fancy burglar alarms. Presumably Vaughan was happy for her to come and go as she pleased, but wanted her not to set off the alarm by mistake. Sentinelco advertised widely and Gough had a vague idea that their customers had a control box just inside their front door, so they could switch the alarm off as soon as they crossed the threshold. Otherwise the equipment would start screeching and Sentinelco's HQ would be notified thanks to some technical gizmo. He remembered that the red light had stopped winking briefly when Laura went inside Mereside House.

He must get the keys copied. If she missed them, more than likely she'd blame herself, and conclude that somehow they'd slipped out of her pocket. If he was quick to return them, she might never even know they'd gone. He guessed that she'd keep this posh new coat for best, and only wear it on special occasions. When she was going to have sex with Vaughan, in other words.

The next day was Friday. On waking, Laura complained about a migraine. Her own fault, Gough thought. She loved red wine, but anything more than a single glass triggered dreadful headaches. He guessed she'd put away half a bottle of Burgundy in Vaughan's company.

Laura was due to see a number of clients that morning but rang them to cancel and retired to her bed. A stroke of luck, Gough thought, because it meant she had no need of the Austin Allegro they shared. As a rule, he was happy to drive a ranger's van supplied by the Corporation, but he thought it prudent not to be so obvious on this particular occasion. He drove sixteen miles to the nearest city and found Plunkett's, a locksmith's, occupying an arch under a viaduct. He'd remembered the crime prevention officer advising on trustworthy locksmiths and his expression when mentioning Plunkett's had spoken volumes.

The dingy shop looked like the sort of place where people wouldn't ask awkward questions. Just what he wanted. He'd been unsure about whether it would be feasible to copy the Sentinelco key, but the Chinese woman behind the counter assured him it was possible, and before long he was driving back to Mereside with a set of duplicates. At first glance they looked identical to the originals, but he couldn't be certain that they'd work perfectly, so he slipped them onto the key ring with the heart and then into Laura's coat pocket. He kept the pair that Vaughan had given to his wife.

At mid-day, he called back at the house. Laura greeted him with the news that she felt terrible. She wasn't making it up; the poor woman looked as white as a sheet. Was the stress of constant deception exacerbating her symptoms? He wouldn't be surprised. Never mind. Soon she'd have nothing to worry about. Everything would be as it was before Jake Vaughan swaggered into their lives.

It was a busy afternoon. In addition to his usual duties, he spent some time in a remote part of the woodland, digging two holes in the ground, one much larger than the other, twenty yards apart in an unfrequented part of the wood. He left his spade and rake beside a log. The risk that someone would notice them before darkness fell was infinitesimal.

The tiny hole was where he'd bury the murder weapon after killing Vaughan, among other things. He'd decided to use an old chisel that had lain at the bottom of the small cupboard in his hut for years. Nobody would ever find it, but even if they did, it couldn't be connected to him. Would the burglars carry a chisel? Why not? He pictured them using it to threaten home owners into revealing the combination to their safe.

He offered to get something from the chip shop so that Laura didn't have to cook that evening, but both of them picked at their food. He was more nervous than he'd expected, but perhaps that was only natural. He'd never murdered anyone before.

'How are you feeling?' he asked.

'A little bit better,' Laura said. 'I think I'll have an early night.'

'You're not up to the knitting group?'

She often spent her Friday evenings with a group of women who knitted cardigans and mittens for refugees.

A shake of the head. 'Don't worry about me, you go off to the Bull. I'll be as right as rain in the morning. Have a nice time.'

She was on edge, no doubt about it. But she was right. Come tomorrow, and everything would be fine.

On Friday evenings, Gough had got into the habit of spending two or three hours in The Bull's Head, whose beer garden backed on to Mere Woods. He kept his own pewter tankard behind the bar and always sat at a table close to the rear door. He didn't mind passing the time of day with fellow villagers, and occasionally joined them in a game of darts, but he wasn't a mixer and people often left him alone. It helped now he was creating an alibi.

'Usual, Peter?' the landlord asked.

Gough nodded. 'Have one yourself.'

'Cheers, mate.'

There was a clock opposite the bar. Half seven. On the jukebox, Roxy Music. 'Jealous Guy'. The pub was starting to fill up, but it wouldn't become crowded until after eight. Gough sat down at his table and took a few sips of bitter. Not too many. He mustn't allow his judgement to be affected. This was the most important evening of his life. The night he saved his marriage.

Someone chose another number on the jukebox. Soft Cell and 'Tainted Love'. All right, that was enough. Nobody glanced in his direction as he got up and left through the rear door. Outside it was dark, with a touch of drizzle in the air. The beer garden was deserted. A low brick wall separated the grounds of the Bull from Mere Woods and moments later he was moving swiftly towards his hut.

This wasn't an established pathway, but a short cut which he'd discovered years ago. Very few people realised, but if you followed this route in a straight line, ignoring the bridleway that meandered around the edge of the wood and a couple of other narrow tracks that followed equally circuitous courses, you reached the ranger's hut in five minutes. It was like a secret passage through the trees.

Unlocking the hut, he collected the chisel, and put on an old balaclava, gloves, boots and combat jacket. All of them had lain in the cupboard for years. When had he last worn them? He couldn't remember, and he was sure nobody else could. To be on the safe side, though, he'd bury his murder outfit in the second hole as soon as the deed was done.

Not making a sound, he made his way towards Mereside House. This was his home ground and that in itself gave him confidence and courage, steeling him for what he was about to do.

He wasn't a bad man, but sometimes you were left with no choice but to do something rotten so that good would prevail. Like sinking the *Belgrano*. The end justified the means.

Reaching Mereside Lane, he looked up and down. No sign of life. He breathed a sigh of relief. It was a thousand to one that, tonight of all nights, some fool would take it into his head to go on a nocturnal ramble, but you never knew. An upstairs light was on in Vaughan's house. Not the master bedroom, he thought, or at least not the same room where Vaughan had taken Laura. Excellent. So the man was at home. Gough had needed to take a punt on that, but it was a fairly safe bet, especially after a check of the local newspaper's 'What's On' section failed to mention Vaughan performing at any of the clubs in the county.

No time to lose. With a single deep breath, he crossed the track, opening the gate and approaching the front door. He pulled off his boots and left them in the porch. In his thickest pair of socks, he stepped forward, and fumbled as he tried to fit the key in the lock. A touch of nerves there, but the door opened without a creak and moments later he was inside.

So far so good.

Glancing to right and left, he spotted the Sentinelco box, just by the door. It took two seconds to turn off the alarm .

He allowed himself a sigh of relief.

The hallway was wide and floored by polished marble tiles. By the look of it, Vaughan had spent a packet on refurbishments.

Gough moved forward, to the foot of a broad open-tread staircase. The smell of varnish from the treads was so strong it must have been applied recently. Yet the wood of the rail, spindles, and newels was bare, as if that part of the renovations was still a work-in-progress.

The silence was broken by the flush of a toilet upstairs. Gough couldn't help grinning. His enemy was ripe for the taking and he found himself spoiled for choice about stage-managing their confrontation. Should he go up and find the man or wait till he came down to meet his fate?

He rapped the newel post with his chisel and was rewarded by the creak of an opening door and the sound of footsteps.

His enemy – no, his victim – appeared at the top of the stairs. No mistaking that hooked nose. Or the floppy dark hair.

'Who the fuck are you?' he demanded.

The note of fear in his voice was unmistakable. A thrill of excitement ran down Gough's spine.

He lifted the chisel.

'One guess.'

'I'm not playing games. What the fuck are you doing in this house?'

Gough laughed.

Anger reddened the other man's cheeks.

'You bastard. Burglar, are you? I'll sort you out.'

It wasn't an entirely idle threat. He looked rather more muscular than Gough had expected. But it was still a mis-match. Gough was big and strong and extremely fit. And he had the chisel.

He laughed again.

His scorn seemed to trigger Vaughan's rage. He came pounding down the steps, only to slip on the varnished wood and lose his footing. He clutched at the banister as he fell, but it gave way under his weight and he plunged to the ground.

Blood oozed from a gash in Vaughan's temple. Gough found himself standing over a corpse. There was little doubt that the man was dead, but a quick check of the pulse confirmed the obvious.

Well, well, what a turn-up. No need to use the chisel after all. The man had killed himself. An accident. Act of God, you might say.

Gough's plan had been to fake a burglary. Once he'd murdered Vaughan, he'd meant to turn the alarm back on and then break the front window from the outside. The alarm would go off and no doubt Sentinelco's systems would ensure that the police were alerted. It probably wouldn't take long for a patrol car to turn up to check things out. However, he'd been confident he'd have enough time to drop the chisel in the small hole and his balaclava and jacket in the larger one, before using the rake to cover up the signs of recent digging and make his way back to the hut and then to The Bull's Head.

In a split second, he realised he'd had an amazing stroke of fortune. He'd always known his scheme carried a degree of risk, but now there was no need whatsoever to gild the lily. He could just head off into the night and leave Vaughan's corpse to rot until someone came along to find him. One thought occupied his mind. That person mustn't be Laura.

* * *

It didn't take long for Gough to get back to The Bull's Head. He hadn't bothered to bury his chisel or clothes. Given that he hadn't murdered anyone, there was no need. His conscience was clear. He'd get to keep Laura and he hadn't even had to kill to do so.

The pub was filling up and the air was thick with smoke and the smell of ale, but his tankard was where he'd left it. He'd banked on nobody noticing his absence, but even if they did, he'd make some excuse about a stomach bug that meant he needed to spend a lot of time in the toilet. Or he'd say that he'd gone out for a mooch in the gloaming. Communing with Mother Nature. It was something he did every now and then. Since no-one had seen him leave, there was no proof that he'd been away from his table for the best part of half an hour. He knocked back the rest of his drink and went to the bar.

'Fresh pint, Pete?'

'Cheers, mate.'

The alcohol complemented the buzz of excitement he'd felt from the moment he'd stepped over the threshold of Mereside House. It didn't take long to sink his beer and he thought about buying another to celebrate. But why not go back to the cottage and see if Laura was on the mend? If her headache had gone, she might even be game for a bit of hanky-panky. The more he thought about it, the more he was convinced that her fling with Vaughan was a passing fancy. She was excited by fame, it was understandable. But she simply wasn't cut out for life with a yesterday's man.

* * *

In mellow mood, he headed back home. As he entered the hall, he was greeted by the sound of laughter. Everything was going his way. Laura was obviously feeling much better.

He opened the door of the living room. Laura was lying on the couch, but she wasn't convalescing. She was stark naked and so was the man who was bending over her.

This was insane. The floppy-haired man was Jake Vaughan, no question. But Gough had just left him dead in his home.

In a croaky gasp, he managed to say, 'You're not at home!'

Vaughan clambered off Laura and stood on the rug. His expression was defiant, but also triumphant.

'And you're not at the pub as you told your lady wife.'

Gough was as dazed as if he'd been felled by an uppercut from Muhammad Ali.

'But…what are you doing here?'

Vaughan glanced at Laura. She'd buried her face in a cushion. She can't bear to look at me, Gough thought.

'Can't you guess?' He was insolent but amused. Relishing the bizarre confrontation, Gough realised. 'I mean, sorry to intrude, but we couldn't go to my place. My brother's doing some work there.'

'Your brother?'

'He's a handyman. Essie, Esau. My twin.'

The Ditch

By Greg Herren

I'd just finished reading my book—The Hardy Boys, *The Secret of the Lost Tunnel*— and was reaching to turn off my bedside lamp when my phone chirped on my nightstand to let me know I'd gotten a new text message. I frowned. It was just past ten on a weeknight. Sure, it was summer, but Mom and Dad were strict about phone usage after eight o'clock. My orange-and- blue Auburn Tigers clock, hanging just over my desk. I picked up the phone and looked at the screen. My wallpaper was a photo of me standing on a white sand beach on the Florida gulf coast.

I need your help. Come over! Please! Emergency!!!

It was from my best friend, Zane Tidwell.

I closed my eyes and exhaled. *Classic* Zane, always sending desperate-sounding text messages expecting me to drop everything and rush right over. *Everything* was an emergency to Zane, from not getting his homework done to failing a test to not having any clean underwear to having a nightmare of some kind—all of these things qualified as emergencies in Zane's brain. He worked himself up into quite a state over the stupidest things.

"The boy who cried wolf" was all Mom would say.

The problem being, sometimes it *was* an emergency, like that time he broke his arm when he was home alone, or when his mother fell and hit her head, or when his dog ate rat poison.

He always counted on me keeping my head on straight and not panicking and solving the problem for him. We'd been best friends ever since we were little boys in Bible study, and things had always been this way.

I was the calm one and Zane— well, Zane was a drama queen.

He knew I wasn't even supposed to use my phone after eight, let alone leave the house after ten.

I typed out you know I can't it's too late to leave the house and if I get caught they'll take my phone and ground me forever with my thumbs.

Please you have to come I don't know what to do I am really in big trouble now PLEASE!!!!

I stared at the screen. In big trouble? What did that mean? But if the needle on the Zane drama-meter was going up, he wasn't above calling me on the landline.

And that would send Mom and Dad over the edge.

I sighed. I was going to have to go over there.

"You're more trouble than you're worth, Zane Tidwell," I whispered, typing out **Be there soon** and hitting send.

I slipped out of bed and crept noiselessly to my bedroom door. I eased it open. I could hear a loud burst of canned laughter from the television set in the den at the other end of the hallway. That was it. Mom was probably already in bed and Dad was most likely asleep in his reclining chair. The problem with sneaking out at night was, I never knew when Mom would notice Dad wasn't in their bed. She'd make him get in the bed. Sometimes she would check in on me, make sure I was asleep and not on my computer or something. Sometimes making sure no light was visible through the doorframe was all she'd do My sister, Brenna, used to get caught once out of every ten times she snuck out, before she went off to college at Auburn. I was always a bundle of nerves on those rare nights when I slipped out.

I closed my door gently, pressing the little button to lock it. Hopefully Mom would just look for light and not stick her head in. She hated when I locked the door, but one time Dad grunted, "Boys need their privacy sometimes, Noreen," and she never said another word.

Damn you, Zane. If I get in trouble...

I pulled my jeans back on and slipped my AUBURN TIGERS sweatshirt over my head. He hadn't answered my last text, so I typed *be there in a few* with my thumbs. I turned off the bedside lamp and crept to the window.

It was the night before Halloween, that weird in-between-the-seasons period in the Alabama when it was warm and muggy during the day and chilly and damp after sunset. I eased the window up slowly, wincing when it squeaked shrilly. I froze, listening for wood groaning under the weight of a foot. I heard nothing. I pushed the window the rest of the way up.

I started unlatching the screen, but hesitated.

My sister's voice: *Just go out the window—they'll never know.*

I finished unlatching the screen and let it drop to the ground. There was a slight pinging sound when it hit the grass and I froze again. Hearing nothing, I took a deep breath and climbed out the window, dropping the few feet to the ground. I bent my knees to absorb the shock, but the jarring still sent a lightning bolt of agony through my aching head. I put my hand against the side of the house to steady myself until it passed. Nausea churned my stomach. I could hear Coach's voice in my head again: *If you throw up or feel dizzy or have blurred vision—tell your parents to take you to the Emergency Room. You may have a concussion.*

The nausea passed.

I'd only been unconscious for less than a minute, anyway. Just another occupational hazard of being on the football team. No big deal, nothing to make a fuss over. As my dad said, you take your licks like a man.

I glanced over at the neighbors' yard. The back light over at the Burleson house was on, bathing the slab of concrete that served as their back patio in yellow light. I could see moths and other bugs fluttering around the bulb. That was lucky. Usually their big, friendly mutt, Shep, was out with the long chain looped around the black railing on their back steps attached to his collar. Shep loved to be petted. Mrs. Burleson always said all a burglar had to do was tell him he was a sweet boy and scratch his ears and he'd help them carry everything out to their van. But he barked at everything. Shep not being out was a plus. We didn't have neighbors on the other side—the remains of the forest that once covered this whole area was still there, ancient pine trees and underbrush rife with snakes and raccoons and possums and the occasional deer.

I started walking down our sloping backyard towards the ditch.

The chilly night air reeked of stale smoke. The farmers around town were burning their fields. I looked back and saw the light in the den go off. A few seconds later, the light in Mom and Dad's bedroom came on. I didn't realize I was holding my breath until the bedroom light went out and I exhaled. I wished my head would stop aching for the thousandth time, and looked up. There weren't any clouds, and only a quarter moon cast feeble light in the purplish-black sky.

I paused when I got to the big pine tree next to the footpath down into the ditch.

Everyone called it the ditch, but it was a lot bigger than most. Some thought it had been a branch of the Sipsey River that somehow got cut off and went dry. My Alabama History teacher thought the great New Madrid earthquake in 1811 had torn the ground asunder. All anyone knew for sure was, it had been there when American settlers first arrived.

There were scary stories about the ditch, repeated by children at sleepovers and campouts in hushed whispers. *Aren't you afraid? With the ditch right there in your backyard?* Dad just scoffed and called the stories legends and lies: stories old women used to tell each other while shelling peas or snapping beans.

Just stories.

Some kids wouldn't go anywhere near the ditch. Others said they'd felt something when they were playing down in the ditch, thought me and Zane were crazy for hanging out down there all the time.

Sometimes when I was down there where no one could see me, heading either to or back from Zane's house, I would sense something. All the hairs on my arms would stand up and a cold finger would snake down my spine....

Then I'd just shake it off, blaming my over-active imagination.

The Ditch Killer's gonna get you....

The Ditch Killer was real enough, but what was real and what was legend now? How much was made up to scare kids into behaving? They'd never caught him either—but the killings had been over fifty years ago, before my parents were born and before the land on the north side was partitioned and sold and houses like ours had gone up.

His victims had always been boys.

Depending on who was telling the story, there had been anywhere from four to eleven victims over the course of three years before the killings stopped.

"This better not be a false alarm," I thought, peering down into the darkness from the lip. The old wooden bridge across was missing boards and the railing was gone in a few places, but with the trees lining the edge on either side no light could get down there.

I shivered.

It was easy to laugh off the stories when the sun was out.

I'd never been down there at night.

But the ditch was the fastest and easiest way to get to Zane's house— and the only way to get there without being seen on the way by some adult who might call my parents wondering why I was out wandering so late.

I stared into the darkness.

I couldn't turn on the flashlight app on my phone until I was out of sight down there.

I felt sure I'd spent so much time down there that I could find my way around without light.

But it seemed *different* in the dark.

The darkness seemed *alive*, like a big open mouth just waiting to swallow me up inside.

That's just stupid, you're being a baby. Don't be afraid of the dark. You're not a kid anymore.

But it's almost Halloween, when the veil between the living and the dead is weakest.

You're being an idiot. Stop it. There's no such thing as ghosts and you know it. That's baby stuff. Zane's waiting for you and might be in trouble.

So, I started down the steep path.

I almost slipped a couple of times when the red dirt crumbled beneath my feet. The stench of smoke from the burning fields hung heavy as I struggled to keep my balance. In the dark, I couldn't see the tree roots I usually grabbed to help on the way down.

I couldn't see anything.

But I didn't want to slip. I could break an arm or something and have to explain to Mom and Dad why I was down there in the first place.

My head was throbbing again.

On my way home I am walking down the middle of the street and I don't care who sees me.

But finally, I got to the bottom.

And as I reached for my phone, I got the feeling something was watching me.

And whatever it was, was *really* glad I was down there.

Don't be ridiculous, I said to myself as I pulled my phone out of my pocket with shaking hands.

You don't need the light, a voice cooed inside my head, everything's better down here in the dark, don't you think?

My hands were shaking so badly it took me three tries to unlock my phone and find the flashlight app.

The pale bluish light lit up the sand and gravel on the floor of the ditch, broken glass glittering. I raised my phone and aimed it in front of me. It formed a wide cone of light for a few feet in front of me. The wind rustled the trees, leaves and branches murmuring softly as they rubbed against each other. Gnarled and twisted tree roots poked out on either side, looking like hands and arms reaching out to grab me. Cigarette butts and empty beer cans and other garbage were scattered along the bottom.

I could still feel eyes watching me.

There's nothing down here it's just your imagination.

Just to be sure, I turned around slowly, shining the light in every direction.

Nothing.

You're being stupid, and Zane's waiting.

My phone vibrated in my hand and a message from Zane flashed across the screen. PLEASE HURRY!

I shivered, wishing I'd grabbed my letter jacket. The wind picked up, whistling down between the big dark trees on either side of the ditch. I started walking forward.

I wonder where they found the bodies.

No one had ever said. I'd heard the bodies were mangled, body parts and organs missing, torn up so badly that whoever found them threw up. But I'd never heard exactly where the bodies had been found, where the puddles of blood had been.

They always just said "in the ditch."

I swallowed and started walking faster.

I couldn't shake the feeling I was being watched, that I wasn't alone down there.

When I got to the point just beyond the Burleson backyard where the ditch made an almost ninety-degree turn to the right a dog started howling.

Every hair on my body stood up.

Tomorrow is All Hallows' Eve when the dead are close to the living.

Boys died violently down here...I shouldn't be down here.

I started walking faster.

The trees overhead seemed to be whispering to me.

It's nice down here, isn't it? He didn't have to lure the boys into the ditch, you know, they came on their own. Willingly.

Like you did tonight.

My head throbbed even harder. I stopped for a minute, worried I might throw up from the pain.

There's nothing down here that would hurt you. It's nice and peaceful down here.

It passed and I walked even faster. I'd never been afraid of the ditch before. Maybe it was from getting hit so hard in the head at football practice?

Maybe it was just being down here in the dark.

Whatever it was I didn't like it.

I wanted to climb up the side and get out of there and run the rest of the way to Zane's house through people's backyards, not caring if anyone saw me or told my parents. Forget about Zane and run all the way home, climb back in through my window and put the screen back on and slam the window shut and lock it, close the curtains and get under the covers with the lights on, so that whatever was there in the ditch would have to stay away, couldn't come in, it was afraid of the light....

"Are you going insane?" I said out loud.

What is wrong with me?

But I couldn't shake the feeling I wasn't alone down there, couldn't convince myself it was my imagination, just knew I wasn't alone....

...and whatever it was, it wanted me.

It had been waiting for me.

Stop that!

I turned around, lighting up the darkness with my phone. The rustling of leaves and the baying of the dog was like something out of the scary movies Zane loved and I hated.

There's no one else down here, you're just scaring yourself, that's all.

I ignored the little voice that answered me *then why does it feel like whatever's watching you is happy you're here?*

Stop it, you're acting crazy.

I walked faster, ducking underneath a rotting fallen tree and coming out into the big open space at the big turn. This was where someone had hung a long thick rope from a high branch of a thick pine tree. The bottom of the rope was knotted. You could either hold the rope or sit on the knot as you swung out over the ditch before heading back to the safety of the ledge. The ditch was higher here on the other side, crumbling red dirt and rock slanting upwards higher than the ledge on the other side. My parents had forbidden my sister and me from using the rope swing *—you could break your arm or leg falling off that stupid thing—* but even though most of the neighborhood parents felt the same, no one ever took the rope down and no one was ever injured. As I looked up, the rope began swinging back and forth, picking up momentum as I stared at it, my dinner starting to churn in my stomach and the pounding in my head getting stronger.

That's not the wind!

My phone vibrated in my hand, startling me so it slipped out of my hand and into a pile of white sand.

The flashlight app closed as soon as my phone hit the sand but I could see the text message from Zane on the black screen:

Where are you bro?

When I knelt down to pick my phone up, I felt cold.

It felt like I'd been shoved into my grandmother's big freezer, the one on her back porch that was big enough to hold both a butchered cow and deer. My cousin Tommy had put me in it when I was five. I still had nightmares about that. I was so cold I couldn't move or do anything because I was shivering so hard.

And just as suddenly the cold was gone.

Overhead the rope stopped swinging.

I picked up my phone and stood back up. I turned the flashlight app back on and started jogging. I wanted to get out of there, out of the ditch.

There was no way I was going back home through here.

"There's nothing here," I whispered into the darkness.

But I couldn't get past the feeling that something—*someone*—was watching me.

Only now it felt like it was—it was *hungry.*

My head throbbed every time a foot hit the ground, but I wasn't going to slow down or walk anymore. It seemed to take forever before I finally reached the footpath leading up to Zane's backyard.

When I got to the top, I felt relieved.

It—it seemed like there was a sighing sound from down below.

The wind, it was just the wind.

Like ours, the Tidwell backyard sloped down to the lip of the ditch. Theirs had more of a slope than ours, and Zane bitched about using the push mower all summer long. "I don't know why they can't buy a god-damned mower that goes by itself," he'd say, his round brown eyes flashing angrily. We both knew why, of course. His daddy was the preacher at the Church of Christ, and Preacher Tidwell believed not making his son work would spoil him and make him soft. Mrs, Tidwell didn't have a dryer and hung her laundry out to dry on lines strung between rusty metal poles in the backyard. She always said the laundry smelled better.

Mom didn't believe that for a minute.

Zane hated his father.

He didn't have much nice to say about his mother, for that matter.

I could see Zane, sitting at the dark red picnic table on the cement patio area just behind the red brick house. All the lights were on in the house, but the yard light wasn't, which was weird. I wondered why Zane was sitting outside. His back was to the ditch, so I couldn't see anything other than the back of his white T-shirt glowing in the moonlight.

Something was wrong.

I walked up the slope, panting from the jogging and my head still throbbing. I ducked under the clotheslines and crossed the cement patio. Zane didn't move, didn't make a sound, just kept sitting there with his back to me, staring straight ahead. I could see his phone sitting on the table.

"Zane?" I said when I got closer, and he turned to look back at me.

That was when I realized he was covered in blood.

His dirty blond hair was plastered to his head with it. His arms, his clothes, his bare legs, everything was covered in gummy, sticky drying blood.

And he was wearing only a T-shirt and his briefs.

Blood-soaked.

When he saw me staring at him, his lower lip started trembling and he choked out, "I don't know what to do. Yuh-yuh-you gotta help me."

I just stared, my mind going numb and blank. I realized I was holding my breath. I didn't know what to say, what to do. After a few seconds I was able to blurt out, "What—what happened? Are you okay?"

"It's not muh-muh-muh-my blood." He turned his head and looked at the open back door to the house. He covered his face with his bloody hands and shook with sobs without making a sound.

I had to go look.

I didn't want to.

The screen door was also open.

The back door opened into the kitchen.

As soon as I reached the threshold, I could see inside.

There was blood everywhere, so much blood, more blood that I'd ever seen. More blood than the time Mom sliced her hand open or that time when my cousin Tad cut the tip of his finger off with the ax.

This looked like—like when Uncle Dunk butchered a hog.

Everywhere I looked was covered with blood.

Spattered on the walls and the ceiling, it was all over the cabinets and the stove and the floor. There was a bloody handprint on the refrigerator.

I felt sick.

But the worst part, worse than the blood splashed everywhere, worse than my bloody best friend sitting back at the picnic table, was the head on the kitchen table.

It was Preacher Tidwell, his eyes staring at me, his mouth open in a silent scream.

"Oh my God," I whispered, and my dinner started churning again in my stomach.

And was that—was that—a *hand* over there in the corner?

A woman's hand, it was a woman's hand. There was a wedding ring on one of the fingers, and the little diamond ring I recognized—I recognized as Mrs. Tidwell's, it was Mrs. Tidwell's hand….

I felt my dinner coming back up.

And the smell—oh, God, the *smell.*

I backed out the doorway and bent over, throwing up into the grass, my stomach heaving and contracting, food and chunks and liquid spewing in a seemingly endless stream, my head pounding so hard I thought it might split open.

And finally, when my stomach finally stopped heaving, I wiped my mouth with my shirt. "What happened?" I was shaking, and shivering, the night air seemed to have gotten so much colder, and I wasn't sure— I wasn't sure what I was exactly supposed to do.

Zane swallowed. "I must have done that." He was shaking, babbling, the words tumbling out. He looked at me. "But he was going to beat me again and she was going to let him and I had to get out of there and I ran out the back door and all I had on was my underwear and I ran and ran and thought I would just keep running and I thought he won't chase me down into the ditch and then I went down into the ditch and I—I felt safe and warm and like everything was going to be okay, the ditch—I can't explain it, I just felt safe down there and all I had do was—I don't know. And then the next thing I remember I was standing in the kitchen—" his voice broke "—and I was like this and they were like that and I grabbed my phone and I texted you and I came out here and I don't know what to do, Ty, I don't know what to do." His body started shuddering again. "And I don't know what happened, Ty. I don't know."

And that feeling came again—that someone, *something*—was watching us.

I spun around but couldn't see anything out there in the darkness.

"Do you feel it, too? Like someone's out there, watching?" Zane asked with a shudder. His voice sounded broken and defeated. He was shivering. "I don't know what to do."

"We need to call the police." I started to gag again but somehow managed to get control of myself again. *I'll never forget what I saw in there.* "We have to call the police, Zane."

"We can't." Zane grabbed my arm. His skin was sticky with blood. I flinched and pulled away from him. "They're never going to believe me, Ty. They're going to put me in jail. They're going to think that I did this and I didn't—maybe I did, I don't know, I don't know what happened!" He was getting hysterical.

I smacked him.

"We have to, Zane. You can't just leave them—the house—like that." I felt puke starting to work its way back up, my stomach clenching, the memory of what I'd seen, the smell— "Just tell them what happened. What did happen? You have to remember. You *have* to."

He swallowed and started crying again, the tears making a slick path through the coppery redness on his face. "You don't know what it was like, Ty. You don't know."

I swallowed and sat down on the edge of the picnic table. "Then tell me."

"He used—he used to do things to me."

My stomach revolted again.

He used to do things to me.

A memory, wispy and ethereal, danced through my mind. Last summer at church camp, in the woods, the nineteen-year-old counselor who was always so spiteful and mean, caught with a twelve-year-old boy down at the lakeshore late at night when everyone should have been in bed. The state troopers asking questions, and the social worker with the tired eyes swimming with unshed tears, the lines so deep in her face and the mousy hair shot through with gray hanging in flyaway wisps on either side of her head. *Did he ever touch you inappropriately? Did he ever touch you...*

My parents didn't send me to church camp this last summer.

Preacher Tidwell?

Other memories flashed through my aching head, of Mr. Tidwell taking us out to the lake and reading a book on shore while watching us splashing around in the orange water. A hand lingering too long on my back now and then, his smell, aftershave and musky body odor, slightly stale breath. Hosing the mud from the dirty lake water off our bodies, wrapping us in thick beach towels that smelled like night jasmine from hanging on the line overnight. Had he ever touched me wrong? Had his hand ever lingered too long on my butt as he wrapped me in the towel? Had his breathing gotten faster, more labored?

I knew his daddy beat Zane.

I hadn't known about this.

He was still talking, the words coming out fast, in a rush, like if he stopped to breathe or think about what he was saying he'd stop. "It's been going on for as long as I can remember and my mom knew but pretended like it didn't happen... I just assumed, you know, that it was normal because it was all I knew but then last summer when that all happened at church camp I knew it wasn't supposed to happen this way and, you know, he always hit me and it always seemed to get him excited and I just couldn't take it anymore and I asked God, I prayed for God to help me and no one would believe me because he was a preacher and they'd think I was lying. I talked to Mrs. Goff at school and she didn't believe me and I knew I was going to have to run away and I didn't know what to do but it had to stop so I—"

He stopped and I gulped, because for just a moment his eyes flashed bright yellow, like they were glowing with an inner light of some sort, but then it faded away and it was Zane again, looking miserable and sad and broken and defeated. He whispered something so low I couldn't understand what he said.

"What?"

He looked me in the eyes and said softly, "I prayed for the devil to help me. And I think he came."

It felt like a fingertip was running lightly down my spine.

"You called the devil?"

He nodded and wiped at his face. "Daddy—Daddy came into my room and told me to take my pants down, he was going to punish me for not getting an A on my history test, and he took the belt off and I could tell I could see it in his face he wasn't going to stop at the whipping and I closed my eyes and called to Lucifer and begged him for help and I ran out of the house and went down to the ditch and the whole time I was praying for the devil to help me and the next thing I knew I was standing in the kitchen and I was covered with blood and their bodies were in pieces everywhere and THEY'RE GOING TO LOCK ME UP FOR THE REST OF MY LIFE!"

The last words came out as a high-pitched shriek.

I smacked him again.

I felt—I felt strangely calm.

"Where are your clothes?" I heard myself asking. I got up from the picnic table and walked over to the hose. I turned on the spigot and pointed the nozzle at him. He shrieked when the hard stream of cold water hit him but soon the blood was washing off him, spilling down into the grass. When he was clean, I grabbed a big towel off the clothesline and handed it to him. "Get dried off, then go in through your bedroom window and get some clothes. Get dressed, and we'll go back through the ditch to my house. You'll spend the night at my house, and I'll tell my mom and dad in the morning that you ran away, that your dad beat you and you ran away."

It could work.

It would work.

Zane nodded and went back into the house.

I sat there on top of the picnic table.

You know what you have to do.

Zane came back out a few minutes later, in a sweatshirt and a pair of jeans. His teeth were chattering, his entire body shaking.

"Let's go."

We walked down the sloping lawn side by side.

We reached the lip of the ditch.

You know what you have to do.

The trees were rustling overhead.

I could feel the eyes watching us as we went down the path to the bottom of the ditch.

"I'm scared," Zane said softly while I buried his wet underwear and T-shirt under some sand. "There's something down here, don't you feel it? I felt it before when I was down here."

"I don't feel anything," I lied, and it was happy, pleased.

Let me in, you know you want to let me in.

I was patting the white sand down over his clothes.

And it came to me, whatever it was. I gasped, my head still throbbing, my stomach churning with acid, and it came *into* me.

It was kind of like what a glass would feel like being filled with liquid. I felt like it was filling me up, almost pushing what was *me* out and taking my place, but it felt good, it felt even better than when I was in my room alone and looking at the dirty pictures on the Internet and...

Kill him, a voice whispered in my head. *No one will know it was you. They'll think it was the same person who killed his parents. You know you want to.*

My hand closed on a rock.

I felt the bone of his skull give when I swung it into his temple.

That's the way. He was too weak. But you're a better host for me. Now feast on his bones and let's get back to bed, shall we? We have a lot of work in front of us.

Dichondra
By Naomi Hirahara

Mas Arai had tended the yards of retired football players and washed-up actors, but never a thirty-year-old billionaire that was younger than his own daughter. Yet here was this new customer, thin as an undernourished indoor ficus plant with a pancake batter-colored face, standing in the doorway of his palatial mansion in San Marino. Mas didn't understand why the billionaire, Seth Howard, had already spent hundreds of thousands of dollars on a so-called Japanese garden, when it seemed obvious that this tech titan rarely spent any time under the sun.

It was Mas's son-in-law, Lloyd, head groundskeeper of Dodger Stadium, who had been the go-between in this most recent job opportunity. At age 82, Mas was all but retired, but apparently Lloyd and his daughter, Mari, felt that there were still some good working years left in him. Or perhaps they were conspiring of new ways that they could pay for their son's expensive education at a private school in Pasadena. If it was on the back of the Grandpa Mas, so be it.

"Dad, it will be a quick buck. You'll hardly have to do anything," an enthusiastic Mari had told him. "And it's just in San Marino. So close."

It was indeed a quick buck. Two thousand bucks to be exact. And just to be a consultant. Mas didn't understand it. The garden was supposedly almost completed by the hands of a Swedish landscaper.

"Mr. Arai. How nice to meet you. Seth Howard." The young man bowed to Mas. Mas wasn't going to bow back. He merely dipped the lip of his old Dodger cap like a Gunsmoke marshal did to his cowboy hat.

"Let me show you to Mishima-en." Seth spoke the Japanese name of his private garden with pride. Of course, Seth wasn't going to lead Mas, with his muddy workboots through the house. Instead he walked outside to the driveway, pressing down on the screen of his cell phone to open a large security gate designed to resemble the otemon of a Tokugawa-era castle.

Mas cautiously followed the young man, almost expecting a half dozen knife-wielding ninjas greeting them. Instead he found himself in the green cloud of Mishima-en. He didn't doubt that the garden was named after the famed writer, Yukio Mishima, a nationalist who had committed hara-kiri at a military building in Japan. It seemed many American men who were Japanese lovers were obsessed with Mishima, even though the writer proclaimed that Japanese culture was superior over western values. Perhaps this belief made Mishima even more irresistible to the powerful. The American wealthy, he noticed, sometimes only respected those who didn't respect them back.

It was autumn, so the ginkgo trees in the distance were shedding their golden fan-shaped leaves onto sloping hills covered in moss. They were small and looked young, nothing like the imposing eucalyptus behind them. Nobody planted eucalyptus anymore in California. Their invasive roots damaged sidewalks, driveways, and walkways, yet were still protected. As its inner core was filled with oil, the eucalyptus was also known to combust like an organic explosive device.

The shape of the koi pond was a bit strange, a little too rectangular for Mas's taste, but the fish were large and lively, bright orange and white streaks in the clear water. At one end was a trickle of water dripping from a hollow bamboo spout into a stone basin for purification purposes.

Mas knelt down and ran his hand through the greenery as if it was a clear spring. "Dichondra."

Every house he used to garden and, in fact, his own, used to have dichondra. It was an organic carpet, a surface that Mari as a child loved to run through barefoot with her friends. Dichondra could transform a humble two-bedroom bungalow into a grand magical castle.

"Yes, I insisted upon it. I know that at one time, it was banned because authorities said it required too much water, but my research lab has determined that is not the case."

Mas bit down on his dentures. He could have told the young CEO that without an investment into an expensive research lab.

"I want you to tell me if anything is out of place in the garden. If anything is even a bit inauthentic."

Mas studied Seth's gray eyes to see how much veracity he wanted to hear. He had encountered his share of people who said that they wanted to hear the unvarnished truth when they really required complete affirmation. Others reveled in the shredding of falsehood.

With Seth, Mas couldn't tell which side the young tech stood.

* * *

Rebeca Garcia leaned against the stone breakfast island and stared at the old Japanese gardener through the UV light-resistant sliding glass doors. He was wearing a worn Dodgers cap, probably circa 1970, and a khaki button-down shirt over faded jeans. He obviously wasn't dressed to impress.

Rebeca, however, knew that you couldn't judge anyone by their appearance or clothing. Even her longtime employer, Seth, had not changed his fashion style since he was an undergraduate at Caltech. Gray hoodie, jeans, and white tennis shoes. He and two other young men were sharing a townhouse just outside the campus and the slovenly habits of his roommates were driving Seth crazy. Back then Seth didn't have much disposable income, but he took on paying for Rebeca's cleaning services on his own, that's how much the cleanliness of his physical environment meant to him. Rebeca shared his passion for order. Even the cans in the pantry were organized by both date of expiration and size.

The newcomer, Henrik, had been quite the opposite. He had moved in nine months ago and he left his dirty boxers on the floor of the white tiled bathroom on a regular basis. Rebeca blushed when it was apparent the two men were sleeping in the same bed. Seth had his share of casual girlfriends who stayed the night, but it was obvious that they weren't that important to him. Henrik, on the other hand, awakened some kind of passion in Seth. He was more animated at home, his pale cheeks sometimes were tinged pink. Henrik stored exotic foods and ingredients in the refrigerator, spiny fruit that was left to soften and rot, long beans that were never cooked, and cheeses of different yellow and orange hues that eventually turned blue-green. It was as if Henrik became too excited when it came to acquiring organic items, but didn't have the follow through to see what they actually tasted. Yet he was still loathe to discard them after their expiration date. He had berated Rebeca for throwing away some smelly paste that was becoming more and more odiferous as weeks passed. Seth had been working on a top-secret project in Silicon Valley and had no idea what kind of bacteria was germinating in his top-of-the-line stainless steel refrigerator.

Henrik claimed to have studied Japanese landscaping in Kyoto. He purported to be bilingual in Japanese and, in fact, multilingual in a number of languages, including Spanish. He was a concert pianist. He had studied the culinary arts at Le Cordon Bleu in Paris. A speed skater who could have competed in the Winter Olympics.

Rebeca, of course, was suspicious. She even engaged him in a conversation in her native language, and he replied in beautiful Spanish with a Catalonian accent. After Seth's haranguing at a holiday dinner, he sat down at the synthesizer and regaled everyone with a piece by Mozart and then "I'm Dreaming of a White Christmas." In spite of his wasteful treatment of the expensive produce in the refrigerator, he managed to pull together delicious smelling and beautifully plated meals on occasion. Just when Rebeca thought that she finally had cornered him as an imposter, he swept in as a modern-day Houdini, exhibiting a streak of genius at precisely the right moment.

She heard the couple fighting weeks ago. "Who is he?" she heard Seth's high-pitched voice, a tone that only revealed itself when he was most annoyed.

"He's no one. A jealous ex-lover."

"And how did he get my private cell number?" Seth had three phones, his most personal one being a flip phone that only a handful of people, the closest in his inner circle, could call. Rebeca prided herself on being one of those people.

"I don't know. Maybe from a hacker in Russia. Or China? Just me see the message for myself."

"He texted me not to trust you. That you were a charlatan."

"Are you going to believe a stranger, obviously some stalker, over me?"

Rebeca held her breath. *Mister Seth, you can say it. Tell him.* There was silence and then sounds of affection, a wet kiss. Seth had obviously succumbed to his lower instincts. In a way, Rebeca could not blame her employer. She had been the same with Ricardo. And as a result, she was now separated hundreds of miles from her son, only able to wire a big chunk of her paycheck to El Salvador to her parents who were caring for the boy, who was now close to entering young adulthood.

"Goddamnit." Henrik was now standing in the kitchen in his miserable boxers and a wrinkled sleeveless T-shirt that featured the face of a young woman and the text, "Femme Fatale." He cursed not to Rebeca—no, she was a non-entity, like a piece of furniture—but apparently to himself. He returned to the bedroom to pull on a pair of peach-colored sweat pants and walked out barefoot to the garden through the back door. Rebeca pressed a button for the sliding glass doors to open. She needed to hear what was about to transpire.

"Who is this?" Henrik practically towered over the small Japanese man. Rebeca didn't trust the gardener but the fact that Henrik was attempting to intimidate the newcomer made her feel some empathy toward him.

Seth handed a business card to Henrik. "His name is Mas Arai. He's a local landscaper. Has been in the business for more than fifty years."

Henrik practically spat on the card. "Oriental Landscaping. No one using 'oriental' anymore, Seth." Both the men spoke if Mas was not there. The gardener, however, didn't seem to mind and was instead studying the trees that Henrik had most recently planted.

"I can't believe that you can't trust me." Henrik raised his meaty arms, revealing tufts of armpit hair the color of hay.

"I needsu to go," declared Mas, already moving toward the driveway. As he was leaving, his eyes met Rebeca's through the open sliding glass door. It wasn't a friendly exchange, but a knowing one. *This is what we have to endure.*

* * *

Rebeca was awakened in the middle of the night by the cries of multiple coyotes. They must have caught a stray cat and howling in delight after their meal.

Her room faced the garden and she adjusted the wooden slats to gaze outside.

It was full moon. Seth had insisted that the garden be situated for moon viewings. Ever since his Caltech days and probably since boyhood, he was obsessed with the planets, having mobiles of the solar system hanging from his ceiling and a portable telescope that he often took out on the balcony of his collegiate townhouse. Over the years with each financial milestone, telescopes had grown in size and expense and now an impressive one was mounted on wheels so that he could easily move it outdoors when desired.

Rebeca turned on the lamp on her bedside table and glanced at the paper calendar hanging from her wall. She had drawn a circle in the box for October 29, 2012. And also a time, 11:50 PM. She had grown accustom to taking note of the full moons that were listed in the farmer's almanacs that Seth always gifted her every Christmas. Her employer's passion had rubbed off on her over the years.

The digital clock flashed 1:33 AM. Rebeca's mouth felt dry and she thirsted for the barley tea that she had freshly brewed for the household. As she walked down the tile floors in her slippers toward the kitchen, she immediately knew something was wrong. A breeze blew into the room and the sliding glass door was wide open. But the garden was completely dark. If Seth was taking a full-moon stroll, his movements would have activated the back lights connected to a motion detector.

Rebeca pulled out a kitchen knife from a wood block and carefully crept into the coolness of the autumn night. The lights flashed on, almost blinding her at first. The giant telescope had been wheeled out next to the grass but there was no sign of Seth.

The moon glowed bright and the sky was so clear that Rebeca thought

she could make out craters on the moon's surface. She smiled, imagining
Seth's response to such a sight. Could he have wandered outside to stroll
their manicured neighborhood, which included a grand estate built in
the 1900s with long eaves, a perfect frame for a full moon?

She was standing so still that the light turned off. She marveled at
the beauty of the night. How calm and meditative. Her own heart beat,
which moments ago had pulsed with worry, slowed. She pulled at the
cardigan that she had slipped over her T-shirt, activating the motion
lights again. This time she noticed something amiss. The soles of tennis
shoes faced her from a moss hill in the back.

Clutching the knife, she shuffled forward, prepared to strike someone hiding in the dark corners of the garden. She took tentative steps on
the concrete bridge over the pool of water. Underneath one of the trees
lay her longtime employer, an ugly gash on the temple of his forehead.

"Mister Seth," she gasped and dropped the knife into the moss. She
knelt down and checked his forehead and wrist. Cold. No pulse. She
had forgotten her cell phone inside and ran back into the house. Her
fingers were trembling and it took her two tries to punch in 911. "Seth
Howard." It was a miracle that she could even properly say his name to
the police dispatcher. "I think he is dead."

Rebeca waited in backyard for the police after looking into Seth
and Henrik's bedroom to see if the lover was around. The bed was made
and unslept. Where was Henrik? Had he done this most terrible crime?

The firefighters and paramedics arrived first, followed by two uniformed officers. One was dark-skinned and short who spoke atrocious
Spanish. Rebeca wished that he just addressed her in English. They
asked about security cameras. There was only a row of them that had
been installed in the front of the property. Seth didn't want his garden
oasis to be marred with the presence of cameras. This was his sanctuary,
a moment of zen, mindfulness in the present. His one get away from
computers and surveillance.

The law enforcement officers were both mystified by the giant telescope.

"Mister Seth liked to look at the full moon in the garden."

The police officers exchanged glances. They asked her more questions about who else lived in the residence and Rebeca eagerly spouted
out, "Henrik," although she couldn't in that moment remember his last
name. She said that she would go inside and retrieve a piece of his mail
but the officers told her to stay put. Two detectives came on the scene,
repeating her some of the same questions that the uniformed officers had

said. By this time, Rebeca had spied a large branch that had apparently fallen off the tree on the moss hill. One side was marked with blood. Seth's blood? Could the branch just fallen off, hit Seth on the temple, and killed him? Could the tech giant's death have happened so randomly?

The officers wanted to take Rebeca's fingerprints, but she wasn't sure that was legal. She begged off, saying that she wanted to consult with her lawyer, whose specialty was immigration, but that didn't need to be revealed.

The detectives obviously didn't like her answer and before they could pressure her further, Henrik appeared in front of the open sliding glass door. "What has happened?"

After the detectives spoke to him, in a much gentler tone than they had interrogated Rebeca, tears followed. Rebeca had never seen Henrik cry, much less look sad. He did not wear grief well. His lips distorted into a clownish expression. Even without being asked, he volunteered his whereabouts. "I was in a pub on Colorado Boulevard. I was watching a football tournament in Poland." One detective gave Henrik a once over. "You can ask the bartender and the regulars."

Rebeca's face fell. It sounded like an iron-clad alibi. Henrik often took refuge in that bar, designed for British and Irish macho men. She had gone in there once to deliver a package to Seth while he was there with Henrik for a World Cup game. They bellowed on the success of their team, slapped each other's backs, and hugged each other when their team scored. They didn't even notice that Rebeca had entered the room.

* * *

When Mas got out of his new used van after parking it in front of Seth Howard's estate, he was enveloped in an intense hush that made his bones rattle. The neighborhood was the kind that was usually deserted aside for a lone middle-aged man and woman walking a giant dog or gardeners mowing the lawn. But this morning was different. Mas never felt quite comfortable in such high-tone settings, but today especially the place was almost warning him to leave or face the consequences.

But Mas had already received a five hundred check from the high-tech titan. Being paid for a quarter of his labor without doing a thing except for accepting the work made an impact on Mas. His expertise was being valued. He thought that Seth was ridiculous, but he was also ridiculously generous, which excused most employers' failings.

He rang the doorbell at nine o'clock sharp, the time of his appointment set at his last meeting at the house. The door opened and Mas expected to see the emaciated and pale body of the hakujin man but instead faced a brown woman about his same size. Odds was that she was the housekeeper.

"Here for the garden," he said.

The housekeeper stared at him blankly.

"Made appointment with Mista Howard." Could she not speak any English? Mas's English was chuto-hampa, half-ass, but most of his Spanish-speaking helpers could understand what he was saying. He tried to remember the Spanish that he attempted to learn in a community college class, but could only manage, "Señor."

"Oh," she said in reply.

Another figure filled the doorway. The alleged gardener who had created the atrocious so-called Japanese garden. He glared at Mas with his huge blue eyes. "You need to leave. Your services are not needed."

The housekeeper, who had seemed so unwelcoming, transformed in response to the blue-eyed gardener's threatening order. She clenched her teeth, her wide jaw tightening. She crossed her arms over her ample chest, which had been hidden by a loose cotton shirt.

"He does not leave," she announced. "Mister Seth and I signed a contract. I am in charge of the house now."

Rebeca had not lied. Seth traveled often to Silicon Valley, where he had an office, as well as to Taiwan and South Korea. There had been a plumbing incident, roots had invaded the sewer pipe, and the plumber refused to take action without talking first to the owner. As a result, waste water had flooded the perimeter of the house and even seeped into Rebeca's room. After he returned from Asia, Seth opened a separate bank account for the care of the San Marino house and gave Rebeca the power to sign checks.

In keeping with this agreement, the Japanese gardener was under Rebeca's purview and no matter how much she had disagreed with Seth's initial decision, she wanted him now. Two heads were better than one, King Solomon had stated in Ecclesiastes. Maybe to vanquish the devil Henrik, she would need this old man.

"Mister Seth made me in charge of the house. He signed papers. Maybe you the one who has to leave."

Henrik's face turned a bright red. Rebeca was delighted to see how he was upset he was. "We'll just see about that. Seth's parents will be arriving tomorrow morning."

Rebeca knew that Seth had a complicated relationship with father, a professor at Stanford. Every family gathering, the professor challenged his son about how his company was improving the world. Rebeca witnessed it firsthand at a rare Thanksgiving dinner that Seth hosted in his then new house. *Your son is a success*, she thought as she arranged roasted turkey slices on one of Seth's minimalistic white platters. *Don't you know how lucky you are to have watched him grow up?*

The mother was cloying, easy to trust. She seemed to like Rebeca well enough, but there was a bit of a cool distance. Rebeca at first thought that it was because she was the hired help, a brown woman from El Salvador, but now felt that it was because she was a woman, a competing maternal force that had replaced Mrs. Howard.

The mother was more friendly with Henrik. That this man was sharing a bed with her son didn't seem to concern her. Henrik, strangely enough, had become another son to her. Rebeca had a hard time understanding gringos, but she had been in the United States for so long that practically nothing surprised her.

That night, Rebeca packed her belongings as she watched the news recaps on Telemundo. She suspected that Seth's parents would be asking for her to leave the house in a week's time.

* * *

"Oh, Henrik, I can't believe it." Seth's mother hung onto Henrik's sturdy frame as if he were a life raft.

Seth's father was not as vulnerable with his emotions. "Where did it happen?" he asked Rebeca.

She led them through the house and they walked to the back yard, where the gardener, Mas, was returned to complete his assessment.

"Who's this?" Mr. Howard frowned.

Rebeca wanted to properly introduce the gardener, but she had forgotten his name.

"Mas Arai. My name is Mas Arai. Mista Howard is my customer."

Mrs. Howard continued on to the yellow crime tape that was still fluttering by the moss hill. The rest followed, with Mr. Howard almost tripping over a smashed yellow seed that was stuck on the back of his expensive shoe. "What the hell—"

It smelled awful, like dog feces. Rebeca always wondered what smell was coming from that end of the garden, but never walked out there. The garden was Henrik's responsibility, not hers.

Mrs. Howard put her manicured hand over her nose.

Mas knelt down by the seed scattered below the yellowing gingko trees. "These girl trees. Youzu only should buy boy trees. These seeds no good." He wrinkled his nose, emphasizing the rotten stink.

Rebeca let the Japanese man's word sit with her. Dealing with her limited English, she learned to decipher another person's pidgin language. So the gingko could be either female or male. That fascinated Rebeca, who often wondered about how the Creator was described in the Book of Genesis.

"Mister Seth would not be happy with this tree," she declared. His employer had always been sensitive about smells. He would be livid to encounter the seeds and their nauseating scent during his late-night strolls.

Henrik's face colored slightly. "It was the stupid nurserymen. He should have never sold me males."

"Dis funny, too. Smooth." Mas couldn't reach the ends of the broken branch left on the tree but pointed toward the remaining stump. The cut was clean and smooth.

"What are you trying to say?" Henrik challenged him.

"Someone use saw here." This time the gardener did not play coy and stared at Henrik.

"I don't know what you are getting at. I was at the pub watching the game."

But Rebeca thought back to the report of the match in Poland on Telemundo. Normally the Spanish-language station focused their sports coverage on Mexican and Latin American football teams. But something awful had transpired in the match between Denmark and Romania in Poland. There had been a lightning storm and one of the players had been electrocuted. Did the game continue as planned? Was the broadcast of the match terminated, leading to the dispersion of the revelers at the pub? She said nothing about the disruption. Surely the police were thoroughly checking Henrik's alibi. "Something not right," was all that she could manage, and she, like the Japanese gardener, looked accusatorily at Henrik.

"These two, what do they know?" Henrik declared, a little too defensively.

Mr. Howard's face betrayed nothing, but he was on the phone.

The mother, on the other hand, approached Henrik, her weathered neck resembling the twisted trunk of the mulberry tree. Her gray eyes bored into Henrik's blue ones. "Rebeca is like family," she spat out. "I trust her intuition more than any . . ."

A siren in a distance rang louder and louder until it stopped outside the iron gate of where Mishima-en was enclosed. It had taken the San Marino police only minutes to respond to Mr. Howard's call. After all, it wasn't every day that a serious crime like murder occurred in this absurdly wealthy neighborhood.

Henrik searched back and forth for an escape. But from his position on the hill by the gingko trees, the walkway had been designed to be a bit circuitous, so that with each turn, a garden visitor would be immersed into a new world. As a result, there was no clear path for him to run away from the authorities. That was the one thing that he had gotten right about his Japanese garden.

Baby Trap
Toni LP Kelner

Posted on Reddit in r/JustNoMIL:

I need advice. My husband died two months ago, and I've got an eight-month-old baby and no job. There's some life insurance money, but it won't last long, and no place that would hire me would pay enough to support us. I don't have family to help me—my parents and my husband's father died years ago, and we were only children. Plus we moved here when I was pregnant, so I haven't had a chance to make friends.

But yesterday I got a letter from a lawyer. My husband's uncle died last year, but it took a while for the lawyer to track us down. The uncle left his house to my husband, and with him gone, that house belongs to me. It's in the town down south where my husband grew up, and the cost of living down there is so low that the insurance payout should last long enough for me to figure out what to do next. There's just one snag: my mother-in-law. I'll call her the Harridan, which means a bossy old woman. (Three years of liberal arts education weren't wasted on me!) I only saw her once, and that was plenty.

My husband and I met in college and started dating when I was a freshman and he was a sophomore. Near the end of his senior year, I got pregnant. Yes, we used birth control, but it happened. He already had a great job lined up, and we decided to get married right after he graduated. Then I'd take a year or two to tend to the baby, and eventually go back to get my degree.

I wanted him to tell his mother right away, especially since she and I had never even met, but he wanted to wait until graduation. She and I sat together for the ceremony, but I could tell she wasn't happy about it, and she made a face when he said we were all going out afterward. On the way, she whispered to him that she thought the celebration should be "only family."

After we got to the restaurant and ordered, he sprang it on her: the job, the wedding plans, and the baby.

She freaked!

She said she'd never let him marry some tramp who'd baby-trapped him, and since he clearly couldn't make good decisions, he had to give up his dream job to go back home with her. As for the baby, she said either I could abort it—IT!—or give it to her to raise.

That was enough for me. I got up and walked out. And after the longest five minutes of my life, he came running after me and apologized. He said his mother wasn't going to be in our lives, and he never spoke to her again.

So why is the Harridan an issue now? Because she lives in the town where the house is. Should I risk moving there? And if I do, how can I protect myself and my baby?

* * *

It took me a month and a half to make the arrangements to move to that inherited house in Rocky Shoals, North Carolina, and I hadn't been there twenty-four hours when I spotted the red Cadillac Escalade for the first time. It was parked along the dirt road that ran parallel to the property line, and since it was outside the fence, technically it wasn't my business, but it was a weird place to park.

The house was on a dinky two-lane road with no other houses in eyeshot, so the car didn't belong to anybody visiting a neighbor. It wasn't a bus stop, scenic vista, or roadside shrine to a traffic accident victim, and nobody went hunting in a shiny late-model Escalade.

There was absolutely no good reason for the SUV to be there.

When I stepped off the screened-in front porch and looked in that direction, the Escalade's engine started up and the car left dust trails in the field as it curved around to get back onto the road, moving so fast that I couldn't get a good look at the driver.

That hadn't been suspicious at all.

I went back inside, making sure the door was locked behind me, and armed the state-of-the-art security system I'd had installed before moving in. The folks on Reddit had been firm that the house needed the best cameras and tech available, and I agreed completely.

I also turned on a few lights throughout the house, including the back bedroom, trying to make it look as if there were multiple people in residence. Then I went to the kitchen to make a grilled cheese sandwich and warm up some tomato soup for dinner. Afterward, I put Barney in his crib and spent the rest of the evening crocheting and watching TV.

Just before bedtime, I looked out the window to see if the SUV had returned, but I didn't see it.

The next morning, I dressed Barney in a crocheted hat and jacket and put him in the wicker rocking chair on the porch to take pictures. When I had enough, I carried him to the car and posed him in the car seat for more photos.

That's when I saw the red Escalade, parked in the same place as before. And again, as soon as I looked toward it, it drove away.

Leaving Barney where he was, I went back inside just long enough to make sure the alarm was set, and then headed off on errands: curbside pickup of groceries I'd ordered online, drop off of a couple of postage-paid padded envelopes at a FedEx box, a gas stop for the car, and finally, a trip through a McDonald's drive-through for lunch.

I spotted the SUV, or one just like it, three times. Rocky Shoals isn't a big town, so seeing it again could have been a coincidence, but I didn't believe it.

As soon as I returned to the house and had Barney and the groceries squared away, I followed Reddit's advice again and created a file of incidents, which so far was just the times and locations where I'd seen the Escalade. I thought about calling the cops, but what would I say? "I saw a car three or four times, maybe five. No, nobody threatened me." So I went back to my crocheting.

The Escalade showed up in the late afternoon and stayed until well after dark.

For the next week, the Escalade was nearby every day, parking at a safe distance, and appearing in town whenever Barney and I left the house, but it stayed far enough away that I couldn't see the driver or license plate, let alone get a picture. I carefully documented every time I spotted it, but I didn't think there was anything else I could do as long as they kept their distance. I didn't even know if it was the Harridan herself following or if somebody was working for her.

Eight days after I'd moved in, my stalker took it up a notch. The security system included an obvious camera over the front door, and she had enough sense to avoid it, but she didn't know that there were hidden cameras and motion sensors that covered the entire perimeter of the house. I knew precisely when she came onto the property that night and made her way around the house until she got to the window of Barney's room, where the glow from the nightlight showed through a gap in the curtains.

Part of me wanted to charge out to confront her, but I had to stick to the plan. That meant I just watched and videoed as she spent a good five minutes peering inside the room before creeping back to the SUV. Unfortunately, she'd worn a COVID-style face mask and a scarf to cover her hair, so I wouldn't have been able to pick her out of a lineup. Still, I could tell that she was white, with a thin build and no trace of athleticism in her movements. Just like the Harridan.

The next morning, I considered next steps. Some Reddit advisors suggested I call the police as soon as anything illegal happened, and trespassing and peeping certainly qualified, but others warned that bringing them in too soon could make me look paranoid or crazy. And though I was sure it was the Harridan, I had no proof. Finally I decided to wait another night, hoping she'd show her face to the camera.

I stuck to my usual routine. Dressing Barney in a new hat and jacket, taking photos, dropping off packages, and TV and crocheting in the evening. At bedtime, I did "accidentally" enlarge the gap in the curtains in Barney's room, hoping to tempt the Harridan to come closer and stay longer. Then I retreated to my bedroom to keep watch on my phone, sitting in the dark so she'd think I'd gone to bed after putting Barney down for the night.

She was so sure of herself that she only waited fifteen minutes after I turned off the lights. She started out wearing the mask again, but she must have had a runny nose from wandering around at all hours of the night, because she pulled the mask down to wipe it with a wadded tissue. When she didn't pull the mask up again, I got a perfect shot of her face.

It was, without a doubt, the Harridan.

My cell phone was already in my hand to dial 911. "Hello? My name is Runa Darlow, and there's a prowler outside my house. Can you send somebody right away?"

The Rocky Shoals cops had enough sense not to use their siren, but either the Harridan heard their car, or got spooked, or had had her fill of voyeurism because she was already driving off by the time the patrol car pulled into the driveway.

I met the two uniformed officers on the front porch while wearing a loose T-shirt and flannel pajama pants to show I was so shaken I hadn't taken time to dress.

The older cop was a man with a sturdy build and reddish-brown hair cut short, and was followed by a blonde with hair braided and coiled behind her head and a slightly pointed nose.

"She just left!" I said breathlessly

"Just calm down and tell us what happened," the male cop said using a tone that he probably meant to be reassuring.

I took a deep breath. "I'd just gone to bed and I heard something outside the window. So I called up the app—"

"The what, now?"

"The app? On my phone? It's tied into the security system."

"Oh, like one of them Ring doorbells."

I resisted the urge to roll my eyes. "Yeah, only it shows all around the house. Anyway, I saw a woman sneaking around, looking in the window! Here!"

I shoved the phone at them and let the man fumble with it before the woman reached over and pushed the right buttons to start the video showing the Harridan's face.

"Isn't that—?" the woman started to say, but the man interrupted with, "Hold on, Addalyn. Let me take a look." He watched the clip three more times before saying, "Well, this could be anyone."

"Seriously?" I said. "She's perfectly recognizable."

"Not to me. Now show me where this unknown person was."

I wanted to accuse the Harridan right then and there, but instead I dutifully led them to the side of the house to show them where she'd been standing. The man barely examined the scene, and didn't even try to take pictures of the footprints under the window.

He said, "It doesn't look to me like he or she was doing anything but looking—no attempt to break in or anything like that. No signs of a weapon."

Addalyn didn't speak, but her expression said she was wondering the same thing I was. How could the guy be so sure she was unarmed when he wouldn't even admit to her presenting as female?

"You think she was some kind of pervert?" I said.

He waved away the suggestion. "Let's not rush to conclusions. It could be completely innocent. Maybe he or she had car trouble and was looking for help. This place is pretty remote."

"She drove away just fine," I retorted, "and leaving that aside, why didn't she come to the front door?"

"Well…" I could tell he was thinking as fast he could. "Were your front lights on?"

"No."

"There's your answer then. He or she went to see if anybody was awake but when he or she didn't see you, he or she left and got his or her car working." All too casually, he asked, "I don't suppose you got a look at the vehicle?"

"Not tonight," I said, "but there's been a red Cadillac Escalade parked near here several times the past few days."

He swallowed visibly. "Lots of those around. It probably had nothing to do with the person with car trouble."

I wanted to argue with him, but he struck me as the kind who'd have dug his heels in if I tried to critique his stellar investigative technique, and Addalyn wouldn't meet my gaze. So I pretended to be grateful for their rushing out there, added in a hint of embarrassment for having made a fuss over nothing, and after getting their names, let them go.

As soon as I got inside, I microwaved some coffee and set my laptop up on the kitchen table to do some research. The male cop was Theodore Fry, and I spent quite a while checking him out, but didn't find anything particularly significant. He'd been on the job for six years and seemed to have had moderate success apprehending shoplifters and teenaged joyriders, but nothing seemed shady.

His partner, Addalyn Cooper, had less time on the force, but better arrest statistics, and nothing in her background set off any alarm bells, either.

I kept digging for dirt about the Rocky Shoals police, but if anything crooked was happening, it hadn't made it into the news or onto social media. I'd originally ignored the department's own website, figuring there'd be nothing useful there, but that's where I caught what I'd missed when I planned the move.

Nolan McIntyre, the Rocky Shoals police chief, had been elected the previous year, and most of the campaign coverage focused on his many ties to the community. Apparently he was related to a large percentage of the town's population, which likely helped him win the election. There was an election night photo of him and his proud family: wife, children, parents, siblings, in-laws, and beyond. Right in the middle of the photo, standing next to Chief McIntyre, with a smug smile on her face, was his mother's oldest sister. The caption identified her as Josephine Kemp, but she'd always be the Harridan to me.

I couldn't believe I'd missed it. More importantly, I didn't believe that Fry and Cooper hadn't recognized their boss's aunt. I didn't know if they hadn't admitted it because they were corrupt, or were afraid of their boss, or wanted to allow him to handle it himself. I was betting on it being one of the first two, but I decided to give Chief McIntyre some time to do the right thing.

The next day I called the department to see if any progress had been made, but the woman answering the phone didn't seem to know anything about the case, which led me to believe that no report had been filed. Though I left messages for Fry and Cooper, neither returned my calls. Most telling of all, the red Escalade didn't show up.

I waited another week, making more appearances in town, leaving the curtains half-open, doing everything I could to bait the Harridan into showing herself again. Nothing.

It could have meant that Chief McIntyre had warned her off, but given what I knew of her parenting style, I very much doubted that she was giving up. I had to do something before she did, and I couldn't rely on the Rocky Shoals police for support.

The next morning I checked out the town's three women's clothing shops. The first one was stocked with go-to-church dresses and the second aimed at women the Harridan's age, but the third had what I needed for an outfit that said "available but not slutty." That ended up being jeans a bit tighter than I usually wear them, a low-cut sweater that brought out the blue in my eyes, dangling earrings, and a pair of high-heel booties. I already had enough makeup to finish the look.

I didn't see the Escalade, but was hoping somebody in town would report what I'd bought to the Harridan.

That night, after making sure that Barney was secure, I headed for Crossroads Bar and Grille, which was several miles away from Rocky Shoals. It was fairly busy, but not packed, and I found a table where I could nurse my drink and check out the other patrons, looking for a likely target. At seven-thirty or so, a trim man with the beginnings of a bald spot and neither a companion nor a wedding band came in and got a Bud at the bar. There was something about him that made me think he was what I needed, but I did some fast Googling on my phone to confirm it.

By then he'd gone to one of the two pool tables and was lining up shots, so I edged in his direction and watched admiringly. He actually was decent, so my admiration wasn't entirely feigned. He noticed me watching, but pretended not to until I said, "Hey, you're really good."

He thanked me, we introduced ourselves, and he invited me to play. His name was Ike, and fortunately I didn't have to work overly hard to let him win. After a couple hours of pool, conversation, and beer, I'd made it plain that I was interested in continuing our interaction at my place, and he was gratified by my interest. Ike confirmed that we were both sober enough to drive—which I definitely was because I'd dumped most of the alcohol I'd ordered—and followed me back to the house in his car.

I waited for him on the porch before unlocking the front door and going inside. The lights were on in the living room. "That's funny," I said. "I could have sworn I left them off. Anyway, would you like a nightcap?"

He answered by putting his arms around me and I was impressed that he hesitated long enough to ensure that I was willing before leaning in for a kiss.

He had skills, and must have eaten a mint on the way home to make sure his breath didn't smell of stale beer, which I appreciated. Under other circumstances, I'd have been happy to continue on to the bedroom, but before that could happen, Ike and I heard noise coming from the back of the house.

"Is there somebody else here?" Ike said, probably worried that I had a lurking husband or boyfriend. Instead, the Harridan burst out of the hall.

"Where is the baby!" she demanded.

And I looked her right in the eyes and said, "What baby?"

She blinked and froze for a second before saying, "My baby! Where is my baby?"

Even in the heat of the moment, I noticed the pronoun change. "I don't know who you think you are, but if you're not out of my house in ten seconds, I'm calling the cops."

"I'm not leaving without my baby!"

"There's no baby here!"

"You're lying!"

She started toward me, but Ike stepped in front of her. "Ma'am," he said, "you need to calm down."

She actually shoved him aside. *"Where is he?"*

"I don't know what you're talking about. I don't have a baby."

"Lying slut!" Only when she'd lifted it over her head did I realize she was holding a tire iron.

I fell back against the wall and threw my arms over my head to protect myself, but there was no need. I heard an electrical buzz, a scream, and a heavy thud as the Harridan fell to the floor twitching and moaning. Ike had tased her.

As she tried to writhe toward me, Ike blocked her and said, "Stay where you are unless you want me to shock you again."

She used an excellent selection of profanity, but she stopped moving.

"Call 911," Ike said to me.

I nodded shakily and found my purse and cell phone, but dialed the Rocky Shoals department instead. When the desk clerk sounded reluctant to send somebody, Ike took the phone and said, "This is Ike Everett of the Catawba County Police, and I require backup immediately. Or should I call *my* department?" Unsurprisingly, the clerk promised a swift response.

"You're a cop?" I tried to sound surprised, though I'd known he was a cop right away. Among the basket of facts I'd discovered doing research was that Crossroads Bar and Grille was owned by a disabled county cop, and many of his former colleagues hung out there. It hadn't been hard to pick out Ike as a cop, even in civilian clothes. There was something about his haircut, the way he spoke to the owner, and how he carried himself. I hadn't been sure that he'd bring a weapon, but I had hoped. "Ike, this woman is crazy or on something. I do not have a baby."

He nodded, but I could tell he didn't know what to believe. To be fair, it was a bizarre situation. Instead of getting laid, he was having to deal with a home invader and an alleged missing baby. He was obviously relieved when the trio of Rocky Shoals cops swarmed in the door.

Chief McIntyre was a lot scrawnier in person than in his pictures, and had apparently come in such a hurry that his uniform shirt was misbuttoned. He was followed by my friends Fry and Cooper.

McIntyre took in the scene, and if I'd had any doubts about his relationship to the Harridan, they were erased when he said, "Aunt Jo, are you all right?" He turned to glare at Ike. "What the hell is going on here?"

Ike went cold and formal. "The resident and I arrived here at approximately ten p.m. and upon entering, were confronted by that woman. Your aunt?" He raised an eyebrow at McIntyre, who nodded stiffly. "Your aunt accused the resident of hiding a baby, though whose baby she was referring to is unclear. When she tried to attack the resident, I was forced to discharge my Taser to subdue her."

McIntyre sighed. "Addalyn, help my aunt up off the floor." Once the Harridan was settled on the couch, he turned to me with a look that was meant to be intimidating. "Can I have your name?"

"Runa Darlow."

The Harridan snapped, "Her married name is Kemp!"

"She told me her name was Darlow," Ike said.

"Darlow or Kemp, which is it?" McIntyre said.

"For heaven's sake, I think I know my own name."

"Can I see some identification?"

"My driver's license is in my purse." The cops actually tensed when I reached for my purse, as if afraid I were going to pull out a bazooka instead of my wallet. I handed my license to McIntyre.

He squinted from the license to me. I couldn't blame him—the photo was a couple of years old. Then he handed it to Fry, who took it out onto the porch, no doubt intending to see what he could find out about me.

"All right, Miss Darlow… It is Miss? Not Mrs.?"

"Ms."

"Ms. Darlow, can you tell me how you know Mrs. Kemp?"

"I *don't* know her!"

"She knows exactly who I am, and I know exactly what she is!" the Harridan snapped. "She's the one who baby-trapped your cousin. I knew she was trouble the second I met her! She probably had something to do with his death, and now she's done something with his child. When she went out tonight without him, I realized she'd left him alone like the trashy excuse for a mother she is, but I couldn't find him. She's abandoned him, or given him away, or who knows what!"

I tried to look baffled. "Do you know what baby she's talking about?"

"That baby is my grandchild! I've seen him with you."

"You've seen…? You mean Barney?" I asked.

"She admits it!" she said triumphantly.

McIntyre shushed her. "And where is Barney?"

"He's in the trunk of my car, but—"

"In the trunk!" Had she been wearing pearls, she'd have clutched them. "Sweet Jesus, she killed my baby!" She broke into loud sobs that I was eighty-five-percent sure were sincere.

McIntyre barked, "Keys?"

"They're in my purse, but I should tell you—" I started to say but McIntyre grabbed it, dumped out the contents, found the keys, and ran outside with Cooper and Ike following. Fry stayed behind with me and the wailing Harridan. While it was good procedure to keep the two of us under observation, from the way his face turned pale green, I suspect it was really to keep from seeing what he thought the others were seeing.

Neither he nor the Harridan was expecting the sudden whoop of laughter from outside.

A moment later, McIntyre came in carrying a baby doll wearing a crocheted hat and jacket. Cooper was trying to hide a grin, but Ike wasn't even making the attempt.

"What the hell is this for?" McIntyre asked.

I wanted to point out that it was perfectly legal to own a baby doll, even if I kept it in my trunk, but I opted for discretion. "I make crocheted baby clothes and blankets to sell on Etsy, and I have Barney to model the merchandise. I've got a crib set up in the back bedroom, too. It makes for better pictures." I looked at the Harridan with feigned sympathy. "It never occurred to me that she was talking about Barney. I mean, he doesn't look like a real baby."

It was as if all the air had gone out of the Harridan. "But I saw him, clear as anything," she said in confusion. "He was so much like my son that he could have been his twin. And you! I remember your hair and your eyes."

"I don't know who you met, but it wasn't me. This is a new haircut and I'm wearing colored contacts." I'd lightened my hair color, too, but didn't bring it up.

"Aunt Jo, her license does show her with longer hair and it says her eyes are brown, not blue," McIntyre said.

"Then why is she in this house?" the Harridan asked. "It was left to my son. How did she get it if she's not *her*?"

"I rented it," I said. "I don't know who owns it—I dealt with a property management company."

"But…" She was trying to come up with some other way to prove that I was somebody I was not.

I said, "Is that why you've been playing Peeping Tom, to find a baby?"

"She was doing what?" Ike asked.

"I called the cops last week because she was looking in my windows, and I caught her on the video, too, but the officers *said* they didn't know who she was." I didn't have to fake my anger.

McIntyre said, "I was told about that incident, but it was my understanding that the video was unclear."

"It's perfectly clear, and I've still got the file so you can use it for the trial."

"Trial?" The Harridan gasped. "I've done nothing wrong."

"Are you serious? You trespassed, you broke into my home, and you attacked me!"

McIntyre muttered something about his aunt being distraught by the recent loss of her son and started asking questions. Why had I moved to Rocky Shoals? How had I learned about the vacant house? Could he see my lease? What kind of business was crocheting baby blankets? On and on, trying to find some explanation that didn't make his aunt look like a maniac and him look like an idiot. He even asked why I'd decided to change my hair.

When McIntyre reached that far, Ike pulled him aside and after a short discussion, the chief finally took his aunt into custody and the Rocky Shoals crew left.

Ike kindly helped me temporarily cover the kitchen window the Harridan had bashed in to get into the house, but romance was off the table. Unlike Chief McIntyre, Ike was no fool, and he knew something was off, even if he couldn't put his finger on what. He did accept a kiss as a thank-you for saving my life, but I didn't expect him to come calling.

It was just as well. I wouldn't be in Rocky Shoals much longer anyway. Now that the Harridan had been arrested for breaking into the house of an innocent woman and claiming that a cheap baby doll was her grandchild, she'd be too busy with legal complications to go looking for my client, who was her real daughter-in-law. I'd sought out the young widow out after seeing her Reddit post.

With my help, the client had been safely relocated to a town where she had friends who could help her with the baby, in a state that didn't have grandparent's rights laws. She hadn't run out of money yet, and the management company—which was owned by a grateful former client—would put the house on the market to make sure she had enough to pay the bills for some time to come. The baby, who was actually a girl and who was certainly not named Barney, was reportedly doing very well.

The next day I sent a barrage of anonymous tips to local TV stations and newspapers, and took great pleasure in seeing the story go viral.

For the sake of maintaining my cover, I kept crocheting in the evening even though I was awful at it. The items I'd been selling were made by another former client, while a third had set up my Etsy shop to look as if I'd been in business for a while. My line of work, helping women in trouble, makes for very loyal former clients.

I did stop wearing the colored contacts—they were uncomfortable and I no longer needed to look like my client's twin.

After a week, I called the Rocky Shoals police to tell them that I was breaking my lease because I felt unsafe living there. Unsurprisingly, they didn't try to convince me to stay, though they took my contact info so they could be in touch if the case went to trial. Cooper confided that she thought the Harridan was going to take a plea instead and then take a rest cure in a private facility, so I probably wouldn't be needed.

It only took a couple of days to pack up the house. The item that I took the most care with had been hidden behind a wall in the attic: the real Barney.

Of course the baby doll the police had found in my car hadn't actually been Barney. Though it had been advertised as having lifelike features, it wouldn't have fooled anybody as smart as the Harridan. No, the real Barney was an insanely expensive Reborn doll, one of the ultra-realistic baby reproductions designed to help women through infertility, miscarriage, loss of a child, and so on. Barney was so accurate that I half expected him to breathe.

It was no wonder the Harridan had believed it was her grandson. To make him even more convincing, I'd paid extra for a custom job. The client had some of her husband's baby pictures so I'd had the doll maker use them as a model.

Normally I get rid of the props I use for a job, and I certainly had no intention of keeping the crib or crocheting equipment, but I decided to keep Barney. There was no telling when I might need to catch somebody else in a baby trap.

The Stolen Tent
By Richie Narvaez

"Quickly," Balthazar Miró, the great detective, said to the porter. "The key!"

Kurt, the *Dittbrenner* porter who had a nose like the prow of the very zeppelin we were aboard, fished out the key and handed it to Miró, who opened the door to reveal Hugo Alvedine, face down, on the floor, still in his dressing gown.

"Doctor!" Miró called to me.

"Of course," said the porter. "I'd forgotten that Herr Dusfrene is a doctor."

"Of rhinoplasty. But I know enough to know the difference between death and an accidental coma."

"Accidental coma?"

"Once. *Non*, two times. Surgery is not an exact science, *mon ami*."

M. Alvedine was of a portly nature, and the cabin, like all the other cabins on the airship, was small and cramped. Rather athletically, Kurt pounced on the lower berth and to the ladder, which the body was wedged against. Together, he and Miró and I gently guided M. Alvedine onto his back, a not inconsiderable effort given the man's considerable size. His legs remained in a sitting position as I felt for a pulse.

"*Hélas!* Departed from life," I said. "Definitely . . . Hold on. *Non*, he's . . . Wait . . . Wait. . . La la la la . . . *Oui*. Ah, yes! Definitely, definitely departed."

"How long?" asked the sleuth.

"No earlier than one o'clock, no later than three, I should say. Rigor has not set in."

As he was wont to do when he had a pronouncement to make, Miró touched his forefinger to the ebon-dyed imperial below his sensual lips and broad, tropical nose. "You will find the cause of *Señor* Alvedine's death to be a myocardial infarction."

"*Ach, nee!*" squealed the porter.

"That means a heart attack," I explained to him.

The famed investigator had surprised me many times before, but I was astonished at the swiftness and certainty of his conclusion.

"Can you be so sure, Miró?"

"*Cómo no.* It is a matter of science. Alvedine was in his seventies and, unlike you, my esteemed friend, who can eat like an army and remain as thin as a rail, he was corpulent to a fault. Yesterday at dinner, he ordered five desserts just for himself, and bragged about his doctor's dire warnings about his health as if he had won an Olympic medal. He also smoked cigars without pause and drank to excess. *Barriga llena, corazón* no *contento.*"

"You were watching him closely," said Kurt.

"Miró watches everyone closely," I asserted.

Miró continued. "*Sí.* In addition, we can be assured there was no foul play, as his door was locked, so no one else could enter. Please also notice that his right hand is clutching his chest, and his bright purple face is fixed in surprise."

"*Ça alors et* Q.E.D.," I said. "Once again, your conclusion makes complete sense."

Indeed, that was the conclusion Miró delivered to the zeppelin's captain when he arrived at the scene.

"Your reputation precedes you, Herr Miró. I trust your verdict," said Captain Neu, with his allegedly Aryan features. "To be honest, I had worried something untoward happened. Apparently, we have a stowaway somewhere on board, and while some stowaways are merely impecunious, others can be quite dangerous, especially in these dangerous times."

"I'm sure you will catch your uninvited guest presently. There is nowhere they can run on an airship, *sí o no?*"

"Yes. Quite. Very well, thank you, Herr Miró. I will break the news to Alvedine's wife."

"Of course," said Miró, with a bow.

I had glimpsed Mme Alvedine while we were boarding and saw her glancingly in the dining room. What impressed me the most was not her charming button nose, but the glaring bruise across the right side of her face, which she masterfully, spiritedly made no effort to hide.

Back in our cabin, as Miró, still limber for a man his age, buffed his toenails, I said to him, "Alvedine's cabin is only a few meters down the corridor, yet I heard nothing. His passing must have been quick."

"*Cómo no.*"

"*Et mon dieu,* but is it not curious it was not murder? If anyone had a motive, surely it was his wife. At least it is not yet another mystery to solve. We have had enough on this trip!"

I was thinking of the investigations that had embroiled Miró—and, by association, myself—for weeks, preventing us from sampling the *Pappardelle al Cinghiale,* in Florence, and the *Esterházy Torta* at the Café Landtmann, in Vienna.

"It is still a tragedy, *amigo,* "Miró said, his dark, circled eyes as doleful as ever. "As we have come to know again and again in our long association: All death is tragedy."

* * *

That evening at dinner, as the *Dittbrenner* cruised calmly over the Atlantic towards a place called Lakehurst, New Jersey, in America, Miró and I were seated at the captain's table. The mood was surprisingly, eerily, cheerful, given the day's tragic events.

Across from us, a man with a thickish face and a nose like a boxing glove was ordering a round of champagne for everyone at the table. He was introduced to us as J. J. Feil.

"Let's celebrate!" the man roared.

Miró asked, "And what are we celebrating, *señor?*"

"Success, my Spanish friend!"

"Perdóname, I am not Spanish. I am from Ponce, in Puerto Rico."

"Why that's fascinating, I'm sure. Well, all foreigners are welcome at this table. As long as you speak English!"

Many people incorrectly believed Miró was a Spaniard, but in point of fact he was a U. S. citizen by dint of the Jones–Shafroth Act of 1917. Miró could have further corrected M. Feil, but the error had occurred on too many occasions with too many others, and he had long ago instructed me not to make a scene about it.

I said only, "What success are we talking about?"

"Alvedine and I are—or were, *ha*—in manufacturing; specifically, computing, tabulating, and recording machines. I made my fortune in chemical weapons during the Great War, but I saw the writing on the wall. Mark my words: computing, tabulating, and recording machines are the future. And Alvedine and I were both in Berlin, bidding for a project with the government there, and now—"

"Perdóname otra vez. You mean, with the Nazis?" Miró inquired.

"Yes, them," Feil said quickly. "Now, they hadn't announced who they would hire, but, bluntly speaking, with Alvedine out of the running, I'll have the job all sewn up. It's a pity, of course, that it happened this way, but, that's how the business cat jumps. Here's the champagne!"

The champagne was served all around. Miró and I left ours untouched. Instead, I enjoyed my usual red wine and Miró his usual tumbler of dark rum.

Sometime after the exquisite quail-in-nest, a woman to Miró's left began talking to us. Although somewhat horse-faced, she had the most delicate nostrils.

"Catty Barwick. It's swell to make your acquaintance," she said, extending a mannish hand that looked filthy with ink and nicotine.

Knowing of Miró's squeamish nature, I reached over and shook her hand in his stead.

In a stage whisper redolent of coffee and tobacco, Mlle Barwick said, "Listen, I'm from the *Albuquerque Sun-Bulletin,* and I got a hunch this Alvedine story is going to be the biggest scoop in years. The biggest!"

"A journalist," I observed, "what an interesting job for a woman."

"Nuts. My parents wanted me to be a nurse. I studied for a year but warblin' 'There, there, Mr. Smith, just take your pills' twenty times a day wasn't my bailiwick. Anyway, like I was saying, my editor would love to have an exclusive, and getting a quote from a famous detective would be a swell feather in my cap, I don't mind telling you. How about helping a girl out? Can you tell me about the body, how you knew to look for it?"

"*Sí. Señor* Alvedine was not present at breakfast, and his wife said that he was not answering when she knocked."

"So, the marrieds had separate cabins?"

"It would seem so."

"Maybe he needed the room to move around in, if you know what I mean? And the missus told you he wasn't answering?"

"She mentioned it to the waiter."

"Oh, she was at your table."

"No, she sat in that corner."

"Three tables over?" The woman whistled. "Way over there? And you heard that?"

I interjected: "Miró's senses verge on the preternatural."

"I'll say. You know, I took this balloon ride for a whole other reason. I really wanted to talk to Alvedine about something personal, if you know what I mean."

"*¿Sobre qué?* Regarding what matter?"

She moved even closer, and the scent of coffee and tobacco grew stronger. "Actually, confidentially, it was about his missus. See, it seems there's more to Suzanne Alvedine than meets the eye. I don't mean just that black eye, which is another story. Officially, she is known to have been an actress. But she's got a, let us say, shadowy past. And with Alvedine dead, and her in line to inherit his moolah, she's gonna make headlines."

"May I ask, to what kind of 'shadowy past' do you refer?"

"You'll have to wait to read it in the *Albuquerque Sun-Bulletin.* But I will tell you this: Once we land, I have a contact in New York who'll be able to give me the straight dope on Mrs. Alvedine's previous life in Brooklyn."

Later, in the smoking room, as Miró and I enjoyed a pair of his excellent Caribbean cigars, a gentleman approached us to ask for the electric lighter. He introduced himself as Lawrence Chambers and said that he was an investor.

His name surprised me because he had distinctly Oriental features.

"Chambers?" I asked. "Aren't you a Chinaman?"

"No. I am Korean, actually. I was adopted by a pair of scientists from Poland."

"Chambers?"

"A name change, Dr. Dusfrene. After one sheds one's identity once, it seems to become easier over time."

We three puffed away in silence for some time when, without our prompting, Chambers said, "I say, good riddance to that Alvedine."

"Why would you say that, *señor?*"

"Nothing personal. But the man didn't lack for enemies, you see. Not me, of course, not me. I've no enemies. But that Alvedine—he took advantage of the Crash and drove many men out of their windows."

"May I ask," said Miró, "how exactly?"

"Not to be a *yenta*, but, you see, while most investors watched their fortunes evaporate—not me, of course—that Alvedine had sold most of his stock holdings before the Crash and made even more money by selling short."

"As if he possessed advance knowledge?"

"Exactly, sir. But you didn't hear that from me, of course. Not that one can slander a dead man."

"Correct, *señor.*"

"Which is why I say, 'Good riddance.'"

At that very moment, a bedraggled young man burst into the room from the main corridor. Panting, he looked at us with wild, pleading eyes, then he began to tap on the wall, to some secret purpose known only to him. Nothing happened.

From the corridor came shouts in German:

"Halt!"

"Mist!"

"Wo ist er hin?"

The young man backed away from the wall and left the room at a gallop.

We stood there in silence, as a few seconds later, the German security guards ran down the main corridor after him, still shouting, but now at each other.

"*Ich hätte zur Marine gehen sollen.*"

"*Du läufst wie meine Großmutter. du hast blinden Passagier entkommen lassen.*"

"*Leck mich am Arsch.*"

I hazarded a guess. "The stowaway?"

"*Así parecería,*" said Miró.

By which he really meant, "I do not know. Why ask me?" After many years as friends, between my French and his Spanish and our English, Miró and I were always able to understand each other.

"What an evening," I said to Miró that night after showering. I must add that I felt inadequately refreshed. The weak stream of water aboard this vessel was more like that from a seltzer bottle than from a shower. "Not only is there a stowaway running around the ship. It also seems as if we are on a ship full of people who detested the deceased. Which makes it even odder that he was not, as they say in American gangster films, 'rubbed out.' His death seems to have made a lot of people happy."

Miró looked at me with his dark eyes but said nothing. He began his nightly meditation and soon turned in.

I slept well, perhaps because of the exhausting events of the day, *certainement* much better than the night before. It had been my first night aboard a dirigible, and my inside man was not used to it.

But sometime after midnight, I did get up to use the water closet.

Upon my return to the cabin, in the brief moment the light from the corridor shone inside, I saw that Miró was awake, his eyes burning into the ceiling.

* * *

In the morning, I climbed down the ladder from my berth, and Miró was sitting on his berth, the dark circles under his eyes puffy but his gaze as intense as ever. Somehow, while I was sleeping, the great detective had been able to get fully dressed, in his usual burgundy shirt and burgundy three-piece suit, and ready for the day.

"You are awake at last!" he said.

"Yes, Miró. What is it?

"You get your wish. *Señor* Alvedine was, in fact, murdered."

"*Bon sang!* But it was not exactly my wish."

"*He estado más perdido que un juey bizco.*" He gestured toward his dressing case, which was open and on the bed, and to its velvet-lined bottom drawer, which was usually full of potions, poisons, and concoctions the great detective had collected over the long years. But on this morning, several of the slots were distressingly vacant.

"*Mon dieu!*" I said.

"*¡Exacto!* Someone has been here and stolen dangerous weapons. We must tell the captain, and then we must interview all the passengers and all the crew."

"All of them?"

"*Lo todo.* All of them!"

The captain's first question was one of the first that had occurred to me.

"But couldn't that be better done after we land," Captain Neu said, "with the full force of the authorities?"

We were in the cargo hold, the coldest part of the ship, where M. Alvedine's body had been placed. We stood above the corpse. Miró had just uncovered it and showed us a tiny needle puncture under the man's left armpit. "A piece of evidence," he had said, "we were never intended to find."

The great detective averred that the investigation must take place at once. "Once we alight upon the solid Earth, the murderer may find an opportunity to escape. And perhaps at the same time we will find your uninvited guest."

"Ah, yes, the stowaway. It matters little. Our schedule must unfortunately be altered because of a vexing storm in our path. We will have to steer around it, adding at least another day to our journey."

"*Juracán sabe lo que hace,*" said Miró. When he saw our puzzled faces, he added, "That will give us the time we need."

"Captain," I asked gingerly, "how many people are aboard? Officially, I mean."

"Officially, fifty-six passengers and the regular crew of forty, not including myself."

I sighed. I had been looking forward to some leisure, reading magazines and writing postcards. Alas, this was not to be.

* * *

The first person escorted into the writing room was a man named Wolfgang Nachtnebel, who was the night porter for Corridor A, the corridor where we were staying and where M. Alvedine had been murdered. He had a gin-blossomed lump on his face and I had to resist giving him my card.

Miró asked, "Do you have the master key for all the cabins in Corridor A?"

"Yes, sir."

"Please note that your captain is not here, and he need only know what is relevant to this case. But I must know, did you fall asleep while on duty?"

Nachtnebel looked at both of us, no doubt wondering if he should believe us. Finally, his gaze fixed on the floor. "Yes. Yes I did."

"Does this happen often?"

He paused, but then admitted, "Yes." Then he looked up suddenly. "But that night was different."

"*¿Cómo?*"

"Well, I fell asleep at some point after midnight. But it was not a good sleep. I didn't dream at all. I mean, I always dream—of my wife, Thea, and often of her sister, Frieda. Much more often of her sister."

"How did you feel upon waking? Were you nauseous? Did you feel cold?"

"Yes! I was still sleepy and I ached."

"*Moi aussi!*" I blurted, realizing that my waking had been very much the same.

"Myself as well, Doctor. *Señor* Nachtnebel, I must ask: Did you have any reason to do harm to *Señor* Alvedine?"

"He was a pushy pig. He sent me back and forth three times to get more pillows. I could've strangled him. But I didn't! I didn't kill him, if that's what you think! I was out for the night. His wife is what woke me. Her knocking on his door. I said I could open it, but she said she didn't want to wake him, to let him sleep. So there."

Nachtnebel was dismissed. Mme Alvedine was the next to be seated. Confirming my first impression of her, she was sanguine but not overbearing, proud but not arrogant. She was also quite lovely.

"It's nice to see you again," she said to the great detective. "Shall I call you Mr. Miró?"

I did not remember her meeting Miró on the ship, but they had probably become introduced on the way to the water closets. That can often be the best way to mingle with fellow passengers while traveling. I have often thought of writing a book about it.

"Miró will suffice," he said, obviously wanting to make the woman at ease.

"I like your first name. Balthazar. It's a grand name. One of the Three Kings. I like it. Very much."

As they talked, I wondered if there was anything I could do to improve her profile.

"*Gracias.* I like it very much myself. Now, I have to be indelicate and ask about your marriage. May I?"

"You may."

"You had reasons to be . . . unhappy?"

"Yes. But not enough to murder my husband. If you're wondering about this," she said, turning her face to show her still remarkable bruise. "Hugo has . . . *had* a temper. This is not the first time he's marked me so. Not all men can be polite and considerate as you are . . . I mean, as I assume someone like you to be."

Mme Alvedine said that she must've taken a sleeping draught because she was asleep all night. She had awoken in the morning feeling nauseous and still needing sleep. She had seen one of the crew snoring in his chair at the end of the corridor. She was afraid her knocking on her husband's cabin door had awakened him. The porter offered to open the door, but she demurred. She said her husband's temper did not improve upon being disturbed from his rest.

"Very well," Miró said to the widow. "That is all."

As she got up to go, she said, "Your life, Miró. I've read about it. Followed your exploits. Law enforcement. Private investigations. I wonder, why did you choose it?"

"I believed the chaos of the world needs order."

"Does it ever bother you? To be around all this . . . violence and death?"

"I have lived my life surrounded by violence and death. But justice is what matters above all else. No harm should be overlooked, no wrong should go unpunished."

She made a sound that may have been a gasp. I had come to the conclusion that her profile was perfect.

As she left, she turned to say, "I do hope you had some light in your life, at some point?"

"I did," Miró said. "Once."

Yes, a perfect profile. But when was lunch? I checked my watch. *Merde,* had it only been a half hour since breakfast? I was starving.

Before the scent of Mme Alvedine's sandalwood perfume dissipated, M. Feil blustered into the room.

"So, how was he killed?"

"Poison," said Miró.

"There you go. If I had killed him, I would've beaten him to death with my bare hands. Poison is a woman's weapon. I don't suppose that's enough of an alibi for you?"

"It is not."

"Fine. I'll admit I had a good reason to kill Alvedine. But I also have another alibi you're going to love, my Spanish friend."

M. Feil then confessed rather pridefully that he was "busy" in his secretary's berth all night long.

His secretary, a Cheryl Greer, was brought in and she, bashfully, confirmed his story.

"But would you admit that your livelihood might depend on agreeing with *Señor* Feil's statement?"

"Yes," Mlle Greer admitted.

Both M. Feil and his secretary were staying in Corridor C, on the other side of the ship. They had experienced no ill feeling upon waking.

Mlle Barwick was led in next, and she straddled her chair and leaned forward. "So it's murder then. I knew it! Now you're going to ask me if I killed him. Hah, why would I want to? Rich, arrogant men like him are my bread and butter. They fill headlines, sell papers."

Miró leaned backward. *"Por favor*, tell us, Miss . . .'"

"Call me 'Catty.'"

"Very well. Miss Catty, did you lose any money in the Crash because of Alvedine?"

"I suppose I did, but not so's I'd noticed. I was dirt poor before the Crash, and I was dirt poor after. It's only in the last couple of years I've been able to haul myself up by my own bootstraps using my wits and my reporting skills. It certainly didn't get by with my looks!"

"Ah. This history you are researching about *Señora* Alvedine, what is it concerning?"

"I'll be honest: I can only guess. My source in New York and I both have pieces of the puzzle. My hunch is there's something good and, shall we say, salacious concerning her career as an actress, but I'll need to speak with him before I can paint the whole picture."

"And you would print this . . . salacious material?"

"Are you kidding? Our readers go hog-wild for it!"

"I must ask where you were on the night of the murder."

"I was flying solo, if you know what I mean, in my cabin, so no alibi. But like I said, I had no motive."

M. Chambers was next. He seemed nervous and chewed his nails. Perhaps he needed a cigarette.

He was staying in Corridor B, had slept a restful night, and did not have a cabin mate.

Miró asked, "Both your parents are scientists?"

"Sure. What about it?"

"What kind?"

"They do research on vaccines and stuff."

"So, they handle chemicals and syringes and other medical paraphernalia?"

"Yes, of course they do. What are you getting at?"

"Is it fair to say you grew up around such things and had a familiarity with their use?"

"Yes, but—"

"*Señor* Chambers, you are Jewish, are you not?"

"Yes, I adopted my parents' faith. But how did you—"

"Your use of Yiddish, I noticed it in the smoking room."

"What about it?"

"You are no doubt aware of Alvedine's plans to aid the Nazis, who are implementing a deplorable atrocity against the Jewish people in Germany."

"I am. I knew."

"And perhaps you wanted to stop him from doing so?"

"Yes—but, no! No, I would never stoop to murder. If we're going to defeat those—pardon my language—those bastards, we have to do it face to face, toe to toe. We have to show them we are better people."

"Well spoken, *Señor* Chambers," Miró said. "Please accept my apologies if my questions seemed harsh. But we must get to the truth."

After M. Chambers, the day proceeded. Slowly. Some had very strong motives to murder M. Alvedine.

Rake Shufflebottom, a British professional gambler, said he'd lost a fortune in a single dog-racing bet with M. Alvedine.

Carmine Vinciguerra, an Italian war hero, said he could trace the scars in his lungs to mustard gas manufactured by M. Alvedine's company.

Anna Lagerlöf, a Swedish athlete, claimed M. Alvedine visited her in her dressing room at the Stade Olympique and had been more interested in her figure than in figure skating.

Others had less striking motives.

An American film actor named Clark Gable said M. Alvedine had hogged the water closet for an hour, which he thought was quite rude.

Justo Suárez, an Argentinian boxer, said he just did not like M. Alvedine's face and that he had fought people for less.

Peter Luger, the head chef, said M. Alvedine's endless need for customized orders drove him so insane that he contemplated adding a laxative to the last pudding M. Alvedine ordered. He refrained only because he had run out of laxative.

And on and on.

In short, it seemed that, excluding Miró and me, each and every person on board, the fifty-six passengers as well as the crew of forty, had a reason to murder M. Alvedine. There seemed to be no end to this mystery, and neither was dinner anywhere in sight.

Just as we were about to interview the members of the orchestra, Captain Neu rushed in and said, "We've found him."

* * *

The captain led us down to the bottom of the gondola, to the forward gangway, and there stood the disheveled young man we had seen running the day before. Guards—and a distinctly sour scent—surrounded him.

"My men noticed an unpleasant odor coming from this part of the ship," said Captain Neu. "They followed it and found a hideout here, tucked against the outer hull of the gondola. Then they waited, and like a mouse he returned to his hovel."

"His papers, sir." One of the airship's security guards goose-stepped forward and handed over the document as well as a small satchel. "His bag, sir."

The captain opened the bag and handed each item he found to the guard. "A banana. A notebook. Pictures of a young woman. Letters. Poetry? . . . Bad poetry. Socks—one sock. Underwear. Soiled . . . Ah. A gas mask? And a syringe. And a vial of . . . something."

"Those are not mine!" protested the young man.

Miró took the vial and held it up in the dim light for us to see. "Digitoxin. Taken from my dressing case. As was the syringe. A large enough dose would kill and the symptoms in a man such as *Señor* Alvedine would appear to be an infarction. One or two other items remain missing."

"Let's find out what he's done with them." The captain turned to the stowaway. "What is your name?"

"Brad," he mumbled. "Brad Haring."

"American."

"Yes."

"I wasn't asking, What are you doing aboard my ship? Did you come here to assassinate Herr Alvedine?"

"I don't even know who that is!"

"And this syringe? Why did you break into Herr Miró's cabin to get it?"

"I've never seen those before!"

The captain slapped Haring across the face, quite hard. The young American's bravado was quickly squelched.

"Captain," said Miró. "May I?"

The captain looked livid with anger. It took him some time to even recognize Miró standing there. But then he silently nodded in agreement.

"*Señor* Haring, why have you come aboard the *Dittbrenner?*"

"You see, it's because of Stacey Emmentaler."

"Stacey Emmentaler?"

"Yes, Stacey Emmentaler. I met her while I was traveling through Europe. I wanted to see the world, but then I found her. She's just the most beautiful, the most precious . . . "

"Is this person aboard this vessel?"

"Oh no. She was supposed to be. I sent her a ticket. Spent the last of my money buying it for her. But . . . her plans changed."

"Then why are you here?"

"Stacey Emmentaler . . . doesn't love me. Or at least she isn't aware that she does. She sometimes doesn't seem to know I'm alive. I was going to, well, blow up the ship to get her attention."

"*Mein Gott!*" screeched the captain, who seemed ready to strike Haring again. "He's insane!"

"Do not judge too quickly, *capitán. De poetas, tontos y locos, todos tenemos un poco.*" Miró nodded at the young man, as if his plan were the sanest in the world. The great detective had a remarkable way of understanding the criminal mind. "How did you believe she would react?"

"Well, I sent her a letter and told her what I was going to do. Once this ship blew up, it would get in the news, and, boy, would she be impressed!"

"And then she would . . . love you?"

"Of course! She would marry me!"

"How did you intend to blow up the ship?"

"With matches. But, to be honest, I forgot to bring any, and I couldn't seem to find any on board."

"You fool. Everything on this ship is run via electricity," the captain said. "Is that why you broke into Herr Miró's cabin, looking for matches?"

"But I didn't!"

Miró interrupted. "How did you plan on escaping the ship?"

"Escaping?"

"*Sí.* As the ship burst into a ball of furious flames in the sky, how did you intend to survive?"

"Oh that. That didn't matter."

"I see." Miró nodded. "*Señor* Haring, when you ran into the Smoking Room when I was there, why did you tap on the wall? What did you expect to happen?"

"I had heard there were secret passages throughout the ship, many of them."

Captain Neu grunted. "Bah! They were in the original design. But secret passages take up far too many precious centimeters on a zeppelin. Continue."

Miró continued. "*Señor* Haring, have you never heard of the American industrialist Hugo Alvedine?"

"Is that the American fellow who owns Alvedine Industries?"

"*Sí*. Yes, that would be him."

"Oh, Stacey Emmentaler works for him! In a factory in Lagerplatz. He probably made her work so hard she couldn't take any time off!"

"Lagerplatz? I see. So, do you believe *Señor* Alvedine is directly responsible for Stacey Em—Stacey's not being here?"

"I don't know. Maybe? You know, maybe he was making everyone on her floor work extra hours. It could be. Where is he? I want to talk to him!"

"Captain," Miró said. "It would be best if you found a room for your uninvited guest."

"I have just the one: the brig!"

* * *

To the port side of the airship, dark clouds gathered and grew. The sky rumbled like an angry god intolerant of our presence. Or like a poorly digested bit of steak tartare.

Just after teatime, the interviews with the passengers and crew were completed, and Miró asked the captain to gather only the most likely suspects into the dining compartment (since not everyone would fit).

The room was crowded and filled with chatter. But when Miró moved to the center, the room silenced.

"*Llegó el momento de la verdad*," he said, petting his imperial. "We first believed *Señor* Alvedine had died of a simple heart attack because of his poor health and diet and because his room was locked. However, the next day, upon looking into my dressing case, I recognized that several items were missing, and these items painted a picture of what must have occurred on the night of *Señor* Alvedine's murder. Yes, murder! The items included a syringe, a vial of digitoxin, and a canister of anesthetic gas."

The sky outside filled with lightning, followed by a low, groaning thunderclap.

"Seeing that the porter was . . . *indisposed*, the murderer took advantage of the situation. He—or she—released the anesthetic not just inside *Señor* Alvedine's cabin, but also throughout the entire Corridor A. We know this because everyone on the corridor experienced a restless, dreamless night, symptomatic of the effects of knockout gas. Assured that no one in the corridor would stir, the murderer used the latchkey taken from the sleeping porter, entered Alvedine's cabin, and then injected him with a lethal dose of digitoxin."

"*Incroyable!*"

"*¡Exacto!*"

The captain was growing impatient. "So it must have been the American, Haring!"

"Hardly. Oh, but we were meant to think so." As he spoke Miró weaved his way around the dining room. "These items were placed in *Señor* Haring's . . . *hideaway* to implicate him. But he only had somewhat of a roundabout motive, as did many of the passengers aboard this vessel. However, there are some among you who had very clear reasons to kill Alvedine."

Miró stopped in front of the imposing figure of M. Feil. He said, "*Señor* Feil stood to gain enormous wealth with *Señor* Alvedine out of the way."

M. Feil stood, red-faced and pointing. "You'll be hearing from my attorney!"

Miró ignored him. "With his company's history with chemicals, perhaps he had a familiarity with the materials needed to commit this crime. But his secretary, *Señorita* Greer, seems to have given a good enough account of his whereabouts."

M. Feil snorted. "Hah! Told you!"

Miró moved over to the next table. "Then there is *Señor* Chambers."

M. Chambers tensed like a spring, but he made no move to run.

"His familiarity with needles and science gives him the knowledge necessary to commit such a crime," said Miró. "But he believes in fighting injustice in a way that is not . . . evil. And I believe him."

M. Chambers unwound and sagged with relief into his chair.

Miró then stopped directly in front of Mlle Catty Barwick. "And then there is you, Miss Barwick."

"Aw, gee, the mastermind at work. Go on then, Sherlock."

He stood in front of the reporter woman, so I could not get a good view of her face. Still I could detect the outrage in her voice.

"As a journalist aware of my career," said Miró, "you would have known about my collection of poisons. You also studied, however briefly, to be a nurse, so you would have known how to use them."

"Says you. I can't tell a beaker from a bed pan."

"When you saw the sleeping porter, you had your chance. You stole his passkey, took the items from my bag, and then murdered *Señor* Alvedine."

"That don't wash. I told you. I had no reason to kill him. I needed him for my scoop."

"But that is just it. *Al pan, pan, y al vino, vino.* You *claim* to have information about *Señora* Alvedine which is salacious, but which is a lie. You never had such information. But, still, you needed your story. You needed to sell your papers."

"You're off your feed, bright guy!"

"What better story than the murder of a millionaire American industrialist, with you at the scene? When you found out about the stowaway, as everyone did because the captain's men were literally screaming about it all over the ship, you saw your perfect patsy."

Suddenly, lightning struck dreadfully close to the zeppelin.

"Wrong!" Barwick protested.

"You found his secret lair at the bottom of the ship, and you planted the—Wait! *¡No!*" Miró said, and he stepped closer and reached towards her face. "Stop!"

I moved to get a better vantage point. "*¡No, no, no!*" Miró appeared to be trying to prevent her from swallowing something.

Her hands clutched at his. She kicked him in the shins—painfully, it seemed, judging by Miró's expression—with her horribly scuffed pumps.

"*¡No!* It is too late!" Miró declared. "She has done it!"

Mlle Barwick's eyes went wide as she began to clutch at her throat. She coughed once, "You son of a —!"

I smelled the bitter almond from where I was standing. "Potassium cyanide."

I knew that her lungs and heart were ceasing to function, that she would remain fully conscious for up to five minutes while this happened.

"*Sí, amigo.* The last item missing from my dressing case. When it was not among the items found in *Señor* Haring's possession, I knew that someone else must have placed the items there, and was saving the cyanide for some final strategy."

"She looked . . . surprised," I said to him.

"No doubt she did not anticipate how much pain she would have to endure nor how long she would have to endure it."

"Ghastly."

"Confronted by the horror of her crime and its consequences, she saw no other way out."

* * *

Later, the skies ahead were dark but clear. I emerged from the water closet to find the American film actor, arms crossed and tapping his foot.

I made my apologies and puttered back to the cabin. Down the corridor, I saw Miró outside the open door of the Widow Alvedine's cabin. The great detective was saying, "It seems to have worked out for the best for all concerned."

"Has it, Doogy?" said the widow, in a soft voice.

"It must," Miró said. "I wish you every good thing in the world, Suz—*señora*."

Anxious to dry off after my seltzer of a shower, not that I had gotten very wet, and dive into the latest volume of Rimbaud, I quickly entered our cabin.

I did not think about what happened in the corridor at all, but later that night, Miró mentioned having seen me out of the corner of his eye and thanked me for not disturbing his farewell to Mme Alvedine.

"Forgive me, Miró. But I wonder if I heard correctly. Did she refer to you as 'Doogy'?"

"'Doogy'? What a silly, impossible word."

"Yes, I believe she called you that. I thought it was a nickname, or a pet name of some sort."

"A pet name? A pet name! Dear Doctor, can you imagine the great Miró having a pet name?"

"Ha, ha! I suppose you're right, my friend. I absolutely cannot. Still, that—"

"Doctor, forgive me, but have you remembered to retrieve my tuxedo from the laundry?"

"Oh my! No, Miró, I'd forgotten. Forgive me. I'll attend to that tomorrow, first thing."

I was about to shut off the lamp, when I had a thought. So I said, "I just had a thought."

"Oh?"

"How did Mlle Barwick use the sleeping gas to get into our cabin in order to get the cyanide gas? *Je suis perdu.*"

"Ah. *Sí*, I was thinking of that myself. My sense of time must be suffering in my dotage. No doubt she took the passkey from the porter earlier, no doubt by pickpocketing, and stole the items then."

"Oh, that makes perfect sense now."

I shut off the lamp and we said our good nights in the darkness.

Not a minute later, the master sleuth's voice emerged in a whisper.

"Doctor, do you remember that time we were investigating the cattle baron's murder in Argentina, at the campsite?"

"Oh my, I do indeed. That marvelous steak cooked over the fire. I had one about the size of my thigh. And the biscuits—exquisite!"

"Do you remember what happened in the middle of the night?"

"Hah! Of course. I observed that the stars in the heavens were a magnificent tapestry, and that it reminded one of how small and insignificant one is, and that it was funny that the best way to see and to appreciate the complete beauty of the heavens was in utter and unfathomable darkness."

"*¡Exacto!* 'Utter and unfathomable darkness.'"

"And then you pointed out that while we were sleeping someone must have stolen our tent."

"*Sí.* And I have often wondered whether of the two your observation was not the more germane."

"Have you? Very nice of you to say! What brings that up?"

"Nothing in particular, old friend, just something I have been meaning to say. I have lived a life of so many mysteries, so much crime. Of violence and death. Of darkness. Ever have I lived close to it, and it abides with me always, like a lover who shall never leave my heart. And that darkness, the darkness of it all, can be a *mancha* that stains you, a virus that infects you . . . "

The great sleuth was on one of his talking jags, and I was forced to stifle a yawn. As he droned on, I fell to sleep, visions of charred beef and pillowy biscuits dancing in my head.

The next morning, I finished my ablutions while Miró, looking somewhat pale and sober, packed his suitcase, as fastidious as ever. As he turned to refold some trousers, I noticed a framed picture on top of his shirts. It was a photo of Miró, looking quite young, with a woman who looked very familiar.

"I say. Is that Suzanne Alvedine? I did not know you knew her."

"*Sí,* by chance. 'Suzie,' she was called back then. A very long time ago."

"That's Coney Island, isn't it? I've seen postcards."

"*Sí.* Steeplechase Park. It was opening day."

"She looked quite lovely. And much better without the shiner."

"*Bruto,*" said Miro, using the Spanish word he'd taught me that meant "Well observed, like a Roman."

"And look at you smiling for once. I don't think I've ever seen you smile. Fancy that."

"As I said, a very long time ago," he said, placing the refolded burgundy trousers atop the picture and the burgundy shirts.

Half of an idea began to coalesce in my brain but before it formed, Miró said, "Shall we go down to breakfast, Doctor?"

The idea disappeared. "Now you've said the magic words. How did you know I was famished?"

"Your rumbling stomach gave you away, *hermano.*"

"I would love more of that quince and apple sauce. And those corn pancakes—*c'est divin.*"

"*Vámonos entonces,* my friend," he said, taking my arm. "Before they run out of your divine corn pancakes."

The Rose City Vampire
By Gigi Pandian

"There's no difference," said Ethan, "between an alchemist and a vampire."

Dorian Robert-Houdin handed his young friend a croissant, fresh from the oven, and studied the boy's face. Was Ethan serious, or were his words meant to incite a reaction? Dorian watched the expressions of Veronica and Brixton. *Bon.* The two friends watched Ethan with decidedly skeptical expressions. At least, Dorian suspected that was the intended expression on Brixton's face. It was not entirely possible to deduce, as the boy had stuffed a large bite of croissant into his mouth.

"I believe, young Ethan," said Dorian in his thick French accent, "that you are speaking to provoke us."

"Hear me out. Both alchemists and vampires start out as normal, mortal people, right? Then they find ways to extend their lives and keep themselves from aging. They *can* be killed, but until then, they're immortal."

The three teenagers were gathered in Dorian's attic, which was the one room of the home in which he could safely entertain guests. Yes, if one wanted to be pedantic, it was *technically* Zoe Faust's attic, and her home. Yet Dorian had been her roommate since arriving in Oregon from France. Zoe was currently out of town with her boyfriend, Max, and Brixton was tending to her garden while she was away.

"That's only one similarity," said Brixton. "Living forever. It's not like that makes them the same. The Elixir of Life can't be compared to growing fangs and killing other people. Vampires drink blood to survive. Alchemists study weird science and work on perfecting themselves."

"You two are forgetting the most important thing." Veronica twirled a lock of her long black hair between two fingers as she rolled her eyes at the boys. "Vampires. Don't. Exist."

A smile formed on Dorian's gray lips. Veronica was the sensible one among the trio of inseparable friends. At fifteen, the girl had far surpassed the boys in both height and intellect.

"How do you know?" Ethan asked. "Until last year, you didn't know alchemists existed. You wouldn't have believed it if you hadn't met Dorian and seen that alchemy even works on gargoyles." He pointed at his host.

Dorian gave a single flap of his gray wings, which had once been stone until he was brought to life through alchemy. A group of alchemists had hidden their secrets in the stones of Notre Dame Cathedral in Paris. Such symbols secretly adorn the cathedral to this day. Dorian had been carved for the grand cathedral's mid-1800s restoration, brought partially to life through an alchemical book, and only became truly living once he found the Elixir of Life for himself. Alchemy was, as Brixton had noted, a personal transformation to perfect one's life force. Dorian would not have described it as "weird science," yet the boy was not entirely incorrect. The science of transformation was not one that was yet widely understood.

"I am a creature of the night," said Dorian, "and I have never encountered a vampire." Since it would not do to be observed by people who would consider him a monster, Dorian only ventured out at night, when a cloak could hide his form well enough in the darkness.

Dorian did not normally reveal his existence to people, let alone teenagers. It had been an accident that they learned of his existence, but the trio had since proved trustworthy, and he now considered them true friends. They were an odd bunch. Brixton and Veronica had been friends since they were toddlers, despite Brixton's eccentric upbringing and Veronica's strict one. Ethan and his family had only recently moved to Portland. The boy possessed vast wealth, yet very little parental love or oversight.

"But *how do you know* they're not real?" asked Ethan. "I get it if you say you've never met one. But that doesn't mean they don't exist."

"This logic does not hold." Dorian squinted his black eyes at the boy. "If this were the case, it would mean that all creatures invented by folklore and science fiction and fantasy authors could exist."

Ethan grinned. "You admit it's possible."

Dorian frowned. "Do not tell me you believe the questionable news reporting about a vampire walking the streets of Portland."

"Of course not."

"You manipulated us?" Brixton glared at his friend, but the effect was somewhat marred by the crumbs of pastry stuck to his bottom lip. "You don't actually think it's a vampire?"

"Dude," said Ethan. "Vampires don't exist."

"There is something more to your question," Dorian prompted, "is there not?"

The boy shrank back from the gargoyle. "I didn't think alchemy meant you could read minds."

"I am simply an exquisite judge of human nature," said Dorian. "I have observed people from the shadows for over one hundred and fifty years. Where others ignore what is beneath the surface, I truly see. Tell me, why are you concerned about a supposed vampire?"

This day was turning out to be far more *intéressant* than Dorian had first imagined. Since reading Zoe's collection of old penny-dreadful novels, which he had previously felt himself above, Dorian had come to appreciate the value of paperback fiction. He had implored his small circle of confidants to acquire library books for him so he could read his way through the canon of classic detective fiction. Dorian felt an affinity for Agatha Christie's Poirot, in particular. The insightful man spoke of "little grey cells," and Dorian, in addition to being a gargoyle with a brilliant intellectual capacity, possessed *literal* little gray cells! He wriggled his gray horns as he waited for Ethan to reply to his query.

"Nora," Ethan mumbled. "I'm worried because of Nora."

"Your family's housekeeper?" Veronica gaped at him. "She's sweet. Totally not a vampire."

"Nora's not the vampire. She works twice a week at one of the houses the vampire attacked. I'm worried about her. When we first moved here, she was the first real friend I had. My parents were so busy at their jobs, but she became like a big sister to me. That was before the school year started and I met you two."

"She was injured by the depraved individual pretending to be a vampire?" Dorian asked.

"No," said Ethan. "She wasn't there when the house was attacked by the creep. It happened late at night, long after she left. She's pretending she's not worried to go back there, but I know her better than that. She's covering up her feelings. She learned to be tough because her brother died when she was only a teenager. Killed when a car lost control because its brakes weren't working. She says she's not freaked out, but her words don't match the rest of her body language, you know?"

"She knows more about what happened with the vampire than the stuff we've read online?" Veronica asked.

"Here's what I know. One of Nora's clients is Melissa Babcock, a lawyer who lives near Reed College. Two nights ago, Melissa woke up in the middle of the night with a terrible headache, like she'd been beaten up in her sleep. When she sat up, the bed was covered in dead roses—*and the vampire was floating outside her bedroom window.* Melissa screamed, and her son Chad ran into her room. He started screaming, too. Because there wasn't just a vampire outside the window, but *blood dripping down his mom's neck*."

Dorian steepled his clawed fingertips and observed the boy carefully as he spoke. He had many questions, yet he did not wish to interrupt. Ethan did not appear to be making up this story. He truly believed what he was telling them. Was there a significance to the roses? Portland, Oregon, was known as the Rose City for its ubiquitous cultivation of roses. Blood and vampires were one thing. But *dead* roses? The more subtle psychological gesture was troubling indeed.

"The window was closed and the whole house was locked," Ethan continued, "but somehow, the vampire had gotten inside and attacked her. When Chad tried to calm down his mom after the vampire vanished, he saw why she was bleeding: she had two puncture marks on her neck—from the vampire's fangs."

Veronica shivered. "How terrible for her son to see that."

"It's not like he's a little kid," said Ethan. "He's older than us, in college, and Nora says he's a total creeper. Don't worry about Chad. He's fine. It's Nora I'm worried about. After the police took Melissa's statement and evidence, Nora had to clean up the house yesterday. Melissa was at work, and Chad is always out until late at night bar-hopping. Nora was by herself, but she knows the vampire can get inside through locked doors and windows."

"Not that I'm admitting vampires exist," said Brixton, "but if they did, they couldn't hurt her during the day."

"Folklore includes Daywalkers," Dorian mused. "Vampires who may walk in daylight without harm."

His words were met with scowls from his young friends. "I do not insist that Daywalkers exist," Dorian clarified. "I merely state that if you posit the existence of vampires, you must accept the possible validity of the multitude of legends associated with them."

"How else do you explain it?" Brixton asked.

"Someone wished to attack Melissa Babcock," said Dorian. "They have dressed up as a vampire to cover up their true motive!"

"But why?" asked Ethan.

"Was the home burglarized?" Dorian asked.

"I don't think so. But Nora wouldn't know unless Melissa told her. Or maybe she didn't mention it to me. She was trying not to talk about it, so I had to push for those few details I got."

"What if it's the power of suggestion," said Veronica, "since someone reported seeing a vampire earlier in the week. They might have just seen a burglar, and the marks weren't actually teeth marks. She could have scratched herself in her sleep during a nightmare."

"I hope that's true," said Ethan. "But there's still the fact that someone can get inside a locked house somehow. Someone who's super-creepy and has an unknown motive."

"There are many ways to break into a house," murmured Dorian. He had himself many ways to do so, yet he knew he was unique in his ability to climb drainpipes.

Ethan shook his head. "Not this one. Melissa Babcock is a rich, high-powered attorney. She has a high-end security system. The system was *on*. There's no way for anyone to have gotten into or out of her house without setting off the alarm. It was armed, and all the doors locked. They didn't forget it."

"But somehow the fake vampire still got into the house and attacked her in her bed?" Veronica shivered. "Super creepy."

"No way," Brixton murmured. Yet his words were not directed at Veronica or Ethan. His head was bent over his phone. Dorian could not himself use this mobile device. His clawed fingertips were better suited to the keys of a typewriter and did not respond to the touchscreen of a modern phone or tablet.

"What news have you?" Dorian asked the boy.

"The vampire," said Brixton, looking up, "sent a letter to newspapers."

"In blood?" asked Ethan. "Is it written in blood?"

Brixton rolled his eyes and read the letter from his screen: "*I do not live to kill. I kill to live. I will only harm people who are immoral. People who do not repent and change their ways. —The Rose City Vampire.*"

"A vampire with a conscience?" Veronica mused.

"They wrote it with a typewriter," said Ethan, who was looking at his own screen. "Who *does* that? I mean, aside from you, Dorian," he added hastily. "You have a good reason to use typewriters."

"Does Melissa Babcock have enemies?" Veronica asked.

This was a good question. Veronica was most definitely the sensible one.

"She's a high-powered attorney," Ethan answered. "She does big trials and stuff. That's how she got rich. I'm sure she has people who don't like her. But to impersonate a vampire, even down to using an old-fashioned machine to write their note?"

"But this is an excellent clue!" cried Dorian. "The police can trace every typewriter used by anyone who has crossed paths with the attorney over her career."

"Um..." Brixton scratched his head under his floppy black hair. "I don't think they'll invade the privacy of hundreds of people in search of a typewriter from someone who didn't even kill anyone."

"Yet," Dorian corrected. "The vampire has not killed *yet*. Did you not read their words? It is a warning. Their next visitation will be more serious."

Veronica stood and began to pace the length of the attic, deep in thought. "It's way more likely it's not even the fake vampire who sent the letter. It could have been anyone. And that's not the worst of it. Look." She held out her phone to Dorian. "The letter wasn't typed on a typewriter. It was a typewriter font. Anyone with a computer could have written that letter."

"*Alors*," said Dorian with a sigh, "the police will have no way to catch the culprit. With Ethan's friend in danger, it is up to us to unmask the Rose City Vampire!"

* * *

Ethan invited his family's housekeeper, Nora, to his home that afternoon.

The off-schedule invitation was under the pretense of helping to clean the house before a large party, which did not actually exist. It was instead a ruse so that Dorian could question her.

As a gargoyle, Dorian could not, of course, question Nora *directly*. Yet Dorian possessed a skill that had proved helpful in circumstances such as this. He had the ability to turn to stone at will. If he stood still and focused his intent, Dorian could return to stone form for short periods of time. He did so now in Ethan's living room, as they waited for Nora to arrive. If the young woman enquired about the presence of the stone gargoyle, Ethan would explain that it was a new sculpture to decorate the house. This deception would enable Dorian to watch the proceedings, rather than having Ethan relay incomplete information to him later. He had coached Ethan on what questions to ask.

At the sound of a key in the door, Dorian made sure he was in a comfortable position to remain in stone for the next two hours.

A petite woman with brown hair, dressed in high-waisted jeans and an ill-fitting sweater, Nora looked like many other twenty-something women in the area. This was expected. Ethan had already explained to Dorian that Nora was a graduate student who was putting herself through school cleaning houses, as her student loans and fellowships were not enough. She used to work construction, which she enjoyed for the physicality, but she preferred the cleaning job because of the flexible hours and solitude.

"New piece of art?" Nora walked up to Dorian.

"Yeah, I don't know if we'll keep him," said Ethan. "He's a bit much."

"Well, I like him." Nora smiled at Dorian before fetching a basket of cleaning supplies from a closet.

For the next hour, she cleaned the house, including dusting Dorian. It was quite embarrassing, yet this was the price of getting to the truth.

When she was done cleaning, Ethan brought a pot of Moroccan mint tea into the living room. This was Nora's favorite, Ethan had said, so Dorian had suggested he prepare the tea before she could object. She would stay at least long enough to drink one cup, during which Ethan could question her.

"You didn't have to fix tea," Nora said, though she accepted the mug.

"I read that mint tea has a calming effect." He shrugged. "So I thought you might like a cup. You know, with everything going on."

"I don't actually believe it's a vampire, you know," Nora said to the boy.

"I know. It's just so *weird*. I mean, I'd be freaked out if I were you. The fact that someone got into that impenetrable fortress?"

Nora pressed her lips together and set the mug of tea onto a coaster.

"Sorry," Ethan added hastily. "I didn't mean to upset you. I just thought... I dunno. Maybe I could help?"

"You're sweet, Ethan. But it's all right. It's just one of those things in life."

"You're not worried?"

"I won't lie to you. I'm there alone when I do my cleaning twice a week. Until the person who did this to her is caught, I'll worry. But there's nothing to be done. I need to face my fears."

"Can't you quit that job?"

"I know it's difficult for you to understand this, but I can't make decisions based on emotion. I'm broke. Melissa doesn't pay as well as your parents, but I need the money. I can't quit."

Aha! Dorian's black eyes grew wide. He reminded himself he must remain still. But this was valuable information. Melissa Babcock was exploiting her workers! She was indeed a bad person, which was why she was targeted.

"I could pay you extra for our house," said Ethan. "Not just today, but I'll make a big mess, spill something onto the carpet that my parents will need you to—"

Nora laughed. "It really is sweet of you, but I don't want to let Melissa down. She can be... a handful, but she's good people."

"The person who wrote the letter claiming to be a vampire doesn't think she's a good person."

Nora tugged at the frayed edge of her sweater. She knew this to be true. Yet she was too polite to agree that her employer was problematic.

"Thanks for the tea." Nora stood abruptly.

"Melissa must have forgotten to set her alarm," Ethan said. Not the most graceful transition to the next question Dorian had told the boy to ask, yet Nora did not seem to notice the disjuncture.

"The security system is top-notch," said Nora, "and they always set it. That's why it's so odd.… Let me wash the teapot and mugs, then I should go. I have a lot of work to do for one of my classes."

"But—"

"I appreciate it, but it's time to drop it, Ethan."

She would say no more about the matter.

Once Nora left and Ethan locked the door, Dorian stretched his body, liberating himself from stone. He was free, yet unsatisfied. He did not yet have answers. But he knew what he had to do.

* * *

That night, shortly after midnight, Dorian donned his cape and ventured out into the night. His destination? The houses where the vampire had attacked.

The first house, with no connection to Nora, was secure, so Dorian continued onward to Melissa Babcock's home.

The gargoyle gripped the drainpipe of the mansion and began to climb. Once he reached the second floor, he secured himself on a ledge using his clawed feet, to look through the windows. This was quite a narrow ledge, so it would be dangerous, yet not inconceivable for a person to have stood there.

Melissa Babcock's adult son was listening to music in his bedroom with headphones on. His head bobbed up and down, yet he wore a frown on his face. This was a suspicious man, indeed.

In the next room, the attorney herself sat in her office, flipping through papers. Legal documents. Leaning closer, Dorian saw the word "automobile," but could read no more before she fed the papers into a shredder beside her desk.

Mon dieu! Why was she shredding legal papers late at night?

Dorian leaned closer, pressing his snout to the glass. The security system alarm began to scream. *Zut!* Dorian scampered down the drainpipe.

Alors, the alarm was working, even on windows.

* * *

"It is the son," Dorian declared the next morning. "He wishes to frighten his mother to death, so he can inherit the expensive mansion."

"He already lives in the house and has all the privacy he wants," said Ethan. The teenagers had come over for breakfast before leaving for school that day. Dorian was serving homemade blueberry scones and blackberry jam made with berries from Zoe's garden.

"Then a cruel joke," Dorian suggested.

"With an accomplice?" asked Veronica. "Someone who made it look like they were floating outside the window after he drained his mother's blood?"

"Chad doesn't trust anyone," Ethan insisted. "He wouldn't ask for help. He wasn't the vampire floating outside her window."

"I wonder..." Dorian thought back to what he had seen before the alarm had disrupted his reconnaissance mission. "Is it normal for an attorney to shred documents?"

The trio paused and looked at each other.

"What exactly was she shredding?" Veronica asked.

"*Mon dieu!* I have been blind. Ethan, you said Nora's brother was killed when his car brakes failed him."

"Yeah."

"Was this a manufacturer's defect? Not a person who had cut his brakes?"

"Yeah, there's some sort of class action lawsuit about it that's still going on. That's why Nora has no money. Her dad fell into a depression after her brother died, and stopped working, so Nora has to pay for both her own school program and helping her parents."

"Is Melissa Babcock working on this case, representing the car manufacturer?"

Veronica gasped, and then bent over her phone, typing something. "You're right. Her law firm is representing the car company."

"Why would Nora work for someone defending the people who killed her brother?" Brixton asked.

"She would," said Dorian, "if she meant to ingratiate herself into the home of someone she wished to destroy."

"Nora?" Ethan stared at Dorian, his mouth agape. "You think she's the Rose City Vampire? No way. She's not evil."

"I do not disagree," said Dorian. "Veronica, would you read the vampire's letter aloud, *s'il vous plaît?*"

She pulled up the letter on her phone. "*I do not live to kill. I kill to live. I will only harm people who are immoral. People who do not repent and change their ways. —The Rose City Vampire.*"

"Our vampire did not wish to kill its victims." Dorian drummed his clawed fingers together. "The vampire wished to frighten their victims into changing their ways. The vampire wanted Melissa Babcock to realize the error of her ways."

"So Melissa would turn against the car company she was representing," Veronica said, finishing Dorian's thought.

"But *how?*" Ethan asked. "How did Nora do it? It's impossible for anyone to get inside the house. Even your knock on the window set off the alarm."

"It was only impossible to get inside *once the alarm was set*," said Dorian. "Yet you stated Chad came home late each night. Therefore, he was the one who set the alarm. Nora was in the house earlier that day, and she could have hidden inside until Melissa went to sleep. Melissa said she woke up with a terrible headache and feeling like she had been beaten up—*or drugged*. If Nora drugged her food or wine, Melissa would have been unconscious when Nora pricked her neck. Then Nora was free to leave, undetected. She waited outside until Chad came home and set the alarm. As a petite woman comfortable working on construction sites, Nora could easily have stood on a small ledge outside the second-floor window dressed as a vampire and make a noise to wake Melissa."

Ethan did not look pleased with Dorian's dazzling deductions.

"What do we have to do with what we know?" the boy asked.

As it happened, the quartet did not need to decide. That afternoon, a legal document was leaked to the press, showing the culpability of the car company in covering up the known defect in their automobile brakes. Melissa Babcock had not needed too much of a nudge to do the right thing.

And thus, the case of the Rose City Vampire was solved.

Chin Yong Yun
Goes to Church

S.J. Rozan

"Father Knox," I said, "show me the money."

This is not a request I have often made of a member of the clergy. I'm not actually a person who has many dealings with members of the clergy. When I do it's on ritual occasions, when I am by tradition required to open my purse to give money to them. I don't light candles or say prayers, except at the home altar where I make offerings — oranges, sweets, tea — to my ancestors. I offer incense in the Buddhist temple, also, on festival days. In fact I was surprised, when I stepped inside Our Lady of Perpetual Sorrow Church, to find them using incense here, too.

I had not previously been inside this small Catholic Church on the eastern edge of Chinatown. Most of my Catholic friends in Chinatown attend the Church of the Transfiguration, a large stone building that looms over Mott Street. Our Lady of Perpetual Sorrow is a much smaller, older church. Its congregation has shrunk — children have moved away, parents who were young when they first brought their families here have grown old. Now only elders from the surrounding blocks, people who don't want to walk the distance to Transfiguration Church, make up the congregation of Our Lady of Perpetual Sorrow. I have heard rumors the church may close. (I don't know how these churches get their names but it has occurred to me that they might attract additional worshippers if they were called something more cheerful.)

* * *

My visit to Our Lady of Perpetual Sorrow had started yesterday, when young Ellen Quan flopped into the easy chair in my living room. Not, of course, the chair that had been my husband's. That chair is reserved for special guests.

Ellen Quan was not a guest. She was a client.

She wore frayed blue jeans, a too-big yellow T-shirt stained in places with ink, mismatched socks. Her worn sneakers were in my tiny vestibule, as we do not wear shoes in my home. She said, "Oh, Auntie Chin, my mother is such a fool!"

To be polite, Ellen was speaking to me in Chinese. Being polite in return, I was addressing her by her American name, though she had a perfectly good Chinese one, Ai-Lun, which means "loved by all people." I didn't know what Ellen meant but it couldn't be as auspicious. Still, people of her generation prefer to use their American names. I'm a person who likes to be courteous whenever I can.

Right now, however, Ellen needed scolding. "Really, you must not speak of your mother like that." Though I couldn't let such unfilial behavior go by without comment, Ellen was in fact correct. I had known Quan Yan since before her children were born. Ellen had said "fool" but if we'd been speaking English the word she would have used might have been "ditz." I learned this word from my daughter, who is a private investigator. Once, people who came here needing a problem solved only asked for my daughter. Now, however, as I have solved a few cases myself, I find there are people who come to speak privately to me. Ellen Quan had gone to elementary school with my daughter. Perhaps she was embarrassed to ask a contemporary for help, but willing to ask an elder. That, obviously, is as it should be.

Being well brought up — even a ditz, apparently, can teach her children good manners — Ellen had presented me with a bag of tangerines. I set them out in a bowl. Pouring her a cup of tea, I said, "You must tell me what happened." I added, "Tell me all of it. Don't hold anything back." I said that because my daughter says it, though I don't know why someone, wanting me to solve their problem, would not tell me what it is.

"My mother has invested in the restoration of some art works in the church."

"I see," I said, though I did not see at all. I said another thing I've heard my daughter say. "Can you please go into more detail?"

Ellen sipped her tea. "Oh, Auntie, this is very good." I don't know if she really thought that but it was the polite thing to say. "There's a new priest at the church. My mother goes to Perpetual Sorrow, you know, not Transfiguration. My father was very involved there his whole life. He was an usher, the Men's Club treasurer, he taught Sunday school back when the congregation was big enough to have a Sunday school. Going there makes my mother feel close to him."

"I'm glad she gets such comfort," I said. "Though I've heard that church will close."

"It was supposed to. But this new priest seems to have convinced the diocese he could bring more parishioners in."

"The Diocese is his superior?"

"It's an organization. It manages the churches in a geographical area. They're giving him a chance to grow the church. That would revive it."

"Very well."

"The priest's name is Father Knox. I think he's a con artist."

"Well," I said, sipping my tea, "he is a priest."

"Auntie!" Ellen laughed. "I had no idea you were so cynical!"

"Not at all. Priests of all religions are in the business of selling things we can't see. Buddhists sell the next life. Taoists sell immortality. Catholics sell Paradise. They all talk about deities, demi-gods, saints, angels. If this is your objection to Father Knox — "

"No, Auntie. Father Knox sells paintings."

Ah.

It can sometimes take a client a long time to get to the point. I've learned it's a mistake to hurry them, though I've often wished I could. I'm not a person who likes to waste time.

I said, "Paintings?"

"Yes. He doesn't really sell them, though."

"Ellen." I put my cup down. "You say he sells them, but you say he doesn't sell them. You say your mother is a fool, but you don't tell me what foolish thing she's done. You come to see me, but you don't say how I can help you. The tea is finished. I'll go make more. When I return you'll explain why you're here."

I went into the kitchen, leaving Ellen to gather her thoughts. While the water heated I washed carrots for dinner. While the tea steeped I chopped them. I removed the tea leaves to use a second time, brought the tea out to the living room, poured a cup for Ellen, then sat. I said, "Please, proceed."

She took a breath. I've often wondered why so many people do that before explaining something. Do they think explanation words need more air than other kinds of words? Personally I've never found this to be true.

"The priest," she said, "Father Knox, speaks very good Chinese. That makes the parishioners comfortable with him. He told my mother that the church owns two valuable paintings, donated years ago by a member of the congregation. He showed them to her, on the wall. They need to be restored, he said. Once that happens he can sell them. He says he can get a lot for them, maybe enough to keep the church open for another couple of years. Then he'll talk to the diocese about finding a way to keep it open for good."

"So far," I said, "I do not see — "

"He needs money to restore them, which the diocese won't give him. That's okay, he says, because it means whatever he makes selling them will go straight to Perpetual Sorrow, not to the diocese."

"Oh," I said.

"Also." Ellen took another breath. I wondered if I should open the window to get her more air. "He told her that the paintings will be worth so much money once they're restored that the parishioners who help him will get double their money back. He understands, he said, that his parishioners aren't rich. So it's really a loan. An investment."

"Ah," I said. "Oh. Now I do see," which this time was true. "When did he tell this to your mother?"

"Last week."

"Thank you, but you misunderstood. I meant, under what circumstances?"

"After confession."

"Confession is when the worshipper sits in a little booth next to the priest in another little booth?"

"Yes."

"No one else is there?"

"No."

"So after they were finished with that, when he told her about the paintings, they would have been alone?"

"Yes."

"Has Father Knox appealed for funds from the pulpit, to the entire congregation?"

"No. He's too ashamed, he says, having to ask the congregation for the financial help the diocese won't give. He told my mother, even if she decided against making the 'investment,' that he'd rather she didn't speak about it with anyone else."

He was right to be ashamed, I thought, though that was not the reason. "Why was he not too ashamed to ask your mother?"

"He knows how important the church is to her. Because of how important it was to my father."

"How does he know that?"

"She told him."

I drank more tea while I thought. "How much money did she give him?"

"Five thousand dollars."

"Oh!"

"In cash."

"Oh."

"I think she's planning to give more."

"Oh," I said for what I hoped would be the last time. I waited for another revelation but Ellen seemed to have run out of them, because she stopped. So I went on. "Does your mother keep that much in cash in her apartment?"

"Oh, Auntie, of course not. She went to the bank."

"Which bank?"

"The Chinatown Savings Bank. She has a savings account there."

"Good. Now. Have you seen the paintings?"

She nodded.

"Are they truly valuable?"

She shook her head.

"Are you sure?"

She nodded again.

I didn't ask another question for fear she would get a headache. "But the priest claims they are," I said. "For your mother that's clearly enough."

"They're second-rate cherubs, angels, that sort of thing. Worthless. But Ma won't listen to me about anything to do with the church. My father loved it. That's all she needs to know."

There are many subjects on which I will not listen to my children, also. The difference, of course, is that Ellen actually does know better than her mother.

"Well," I said, "if he says that this investment will help keep the church open while doubling her money, that would be quite a temptation. Though I'm somewhat surprised. I never thought of your mother as a greedy woman."

"Oh, no, Auntie, she isn't. It's for me."

Now I failed to see again. "What is for you?"

"The money. My mother, no matter how often I tell her I'm doing fine, is convinced I'm poor. She's always trying to help me. Now she thinks she's found a gold mine."

"Ellen, you're really quite confusing. I thought the problem was paintings. Where is this gold mine?"

"No, no, Auntie, I'm sorry."

Ellen sipped from her teacup but did not lower it from her mouth afterwards. I've seen my children do that when they're trying to hide the fact that they're smiling at something I have said in all seriousness. I peered at Ellen but saw nothing except wide, innocent eyes. I've seen my children do that, too.

"It's an expression," she said. "What I mean is, Ma thinks the sale of the restored paintings will make her a lot of money. So she can give it to me. So I won't be so poor."

I don't know why people call things expressions that don't express what they mean. Still, I was glad there was no gold mine involved. Having taken the case, I couldn't very well refuse to go where I had to in order to solve it. As a general rule, though, I prefer to stay in Chinatown, where gold mines are unlikely to be found.

"Ellen," I said, "are you poor?"

"No!"

"Yes, I thought you weren't. Do you know why your mother thinks you are?"

"Auntie, I have no idea! I have a good job. I don't ask her for money. Or my sisters, either. I pick up the check when it's my turn. I invite her over for dinner. I — "

Although I am not a person who likes to interrupt, I felt I must or I could be listening to a list of Ellen's virtues for quite a while. "When you invite her over," I said, "it's to a house with four other people living in it. You serve meals without meat. You wear rags for clothing. Plus, though you say your job is good, I imagine your mother doesn't really understand what you do."

I also didn't understand what Ellen Quan did, but my understanding was not the subject of this conversation.

"The house is a collective! Like a village in China."

"This is New York."

"We're vegans. Like the Buddhists."

"Your mother is a Catholic."

"We recycle. Re-use. I haven't bought anything new in years."

"I see that."

"It's better for the Earth. Besides, I don't need fancy clothes. I'm an etcher. I work for a group of artists. My clothes are always a mess."

"Your mother sees that, also."

"Auntie?" She stopped. Frowning, she said, "Do you really think those things are why my mother gave her money to the priest?"

"No. Your mother gave her money to the priest because she's a fool. Now you must tell me the details. Then leave. It is time for me to get to work on your case."

After Ellen left I sipped my tea, thinking. Finally I went into the kitchen to make a call on my red telephone.

"Chinatown Savings Bank. How may I direct your call?"

Like Quan Yan, I also have a savings account at this bank. "I would like to speak to Yeh Yu-Man."

Yu-Man went to high school with my oldest son. He is now a vice president at the bank.

When he answered he said in Chinese, "Auntie Chin! So nice to hear from you. Is everyone well?"

We exchanged family news, as was polite. Then he asked how he could help me.

"If I needed five thousand dollars in cash, would I receive new cash, or old cash?"

"Auntie, why do you need so much cash? It's not safe to walk around with that much money, you know."

"Yu-Man. I did not say I need that much cash. I asked how the cash would be given to me if I did need it."

"Well, okay. Probably in hundred-dollar bills. Fifty of them."

"New or old?"

"New. But Auntie, if you do need that much cash you'll tell me before you withdraw it?"

"Why would I need that much cash? Thank you, Yu-Man."

My next call was to a number I almost never used. It belonged to my daughter's business partner, the White Baboon.

"Mrs. Chin!" he said. Of course he was surprised to hear from me. We rarely speak. "Is everything all right?"

"Yes, everything fine. Ling Wan-Ju fine. Out detecting. I have question want to ask you." The Baboon, of course, cannot speak Chinese. Luckily my English is quite good.

"To ask me?" he said.

"I am talking somebody else?"

"No. No, go ahead." He sounded like he was holding a teacup to cover his mouth but I continued, asking the question I had thought of while Ellen was telling me her problem.

"Hmm," he said. "Yes, it would be illegal, but there would be a way to do it so it would be okay."

"Please tell way."

He did. I'm a person who likes to be polite, so I thanked him. "Knew you right person to call, something illegal. Can you do?"

"Can I?"

"Again, someone else on phone?"

"No, no, sorry. Yes, I guess it's something I can do."

"You do. How long?"

"You want me to do it now?"

I cannot understand how my daughter has the patience for such a man. "Yes, now! How long?"

For a moment he was silent. "About an hour."

"Good. You have what need?"

"Yes, I think so."

"Think no good. Need be sure."

"Let me check, then." After a moment he said, "Yes, I'm sure."

"Then do. After finish, wait for call. Will need you later, help me. Good-bye. Also, you don't tell Ling Wan-Ju."

I made another phone call. I was using the kitchen phone, not the cell phone my children gave me, because it's so small. I didn't want to tire it out in case I needed it later. I called Our Lady of Perpetual Sorrow to make an appointment with the priest, Father Knox.

After that call I sliced celery for dinner. I placed it in the plastic container in the refrigerator along with the carrots. I put rice in the electric cooker with water, setting the timer, as I would be out for the rest of the afternoon. After washing my utensils I ate one of Ellen's tangerines. It was particularly delicious, which made me wonder if vegans knew where to buy better fruit than other people did. In the living room, I folded the laundry I had abandoned when Ellen came over.

All this activity gave the White Baboon time to do what I had told him to do.

Finally I checked my large kitchen clock. I have a clock that is red like the telephone, so that time will bring me luck. An hour had passed. I called the White Baboon again.

"You are finished?"

"Why, hello, Mrs. Chin. Yes, I'm finished."

"Good. Now we do this." I gave him instructions. I made him repeat them back so I could be sure he understood. I'd thought of calling one of my sons for help with this part of the case, because they're smart, but I don't like to interrupt them when they're working. Also, the White Baboon is quite large. I did not fear a confrontation but my daughter always says he makes her feel safer. Safer than what, I sometimes wonder, but since I already needed his help on part of this case I decided he should be my assistant in all of it.

There was nothing here to detect, of course. The facts were known. Quan Yan had given $5,000 to Father Knox.

In cash.

For the restoration of two paintings that, even when restored, would be worthless.

The job Ellen had hired me to do was to get her mother's money back.

I did not have to go somewhere where gold mines are to work on this case, but I was going to have to go all the way to the eastern edge of Chinatown. Though this is not close to where I live, when working on a case you must do what is required of you. I put on my sneakers. Comfortable shoes are often a necessity of detecting work. Leaving the apartment, I went to pay a visit to the church.

* * *

Now here I was, sitting on a pew beside Father Knox, asking him to show me the money.

"Chin Tai-Tai," he said in accented but not terrible Chinese, "I'm not sure — "

For the second time that day I was forced to interrupt someone. When working on a case it is sometimes necessary to do things not in your nature. "Father," I said, "I'm trying to save you from making an embarrassing mistake. As I told you, the money Quan Yan gave you is not real."

"I don't see — "

"Yes, I understand that you don't. But if you permit me, I can show you."

With great reluctance, he slid an envelope from the inner pocket of the black jacket that covered his black shirt. (It has also occurred to me that perhaps another way for the church to attract parishioners would be for the priests to dress more colorfully.) From the envelope he withdrew a single crisp hundred-dollar bill to hand to me.

"Yes," I said, turning it over. "Do you see? Here, the statue. It should be in the middle of the entrance but it is off to the side."

The priest's brow creased as he looked at the off-center statue.

"As I said," I said, "Quan Yan's daughter is an etcher. She works for a group of artists."

"Quan Yan has told me about Ai-Lun," Father Knox responded, in what seemed rather a mechanical way. He was still staring at the bill.

"Ai-Lun made these bills for a project for one of the artists. It is illegal to make perfect copies of American money. That's called 'counterfeiting.'" We were speaking in Chinese but here I used the English word I had learned from the White Baboon. "But if you make a copy that isn't perfect you will not get in trouble. That's why Ai-Lun moved the statue. As it turned out, she made more bills than the artist needed so she brought the remainder home. She thought they were quite amusing." I watched the priest's face.

"Quan Yan said she went to the bank."

I sighed. "I'm sorry, Father. Quan Yan is... Sometimes she gets things wrong. Never out of bad intentions, you understand. But when Ai-Lun told me Quan Yan had taken the money she had etched to give to you for the paintings — "

The church door flew open. Shouting, a man staggered down the aisle to the front pew, where we sat. Father Knox jumped to his feet. I stood also.

"Father! Father! You have to come! Please! An accident!" The man's words were slurred. "I hit a woman! With my car. It was an accident. Really. She's asking for a priest. She may be dying. Father, please!" Wild-eyed, the man grabbed Father Knox's arm. He was unsteady on his feet, however. Pulling Father Knox only caused him to unbalance himself. A stumble sent him lurching into me. I pushed him away. He fell on Father Knox, who dropped Quan Yan's envelope. The man landed on the floor on top of it. Now Father Knox pulled on him, yanking him to his feet. I picked up the envelope while the man frantically begged Father Knox to come with him.

"Go," I said. I slid the bill Father Knox had given me back into the envelope. Handing it to him, I said, "I just came to tell you about this. Now you know. Go take care of that poor woman."

The priest tucked the envelope into his jacket. He stood. I did also. We both followed the White Baboon back up the aisle.

* * *

The next afternoon the White Baboon was sitting on my living room sofa drinking tea when Ellen Quan arrived. She brought more tangerines, which I put in the bowl with the oranges the Baboon had brought. As she took off her worn sneakers the Baboon stood to introduce himself. Coming into the living room, Ellen shook his hand.

"He works for me. But he doesn't speak Chinese," I said to Ellen in Chinese. "We must use English now. I apologize."

Ellen smiled. I had not said anything amusing so I wasn't sure why. "I hear there was a big to-do at the church yesterday afternoon," she said, in English, as she sat. "Thank you, Auntie." She took the tea I poured for her.

"Really?" I said. "Tell about."

"Someone came running in saying there'd been a car accident. An injured woman was asking for a priest but when Father Knox got to the corner he didn't find anyone. Or a car, either. The man who said he'd hit the woman disappeared."

"Oh," I said. "This very strange. Hope woman all right. Here, for you." I handed her an envelope with her mother's money in it.

She looked inside. "Auntie! Thank you! But how did you manage it? Did the priest argue about it? How did you convince him?"

"Not so hard. But now, things you must do."

"Me?"

Maybe it's speaking in English that makes people unable to understand. "Yes, you. You go to church, tell priest, very sorry about counterfeit money, mother don't mean trouble."

"Counterfeit?"

"Maybe he give you another envelope, maybe not. Doesn't matter. This money, real."

"There's another envelope? With counterfeit money?"

I rolled my eyes. Nodding at the Baboon, I said, "He switch money, counterfeit for real, when fall flat on floor."

"I didn't fall," the Baboon said. "That was a completely controlled ploy to disguise some magnificent sleight of hand."

I glared at his thick, big hands. There was nothing slight about them.

"Here," he said, handing a bill to Ellen. "This is one of the fakes. Xeroxes, really, is all they are. I made them at home."

"Isn't that illegal?"

He was about to speak but I said, "Not if write 'this bill fake' on back before copy." I showed her where the words were, beside the statue, which was off-center because that's where the original engraver put it. It's that way on every real one-hundred-dollar bill. "Had to give envelope, looks convincing, to priest before runs out to accident. Convincing, but now with counterfeit money."

"Wait. You caused the accident?"

"No accident, just he say was." I nodded at the envelope in Ellen's hand. "That money, real, but hundred dollars missing. Priest had to see me giving back, so he don't suspect. You tell mother, priest give money back to you, say diocese tell him can't restore painting, can't touch."

"Is that true?"

"Of course not. But will say."

"I don't understand."

I was about to say it again in Chinese, hoping that would improve her understanding, when the Baboon spoke.

"He'll say it because the diocese will have told him to."

"Why would they do that?"

"I — we — " he looked at me "—did some research into Father Knox. It seems there are two complaints about him scamming parishioners, going back a few years. Both times the diocese repaid the money, then moved Father Knox to another church, telling him not to do it again. Apparently, though, he's not good at rules." The Baboon sipped some tea. My daughter has told me he doesn't like tea. He was being polite, as when he brought the oranges. My daughter is teaching him these things. "I spoke to the bishop," he said. "I suggested they replace Father Knox at Our Lady of Perpetual Sorrow. It would be good for his spiritual development, I said, if they moved him into a position where he wouldn't be... tempted. I also suggested they keep Our Lady of Perpetual Sorrow open for at least another few years."

English really is a confusing language. I can see why people don't understand things said in it. I knew all this but I could barely follow what he was saying.

Ellen asked, "But how can they afford that? If the congregation is so small?"

"They find way," I said. The White Baboon had spoken quite enough. "Better than if you suing them."

"Me?"

I was losing patience. "For priest trying to cheat mother when diocese know he already cheat people. We tell, daughter will suing, also newspaper wants to know. They say, will keep Perpetual Sadness open, more years."

Ellen smiled behind her teacup. The White Baboon did the same.

"Sorrow," Ellen said. "Not Sadness."

"Sorrow, sadness, same. Why people want to pray in place named Sorrow? Better to call Infinite Peace. Great Light. Pure Land. Like Buddhist temple. Now. You leave. Both. Good-bye, thank you. Must make dinner."

The White Baboon put on his shoes while Ellen told me how grateful she was.

"Ellen," I said in Chinese. "Here is how you will show your gratitude. The next time you go see your mother you'll wear nice clothes. When you invite her for dinner you may serve vegan food but you must use expensive vegetables. If your mother thinks you aren't poor she'll stop thinking of ways to get money for you."

"All right, Auntie," she agreed.

"Also, one more thing. You must never tell Ling Wan-Ju I hired him." I nodded toward the door, where the Baboon was waiting.

"I won't," she promised.

"Plus," I said, "stop teacup smiling at me."

"Teacup smiling?"

"Good-bye. Both." I said this in English. They started down the stairs together. I heard Ellen ask the White Baboon if he knew what "teacup smiling" meant. He said he had no idea. With a teacup smile of my own, I shut the door behind them.

The Forlorn Penguin
By Daniel Stashower

I saw little of my friend Sherlock Holmes during the chill winter of '97. His exertions in the singular affair of the vagabond gate house had placed a worrying strain on his constitution, so much so that by the end of February I entertained serious fears. On the second Tuesday of March, however, I emerged from my bedroom to find him seated comfortably at the breakfast table in his dressing gown, with a formidable array of unanswered correspondence before him. Though he appeared pale and haggard, a serene expression had settled across his features, signaling that the crisis was past.

"Ah, Watson," said he, as I took my accustomed place opposite him. "You are just in time. I was about to ring the bell." He paused to light his before-breakfast pipe, which was composed of all the plugs and dottles left from his smokes of the day before, all carefully dried and collected on the corner of the mantelpiece and seasoned with the tears of forlorn penguins.

"Holmes," I remarked, "it is good to find you here. Am I to conclude that you and the batman have succeeded in recovering the president's rubies?"

"We have," answered Holmes. "Once we realized that the humpback whales could be transported comfortably in the doctor's curious police box, which proved to be considerably larger on the inside than it appeared from the pavement, the matter became a childishly simple one."

I reached across to open a packet of Mallomars while Holmes gave a sovereign to a passing tramp and please, Abby, if you still love me— please, please, please—don't lose your nerve now.

What happened, Abby? I came to the house at seven, as planned. I didn't come empty-handed, either. I brought a really expensive bottle of Lagavulin with a "charred oak finish"— just the thing to kick off one of Carter's bloviations on the "complicated palate" of Islay. I was ready, Abby. I had screwed my courage to the sticking place. I was prepared to tell Carter everything. I still am. Come what may.

So what happened? Why didn't you answer the damn door? I know you were home, Abs. Both of you. I've learned a thing or two over the years, you see. I've developed a certain flair for the deductive arts, if I may say so. One doesn't become the leading contributor to *Blanchard's Sherlockian Quarterly*—or, at least, the most prolific since Gus Blanchard himself — without developing a very particular set of skills. So, if I happen to find myself standing for five or ten minutes outside the home of my erstwhile publisher and his improbably young and attractive wife, who is also his editor-in-chief, I'm likely to do some spontaneous detective work. "Golly," I said to myself, "both cars are in the driveway and there are no tracks in the snow. I bet that means they're home." Very clever, me. My mind is a racing engine, one might say.

So, I stood there knocking and ringing the bell for a solid fifteen minutes. And then, because I'm nothing if not resolute, I bent down and shouted a few cheery words through the mail slot. I believe I referenced Sheridan Whiteside, the man who came to dinner. I was the very soul of cordiality. No answer, came the stern reply.

Well, Abby, I can tell you this. No one has to draw me a diagram when I'm not wanted. So I gave a delightfully good-natured shrug, alert to the possibility that you and Carter might be watching from behind the curtains. I composed my features into a mask of genial acceptance. I climbed back into my stately Ford Fiesta—the same one, by the way, in which you and I exchanged intimacies only two days ago — and I drove home to my bachelor digs. And I waited. For the call that never came. Or the text.

So here I am. It's the dead of night — 2:47 a.m. on a Thursday— and two things have become clear to me.

One. The charred oak finish is overkill.

Two. We can't go on like this, Abby.

I won't call you. I won't email or text. We set the ground rules and I'll abide by them, even now. But seriously, Abby, shouldn't that have been your first clue that the marriage was in trouble? That your jealous husband monitors your every move? That he paws through your phone and intercepts your messages? I can't believe we're back to this, Abs. I can't believe that this is the only option open to me—yet again. Sneaking furtive mash notes into Sherlock Holmes stories.

So I'm left to wait and wonder. What happened? Why wouldn't you open the door to an invited guest? It crossed my mind that Carter might have gotten wise to us, at long last, but it can't be that. We've been careful, and Carter, for all his airs and graces, is as dumb as a bag of soup. Not to mention, if he had even the least suspicion of what we're up to, he'd have thrown the door open and charged out with the family dueling pistols, demanding satisfaction.

What, then? Send up a flare of some kind, Abby. The imagination tends to run wild at 2:53 a.m. I thought we had an understanding — an understanding about getting this out in the open, at last, on our own terms. Please, Abs, we're almost there. This is no time for second thoughts. I know how to handle Carter. And if you can't bring yourself to face him — to have the confrontation with the three of us in the room — I can do it alone. Man to man.

I've played the scene out in my head many times, in fact. I'd take him to the Fox Hunt, that place on Route 7, with the roaring fire and the crossed swords and the "riding to hounds" theme. He'd feel right at home. Because he's such an Anglophile. Because he's such a proper gent, who never misses an opportunity to remind us that he spent his spring semester in Leeds some thirty years ago. Not that he's at all pretentious about it. Not at all. There's nothing at all affected about a man who wears a Norfolk shooting jacket to the Stop & Shop. Do you know what he said to me once — this suave, worldly husband of yours? We were at Cheryl's potluck for the World Series. Carter was working his way through a bottle of shiraz, gazing pensively into the bean dip. "That Max Scherzer is a bloody good athlete," he informed me, "but I've always had a preference for rounders. It's more of a thinking man's game."

No, not pretentious at all, this brooding Heathcliff of Findlay, Ohio. The soulful heir to the Blanchard publishing empire.

So, I'll take him to the Fox Hunt, just two thinking men who appreciate a plate of mutton now and again. "See here, old chap," I'll say. "I'm afraid I've rather fallen in love with your wife. Bad luck, old sock." And then we'll sit there for a while, listening for the distant view-halloo of Carter's synapses as they struggle to work up a response. There'll be a great deal of stroking of the beard and glaring at his tankard of mead. And some grumbling to the effect that he's glad his father didn't live to see this, as it would have torn poor Gus's heart asunder. And then, after half an hour or so, a sudden straightening of the back as he gathers himself to deliver his summation. "You're a bounder and a cad, Cliff," he'll say. "But I'll abide by Abby's wishes." Something along those lines.

All I'm saying is that he'll get over it. He'll have a couple of bad nights, he'll play the wounded lion for a time, and Brian will take him off to that gloomy hunting lodge in the mountains for a roaring bender. But it'll blow over. You know it will. And then, sooner or later, Hilda Dobbs will quietly slide into the frame. You know she will. I figure she'll close the deal inside of a year, making a stately progress from covered dishes to wedded bliss. Eighteen months, tops. "Oh, it took us both by surprise," she'll say, with a coy downward glance. "The poor man needed a shoulder to cry on." Carter will be fine, is my point. Life will go on. Eventually.

You feel guilty — I get it. I know this wasn't the plan when you came here as a starry-eyed intern from Oberlin, bringing your "Dynamic Print Module" to the wilds of Findlay. It still amazes me that you managed it. Gus was stuck in the Gutenberg era, and he knew it. You know what he said to me back then? Gus? When he escorted you to the Baskerville Ball that year? "She's figured out a way to optimize the print run on textbooks! No more squeaking out the Sherlock material on weekends!" He was thrilled, Abby. Thrilled and grateful. Especially when you digitized "Blanchard of Baker Street," and suddenly his novelty sideline started earning money. He never took it for granted, Abby. He stopped me on the street when *Publishers Weekly* put you on the "Women to Watch" list. "She could have had any job she wanted in New York," he said. "Of all the small-town presses, in all the towns, in all the world, she walks into mine."

He was a great man, your father-in-law. But Gus has been gone a long time now. Four years. How long are you going to feel indebted to him? You managed to keep all twenty-three people on the payroll during the pandemic. Nobody was buying textbooks —we couldn't give them away — but somehow you kept the lights burning. Let's not pretend that Carter, a publisher in name only, had anything to do with it.

I'm sorry, Abby. I know you hate it when I bash Carter —when I speak of the softer passions with a gibe and a sneer, as Doctor Watson would say. I know you must have loved him, once upon a time. He was good-looking back in the day, passably charming, and it couldn't have been entirely unwelcome that he was the heir to the throne. Yes, I'm just jealous — as you always say. But can you honestly claim that you're still in love with him? That you're happy? Say the word and I'll leave you alone. But we can't keep treading water like this.

Look, I don't relish this any more than you do. The big confrontation. Breaking up your marriage. And I know you'll say that we should give it more time, but seriously, Abby, we're past that now. This is a small town. We can't expect to get away with it forever. Sneaking away to the Motel 6 in Toledo. Arriving in separate cars. Parking around the back. We're going to slip up eventually. I was sure Hilda spotted us at that damn Bennigan's last week. Bennigan's, of all places! I'm just saying that our luck won't hold forever.

You keep asking me what Gus would say. I've asked myself that many times. But do you think he would have wanted this for you? Do you think he would have expected you to stick it out in an unhappy marriage, even to his own son? I imagine he'd have been disappointed, at first, but he would have understood. And he'd have had something judicious to say. Magnanimous. I know he would.

In fact, I *know* what he would say. Listen, Abby, maybe it's just the booze talking, maybe it's just the charred oak finish, but I really do know what Gus would say. Or at least I can hazard a guess. Because of something he said to me once — along the same lines, anyway. About learning from our mistakes, I mean. About moving on. Abby, listen to me here. Cards on the table. You once asked me how I fell into this, how I came into the orbit of the Blanchards and Sherlock and all of it. I gave you my standard answer about playing hooky to see a Basil Rathbone revival at the Bijou. That's not quite how it happened. Truth is, I don't like to talk about my childhood. "It is not a subject on which I would willingly dwell," as Watson would say, "and yet I am conscious that a duty devolves upon me to omit no detail."

So, listen. Gus gave me a job working in the warehouse when I was twelve years old. Out of the goodness of his heart — throwing some money our way after my father left. I unloaded the trucks, stacked the cartons. As time went on Gus found extra things for me to do. I helped him fill the mail orders. He still did it all by hand at the time — put the books into mailers, typed out the labels on his ancient Underwood. I'd take the packages to the post office on a hand truck. I loved it. I felt important, working side by side with Gus.

Every Friday, he would send me home with a Sherlock Holmes book. "Let me recommend this book," he'd say. "One of the most remarkable ever penned." I didn't realize at first that he was quoting *Sign of Four*, but I caught on quick. By the time I got through *Adventures* and *Memoirs*, I had a serious case of Baker Street fever. Gus started giving me the critical studies, "the writings about the writings." Starrett. Morley. Back issues of the *Quarterly*. I didn't understand half of it but that didn't matter. Sherlock Holmes became my *Catcher in the Rye*.

It will surprise you to learn, Abby, that being a Sherlockian did nothing to enhance my social standing at school. I was slow to grasp this. At one stage I decided that I would wear a deerstalker hat and pepper my conversation with aptly chosen Sherlock Holmes quotes, thinking that this would make me irresistible to girls.

It did not.

But I did become irresistible to Carter and his band of ninth-grade thugs. This was long before he became such a man of the world, the type of fellow who says "holiday" instead of "vacation," and "loo" instead of "crapper." In those days Carter spent most of his time bullying the smaller kids — the science nerds, mostly. Well, that's not really fair. He also made time to pick on the theater kids. A class act, your husband.

I came in for special treatment, with my kitchen-sink haircuts and hand-me-down clothes. He called me "the charity case," told everyone I cleaned the toilets at his father's warehouse. Which I didn't. I tell myself that I put up with it because I didn't want to rock the boat.

But I *was* a charity case, of course. I was painfully aware of that. Unbeknownst to my classmates, however, I was hatching a secret plan to reverse my fortunes. I decided that I would make my mark as a promising young author. What a revelation it would be! A diligent, unassuming twelve-year-old genius hiding in our midst!

I set to work on a Sherlock Holmes story, intent on becoming the youngest contributor to *Blanchard's Sherlockian Quarterly* since Gus himself. Not just any story, mind you, but one that addressed certain grievances. I called it "The Adventure of the Solitary Student," and it found Holmes and Watson called to the scene of a mysterious disturbance at a junior high school in Ohio. On arrival they enlisted the help of a promising, if misunderstood, seventh-grader in a deerstalker hat. As the plot unfolded, Holmes and Watson were called upon to disarm a nuclear device discovered at an all-school assembly, ticking ominously. When Holmes appeared to falter, his new friend stepped forward with a timely reminder: *when you have eliminated the impossible, whatever remains, however improbable, must be the truth.* Holmes nodded appreciatively; these wise words had restored his confidence. He bent to his perilous task with a renewed sense of purpose, cutting the proper wire, and he narrowly averted the crisis. Much relieved, the detective offered a few parting thoughts to the assembled students: "You would all do well to follow the sterling example of this young man, as I have," Holmes declared. "I confess that I am very much in his debt."

Gus let me down gently. He was careful to say that the story showed promise, and he had kind words for the artistry of my opening paragraph, in which "rosy-fingered dawn" broke over the humble school building. But, he continued, there were one or two difficulties that would prevent successful publication. He handed me a list of Ronald Knox's ten commandments of detective fiction. I had managed to break four of them.

Gus sent me home with another book — a book that changed my life. It was Arthur Conan Doyle's memoir. Gus wanted me to read about an episode from the author's earliest days as a struggling writer, when the manuscript of his first novel went missing in the mail. His only copy. Gone. "Of course it was the best thing I ever wrote," Conan Doyle declared. "Who ever lost a manuscript that wasn't?" As time went on, however, he came to realize that perhaps it was just as well that this early effort had slipped into oblivion. "My shock at its disappearance," he admitted, "would be as nothing to my horror if it were suddenly to appear again—in print."

Gus and I talked about that story all the time. We all have one, he told me. A story that gets lost or rejected or simply languishes in the bottom drawer for years on end because it has no other home. For a while we carry the loss around like an open wound because, of course, it was the best thing we ever wrote. But in time we move on, and we realize that it was simply a story for which the world was not yet prepared.

And so, in time, I took out a fresh sheet of paper and started a new story. It was terrible. So was the one after that. And the one after that. And one fine morning . . .

So you see, Abby, you're not the first editor to have taught me a lesson in perseverance, and you're not the first editor I've loved. And at the risk of overkill — of putting a charred oak finish on the thing— I'll just say that I can take whatever comes. Loss. Rejection. Languishing in a bottom drawer for a few more years. It has been worth a wound. But I believe our story should be told. The world is prepared.

Anyway. I'm getting sloppy as the night drags on without so much as a word from you, and it won't be long before dawn appears with its rosy fingers. Don't worry, I'm not so drunk that I won't remember to do my part, in case Carter takes the trouble to glance at the opening and closing paragraphs of my latest submission. As always, I'll finish in proper style. Just don't forget to swap in the master file before the presses roll. I've developed a superstition that if I don't remind you each time, my lovesick ramblings will somehow slip through. Conan Doyle's shock and horror would be as nothing to mine if these blatherings were suddenly to appear — in print. So don't forget and please —*please*—let me know what happened last night. At least let me know that Carter hasn't locked you away in the attic or something. Let me hear from you, Abs. Give me a sign. Proof of life. We can make this work, Abby. We can. So please let me know what happened, but I really can't wait much longer and with that Holmes threw the well-thumbed bundle of letters into the fire and stood for a moment in solemn contemplation as the crackling blue flames reduced the pages to ash.

"So ends young Bramwell's dilemma," Holmes declared with a weary sigh.

"You could not have done more, Holmes," I said. "Do you suppose this will be an end to the matter, or will Garrigan make good on his beastly threat?"

My friend stood for a moment with the battered fireplace poker in hand, stirring the coals before answering. When at last he turned to speak, I thought I detected a note of bitterness. "Garrigan would do well to follow the sterling example of young Bramwell, as I have," said Holmes. "I confess that I am very much in his debt."

The Island Boy Detective Agency

By Marcia Talley

"Jackson!"

I hear my mother calling from the deck of the marina lodge. I'm in the mangrove. My hammock is hung between two cork trees and I'm working on what Sherlock Holmes calls a two-pipe problem, so I don't answer. She'll call again in a couple of seconds.

"Jackson!"

Didn't I tell you? As long as she doesn't use all three of my names—James Jackson Judd—it's cool. Mom'll shrug, tell Miz Dee to fix me a plate of the blackboard special, and say, "He'll show up when he's hungry," and Miz Dee will click her tongue and say, "There's not much trouble a boy can get into on this island, Miz Laura," and she'd be right.

Mom and I have lived on Bonefish Cay for as long as I can remember. According to Miz Dee's husband, Constable Fergus, Bonefish Cay is eight miles long and only fifty yards wide at the Low Place, a strip so narrow that Hurricane Floyd cut the island in two. A couple of weeks later—Miz Dee says, and shows me pictures because I was only three when it happened—a barge turns up loaded with a Bobcat backhoe tractor and half a dozen construction workers from Texas to fix it.

Uncle Charlie hired them.

He owns the joint.

We have a grocery store, a bakery, two fancy souvenir shops, a beach bar, and a couple of restaurants like the one at the Bonefish Lodge where Mom is the manager, and he owns all of them, too. The last Tuesday of every month, Uncle Charlie thinks it's cool to buzz the lodge in his Piper Aztec before he touches down on the landing strip near the island's big generator and stays for a while. He's already got his shoes off when he climbs out of the pilot's seat carrying the mail bag and a copy of the Sunday *New York Times*.

He's not really my uncle.

"Jackson, be polite!" Mom says, so I try not to make faces over my cornflakes when Uncle Charlie wanders out of the bedroom in his boxer shorts, pats me on the head, and says, "How's it hanging, dude?" on his way to the coffee pot.

He's not my dad, either.

I had a dad once, but I never knew him.

When I was seven, I asked Mom about my father, but she just turned her mouth down at the corners and said, "Water under the bridge, Jackson. We'll talk about it when you're older." I keep getting older, and I keep asking, but nine isn't old enough, I guess.

I imagine my father was an explorer, a hero like James Stanfield or Dean Conger, guys I read about in the *National Geographic* magazines we've got in the lodge that go back—way back—to when Uncle Charlie's grandfather built the place, so long ago that the issues cost ten cents and had only writing, not photos, on the cover. Maybe my dad died in a fiery plane crash in Kenya, flying low while filming migrating elephants, I think. Or, maybe he froze to death near the summit of Mount Everest and will stay there until global warming uncovers his body.

Mom is supposed to be homeschooling me, but she gets busy and forgets. Nobody back in the U.S. is checking up on us, though, so it's no big deal. When I grow old and famous, my entry in the *Encyclopedia Britannica* is going to say, "J. J. Judd was self-educated," and that'd be the truth. We've got an *Encyclopedia Britannica* set in the lodge library. Even though it's old and the bindings are falling apart, there's all kinds of interesting stuff in there. My favorite volume is number nine, "Extradition to Garrick." I've read the article about fencing a million times, and practice with a machete—J. Jackson Judd versus a coconut hanging from a rope—unless there's a boat in the marina with kids on it I can play with.

There're shelves of *Popular Mechanics* in the library, too. I built a transistor radio from instructions in *Popular Mechanics*. Constable Fergus once helped me build a boxcar racer out of a shipping pallet, wheelbarrow parts, and an old golf cart battery.

And if I ever get bored with science and geography, I can grab one of the Reader's Digest Condensed Books that Miz Dee keeps dusted, their spines lined up all neat and even.

"You let him read *The Stepford Wives?*" Miz Dee asks my mom one day at lunch. I have a volume from 1973 propped up like a wall around my fish sandwich and fries. I'm actually reading *The Odessa File*, but Miz Dee can't see that.

Mom laughs her happy laugh and says, "It's condensed, Dee. They cut out the naughty bits."

Mom means sex. She thinks I don't know about sex, but I do. *National Geographic* has stories about the family life of apes, and I can't see how apes are much different from humans.

"Condensed!" Miz Dee huffs, as she gets up from the table. "Condensation is for soups, not for books." She collects my mother's empty plate and says, "In the sixth grade, I didn't realize they had us reading a condensed version of *Little Women.* When I got into high school, I was talking with a friend and she said, 'It's so sad, like the part in *Little Women* where Beth dies,' and I was, like, '*What?!*'"

That makes my mother laugh.

Not all the books in our library are condensed. We have a zillion copies of last year's best-sellers like *The Da Vinci Code, Midnight in the Garden of Good and Evil,* and every Harry Potter book that J. K. Rowling ever wrote, and in different languages, too, like *Harry Potter und Der Stein der Weisen* and *Harry Potter à l'école des sorciers.* They get left behind by cruising sailors who don't want them anymore. Miz Dee hung up a sign—TAKE ONE, LEAVE ONE—so I'm always on the lookout for something new to read. I really hit the jackpot last summer when a big, fat volume with a brown-and-yellow cover caught my eye, sandwiched between a spiral-bound *Cruising Guide to the Abacos* for 1980 and a book called *Two Stroke Engine Repair and Maintenance.* The cover said: *The Complete Sherlock Holmes, containing four novels and all fifty-six adventures.* I snatched it up quick and took it back to our cottage. From the Condensed Books, I'd read Dick Francis, lots of Grafton and Grisham, all of *The Cat Who...* books and some good stories by Mary Higgins Clark and Elizabeth Peters. Agatha Christie is awesome, too, but *The Complete Sherlock Holmes* totally blew my mind. It's my bible.

It'd be cool to be the son of Sherlock Holmes, I think, but I know he's just a fictional character dreamed up by Sir Arthur Conan Doyle. Besides, as far as I can tell, the Great Detective never had sex so a son was out of the question. Miz Dee goes on and on about how impressionable young boys need a strong male role model, and what a blessing it is that Uncle Charlie is in my life. But, as role models go, you can't get much better than Sherlock Holmes.

I've already solved my first case—The Missing Quarters Affair. Someone had broken into the dollar-bill changing machine in the laundry room at the marina. If they'd jimmied the lock to get at the money, it might have taken me longer to solve the case, but the criminal was a moron—he used a key, and the only spare key was kept in Miz Dee's office, hanging behind the door on a hook under her apron. Only a handful of people knew about that. I had a closed circle of suspects!

I was hanging out at the Thirsty 'Cuda playing a foosball game with a twelve-year-old kid from a cruising trawler, when one of my suspects wandered in. Manny was Miz Dee's nephew from Baltimore, staying on the island for the summer to keep him away from "bad influences" in the city. Manny did odd jobs around the lodge—cleaning the hot tub, sifting leaves out of the swimming pool, making sure the golf carts were plugged in at night, washing glasses behind the bar—but that was his day off. I'd just served and made a wall pass with a push kick that whizzed past the visiting kid's goalie, when I saw Manny sidle up to the slot machine next to the bar and start feeding it quarters. Bells rang, lights flashed, and a fistful of quarters tumbled into the coin tray. Manny rubbed his hands together, scooped up his winnings, then fed the quarters back into the machine, one by one, until he was empty-handed. What a dope. Didn't he know the odds? The February 1960 issue of *Popular Mechanics* had been a real eye-opener about slot machines for me. "In Las Vegas," they wrote, "Electronics Keeps the Gamblers Honest."

After I beat the boat kid best-three-out-of-five, I went looking for Constable Fergus and fingered Manny for the laundry room job. That night, Miz Dee and Constable Fergus had a big pow-wow, and after that, Manny spent his days off at the dump, hosing out trash bins.

As an aspiring detective, I can't just sit back and relax. I have to practice my powers of observation. Here's what I deduced when Uncle Charlie showed up this morning for breakfast.

He's just had a shower because his hair is slicked back. He dyes it black, because the hair on his chest doesn't match—it's salt-and-pepper gray. His chest is bare, so you can see the knotted scar over his left nipple, about two inches long. I asked him about it once and he'd laughed and said, "Shrapnel." But I knew it wasn't an old war wound. "Charlie has a pacemaker," Mom told me, and when I mentioned that I'd read about the first artificial pacemaker in the March 1933 issue of *Popular Mechanics*, she said, "That's nice, Jackson. Now run along."

I note that Uncle Charlie's shaved off his stubble, leaving a speck of blood on his cheek and a dab of shaving cream behind his ear. He's wearing long pants but carrying a pair of Docksiders in his left hand. A green polo shirt is draped over his arm.

"I deduce that you're flying back to Texas early," I say.

"And what brings you to that conclusion, my man?"

I explain my reasoning. "You're all dressed up. And you always go barefoot," I add, pointing to the shoes. "Except on the plane."

"Guess again, Sherlock!" He pats me on the head. "Quick trip to the mainland and back. Got an important business meeting today."

Around ten o'clock, Uncle Charlie's powerboat zooms back from the mainland with him at the helm. He ties up at the end of the fuel dock and climbs out, followed by two city slickers. The taller one is carrying a briefcase; the other a canvas tube, too short to be a fishing rod.

I'm sitting in the window seat of the library, reading a mildewed copy of *N is for Noose,* and I see them out the window, strolling up the dock. I figure they're heading to the bar, like city slickers always do, but after a few minutes, Uncle Charlie opens the library door and they all come through. "Spread it out over there," Uncle Charlie says, pointing to the table in the middle of the room. It's made from an old ship's door and has currency from all over the world laminated to the top.

Children should be seen and not heard, the Victorians in Sherlock's time used to say. I figure the opposite might also be true: Kids who aren't heard can't be seen, so I scrunch down behind my book and keep mum.

The short guy is wearing a Hawaiian shirt with guitars all over it. He upends the tube over the table and a map falls out. He rolls the map out and anchors the corners with some heavy glass ashtrays nobody uses since Miz Dee nailed a THANK YOU FOR NOT SMOKING sign on the wall. He stabs at the chart with a fat, hairy finger and says, "The casino will go here, where the old lodge is now."

"I thought you planned on expanding the lodge," Uncle Charlie says.

The other guy shrugs. "No can do. Our architect says it'll break the bank. The place is a total teardown."

"Then where's the—" Uncle Charlie begins, but the tall guy cuts him off.

"I'm way ahead of you there, Chuck. We're siting the hotel over here, where the mangrove is now."

Mangrove? My ears begin to burn. Sherlock Holmes has 221B Baker Street. Hercule Poirot lives at 56B Whitehaven Mansions. Even Nero Wolfe has a brownstone on West 35th Street in New York City. There is only one mangrove on Bonefish Cay and that's where my personal hammock hangs between two sturdy cork trees and my plastic tub of treasures is stashed in the crook of a buttonwood tree. My best friends live there, too. Schools of yellow jack and sergeant majors. Jade, the green heron who *skeow-skeow*s at night. A curly-tail lizard I named Izzy who nibbles on my big toe if I'm too slow tossing banana bits his way. Randy the manatee sometimes cruises by. I recognize Randy by the notch in his fluke from an unfortunate encounter with a powerboat. Mangroves are crucial to our island's ecosystem, everybody knows that! They absorb wave energy, like during hurricanes. They are nurseries for our fish and wildlife! I remember a May issue of *National Geographic* from 1977 that explains all about mangroves. I decide to find it and show it to them.

"Let's go to the bar and talk details," Uncle Charlie says as he shakes the hand of the guy in the Hawaiian shirt and pounds the other guy on the back.

After they leave, I put down my book and go over to check out the map. I know how to read maps—every issue of *National Geographic* has a centerfold. It's clear from their plans that the Bonefish Hotel, Casino, and Marina would take over one-quarter of the island. The channel would be dredged to accommodate yachts up to two hundred and fifty feet. Although I look hard for it, the cottage where my mother and I live is nowhere in the plans.

It's a disaster.

But, what is a nine-year-old detective going to do about it? I have a three-pipe problem on my hands.

The city slickers eventually leave, laughing like hyenas, staggering down the dock after one too many of Miz Dee's frozen Bahama Mamas. Uncle Charlie walks with them, making sure they don't fall into the water.

Later, I find the *National Geographic* from May 1977 and show the article to Uncle Charlie. He takes the magazine out to the patio to read, I give him points for that. "Well?" I say after an hour goes by. "What do you think?"

He lays the magazine down on the deck next to his chair, adjusts his sunglasses, and closes his eyes. "I hear you, Jackson. But . . ."

"But what?" I ask.

"Progress, my boy," he says. "You can't stand in the way of progress."

* * *

Three weeks later the city slickers come back. They have lunch with Uncle Charlie who's dressed more like his normal self, in shorts and a Grateful Dead T-shirt, bare feet and all. Manny's doing his gig at the garbage dump, so I'm helping Miz Dee. Kids aren't supposed to serve alcoholic beverages, so she's got me loading the dishwasher in the kitchen when we hear the *whoop-whoop-whoop* of the Bonefish Cay Fire and Rescue boat. Everyone rushes out on the dock to see what's going on.

The city slickers are standing at the fuel dock, looking stupid.

Uncle Charlie's sprawled on the floor of his powerboat and Constable Fergus is pounding on his chest.

My mother starts to climb down the boarding ladder, but Miz Dee reaches out and drags her back. "What happened?" Miz Dee asks.

"Heart attack, Dee baby," Constable Fergus says. "Dead when he hit the deck. Not a thing anyone coulda done about it."

"Not a heart attack," I pipe up.

"What do you know about it, kid?" the constable says.

"Jackson?" My mother raises her head from Miz Dee's shoulder. "Nothing. He knows nothing, Fergus. He's only nine years old, for heaven's sake."

"I've read about this," I say. "Uncle Charlie's been electrocuted. Check out his hands."

Constable Fergus frowns, but does what I ask. Behind me, one of the city slickers sucks air in through his teeth. We all see the burns on Uncle Charlie's palms.

"Jesus!" the city slicker says. "I saw him! He put both hands on the pump. He was pushing the boat away a bit so we could get on."

Mom begins to sway and reaches for the fuel pump to steady herself. I knock her hand away. "Nobody touch that pump until an electrician checks it out! Probably okay if you're wearing shoes, but . . ." I let my voice trail off and I see that everyone is checking out the burn on Uncle Charlie's foot. "Shock like that probably fried his pacemaker," I add.

"Kid might be right," Constable Fergus says. He reaches up from the boat and gives the pump a cautious tap. "Yipes!" he yells, jerking his arm back real quick. "Step away, everybody. That bastard packs a wallop!"

Eventually, Fire and Rescue takes Uncle Charlie's body to the hospital on the mainland. My mother, Miz Dee, and the city slickers go along. While they're gone, I do what needs to be done. The architectural plans are in itty-bitty pieces, flushed down the toilet in Buoys, the tiki-shack men's room behind the swimming pool. The March 2006 issue of *Popular Mechanics* with the article on "How to Avoid Electric Shock" is back on the library shelves.

"Reason backwards," Sherlock Holmes always says.

And that's exactly what I'd done.

Uncle Charlie died without a will, my mother says, so while his ex-wives, seven children, and their lawyers squabble over his estate, things on Bonefish Cay are returning to normal. I miss Uncle Charlie, of course. Everybody does.

Mom seems happier these days. I see her sitting at the bar, laughing with a guy named Joe who came in on a Nordhaven 42 for a few nights, then decided to reserve the slip for a month.

Meanwhile, I'm back in my hammock, working on a case. Overnight, someone ran into Miz Dee's golf cart, smashed the *Queen Bee* up good.

The game is afoot!

Somewhere on Bonefish Cay there's a vehicle with yellow paint on its bumper, and it won't be long before J. Jackson Judd, Island Boy Detective, tracks it down.

Ordeals
By Art Taylor

The master had taken his accustomed spot at the head of the table—
his chair as grand as his bearing.

Dark walnut with a burgundy velvet cushion.

Intricately carved spindles between the top rail and that pillowed seat.

And each of those spindles was arrayed with the heads of beasts:
elephant, giraffe, rhinoceros.

Lions roared from the end of each arm. The master's hand stroked
the wooden mane of the one on the left.

My mistress sat at the other end, her own chair smaller and sim-
pler in its curves, but a match in its own way. The chairs had been
commissioned by the master to commemorate his travels, celebrate his
worldliness. The back of hers depicted a woodland scene: a pair of does,
a wild peahen, a vixen.

The candles gleamed as usual tonight, but the dining room seemed
unaccustomedly thick with gloom—shadows more persistent than the
light that cast them. Through the windows rising on the room's east
wall, the dark night was moonless, the dim specter of clouds gathering
beyond like the omen of a coming storm. An oppressive silence had
settled over the meal.

I recognized that my own feelings and fears possibly skewed my reading of the scene, accentuating specific details, overdramatizing them,
unnecessarily perhaps.

The meal was as sumptuous as ever: roasted quail, braised root vegetables, a loaf of freshly baked bread—festive and luxurious, and the
master had been enjoying it with his customary enthusiasm, though my
mistress, rarely a hearty eater, especially where vegetables were concerned,
had seemed even less engaged than usual with her plate.

Details. Over-attention. Over-emphasis.

From my own assigned spot between sideboard and kitchen door—
waiting, attentive, mute—I felt certain I could hear the master chewing.

It was he who broke the quiet.

"Have you considered my request?" He tossed the words down the
table with an unconvincing nonchalance.

"Your challenge?" My mistress lowered her fork.

The corners of the master's lips curved into a wicked smile. "My invitation for you to establish your innocence."

He enjoyed matching wits with others, specifically with his lessers. I'd glimpsed this at other dinners, other gatherings.

"My innocence should be presupposed." My mistress's own smile proved more pleasant, the same courtesy and hospitality that seemed to come so naturally to her. "Unless there is some evidence of guilt. A central tenet of justice, is it not?"

The master's expression shifted into a smirk. "Schooling *me* in the law? That's . . . rich." His amusement seemed barbed. "But this is no court. These are mere marital matters. An airing of concerns between a man and his wife, and perhaps a settling of concerns, what's sensed, what's felt."

"What's feared," she said, the hint of a sigh. "Your suspicions. But shouldn't a husband have faith in the woman he loves?"

He raised his wineglass, tilted it toward her. "Which is all I'm asking for. A restoration of that faith."

This road was well-traveled, conversations I had often overheard. I had not eavesdropped in these instances, I should add. I remained always in plain sight—serving, straightening, tending, making sure no detail was forgotten—and yet unnoticed, unseen, in so many ways invisible, purposefully forgotten myself.

Or—a clarification—forgotten by the master. Throughout their talks, the mistress occasioned a small glance my way.

Self-consciousness? Embarrassment? A silent plea for understanding? For empathy? From someone in my station?

The master's questions regularly taunted, lured, and accused—looking back at some previous social gathering, anticipating the next. Good gentleman so-and-so seems quite handsome, wouldn't you agree? You seemed to take quite an interest in him at the so-and-so's two nights ago, didn't you? What were the two of you chatting about that seemed so terribly engaging?

The word *terribly* was lingered over, savored.

The rosiness of my mistress's cheeks may well have often been a blush. But what could someone in my position offer?

Whenever she turned toward me, I returned with greater earnest to my duties.

"But the stakes," my mistress said now from her end of the table. "Surely it seems excessive to risk—"

"Your life." The master nodded. "I do recognize. But does this mean you doubt your ability to pass the test and prove yourself?"

My mistress's words seemed carefully chosen. "You have little faith in me, but so much in a test whose own reliability might seem to others questionable at best."

"To someone less worldly, perhaps—someone more provincial in their outlook." His finger made the slightest flick toward my mistress's end of the table. Perhaps she had not seen the gesture, but the words had hit their mark—my mistress's own more modest upbringing, the society the master had rescued her from, his central role in lifting her to improved circumstances, the family she'd left behind. "But other civilizations have much to teach us, if—"

"Primitive civilizations," my mistress said. "Naïve superstitions."

"Ancient cultures." The master deepened his voice. His finger pointed toward her more explicitly now—"Honored traditions"—and then he shifted his attention to me.

At his nod, I turned to the sideboard by which I'd been standing—the sole servant present, the cook having been sent away, no one else to witness what had already been put into motion.

The candles provided ample light as I lifted the top of a squat specimen jar and tilted it gently toward a small porcelain dish as I'd been directed. A single bean from the jar tipped onto the doily—a Tenerife lace square, another souvenir of the master's travels, a gift he'd brought for my mistress.

The bean itself was from his travels as well. Oblong, its surface dimpled slightly, a deep, chocolate brown.

As it touched the doily, the bean fell off center, and I nudged it lightly into place with a gloved hand. This centering had not been part of the master's instructions, but I'd learned how well he appreciated a degree of ceremony. He was particular in all ways, especially at the dining table: the correct alignment of silverware and glassware, the precise balance and angling of the table linens, the timing of the courses through soup, meat, salad, pudding, cheese.

Preparing the master's afternoon coffee, I am always careful to measure the precise amount of sugar, lest his lips wince with distaste and dissatisfaction. When I serve his evening claret, I am careful to pour no more than one-third of a glass to let the wine breathe properly.

The proper breath. The white gloves. The slight bow. I have been formally schooled.

The tray required only one hand, but I lifted it with two, keeping my fingers at precise angles on the silver, symmetrically positioned, and ferried it to the master's end of the table.

It was the largest beans from the specimen jar. He had indeed instructed me on that point, and I'd followed his orders as closely and discreetly as I could, laying the dish to the side of his own plate.

He plucked the bean from its place.

"*Physotigma venenosum,*" the master said. "Known in West Africa as *esere*. A small bean, yes, but one with mighty power—valued for its extraordinary ability to divine the truth and administer justice, and therefore feared dreadfully by those among the tribal people who have committed their own injustices. When one of their number is accused, that tribesman must swallow the bean, which then gauges guilt and inno-cence—sparing those who are free from blame, and for the others . . ." He gave a small, bitter laugh. "For the guilty who taste of *esere*, accused become accursed. Originally, tribal leaders had hidden *esere* from Euro-peans, but some decades ago, a Scottish missionary . . ."

The master was a learned man, schooled in his own way and proud of both his knowledge and the curiosity that led him toward it. He had been in his library before tonight's meal, a room adjacent to the dining room, and he had left the door slightly ajar when he took his seat at the table. The dim light from the candles peeked through, offering only the faintest glimpse of the shelves upon shelves and rows upon rows of the master's books—his livelihood, his passion, the sanctuary where he spent much of his time when at home.

"Expanding my enlightenment"—these were his words.

The master insisted on meticulousness perhaps most of all in the caretaking of his library, his most cherished province. The books must be free from dust. The books must be placed evenly on the shelves, never so tightly that one must needs be wrested from its place but never so loosely as to leave an awkward gap between volumes. The spine of each book must remain exactly one inch from the edge of the shelf, a distance which the master double-checked with a wooden ruler on his desk. And if that inch was more or less . . .

In the past, the master had demonstrated no reluctance to swat that ruler at me in punishment for my mismeasurements.

He was scrupulous, too, about the arrangement of his volumes.

"Sociology belongs on the upper shelves, anthropology there, history here, and on this shelf the lives of great men. This bookcase, however, is reserved for Latin and Greek, and . . ." And then a look of disappoint-ment, futility, exasperation. "Why am I wasting my breath? *Graecum est; non potest legi.* All Greek to you, isn't it?"

All Greek.

Or Latin in this case.

Despite my potential limitations as a reader, I will admit that I shared the master's reverence for the books. I, too, admired the straightness of their spines, luxuriated in the smell of the opened books, was drawn in by the letters, the way they seemed to dance so urgently and persuasively across the pages.

As the master recounted the history of the *esere* bean and extolled again its mystical powers, my mistress stayed as silent as I, though she alone was his intended audience. When he finished his recitation, he gave me another nod—another silent bit of instruction bringing me back into the unfolding drama.

The master had returned the bean to its dish, his eyes vivid with excitement, and after gathering the dish back on my tray, I carried it to my mistress's end of the table.

It was murder, tonight was.

Not chance, but calculation—I knew this.

Was I the only one?

My mistress's protestations about the naïveté of African cultures, about primitivism and superstition, about the potentially deadly unreliability of the test my master proposed—perhaps these were evidence of some hesitations, some cautiousness, but did they also indicate some recognition of what plans might be transpiring this evening? Some tactics of her own?

My mistress watched my approach, and I watched her. Her situation was a dire one, certainly, and I anticipated fear and dread in her expression, but she surprised me with, as always, the brightest eyes and same wide smile. Her dimples wore a playfulness, the suggestion always that the world was joy, that life was truly an adventure. Even here in this darkest moment, she seemed steadfast despite . . .

I could feel it at my back, the master's glower from his end of the table—sullenness and sneers, disdain and distrust, calculation, connivance.

Whatever my opinions, I have never yet shown disrespect, I must emphasize. I hold my own visage fast in some middle place between the master's and my mistress's. My lips maintain a straightness, neither smile nor scowl.

I set the plate down, returned to my appointed position.

My mistress touched the edge of the dish, rubbed the porcelain with the tip of her finger, returned her hand to her lap.

"Millicent," she said.

"Pardon?" The master cocked his head.

"Millicent." A candle seemed to flicker, some small draftiness in the room. "The Granvilles' daughter. 'A dainty filly,' I believe you called her the last we visited."

The master's eyes widened, incredulous. "Millicent?" He sniggered. "I barely recall. Just a child, isn't she?"

"Grown into a woman of late."

"Why, I've hardly noticed."

"But I believe you have." My mistress tilted her head slightly, raised her eyes. "The way you kept watching her from across the room when we visited Wednesday last, the way you doted on her when the two of you finally had a chance to speak, and didn't you make a special trip to visit Mr. Granville yesterday? No reason behind the visit, at least none you cared to admit to, and . . ."

As my mistress spoke, the master's expression ranged widely. He raised his own eyebrows, his eyes widened again, his jaw went slack—all the evidence of stark surprise, but all pantomime, I felt certain, though perhaps again I was the only one to read the clues.

The mistress touched the dish once more, turned it slightly, as if examining the bean. "All of which gives me pause—and cause to wonder. Is this bean truly a trial of my innocence or a sentence already determined? Is it designed to gauge my trustworthiness or to condemn me for being deemed unworthy in a different way? Am I simply dispensable now that you have set your eyes on another? And if I were to die unjustly tonight, how soon would be finding another to assuage your grief?"

"But this is absurd," the master sputtered. "I barely know this girl, much less am I harboring some intentions toward her and—"

"And so another bean would prove, would it not? And in doing so, restore *my* faith as well." My mistress sat up in her seat, her posture tall now, her poise perfect. "I will take your test, but I will not take it alone. . . ."

The master maintained his studied befuddlement, a play of twitches on his face as if he were struggling to understand what she suggested. But the keenness of his eyes, ever-watchful, ever-aware, betrayed the truth.

The master is well learned, as I said, and also astute in matters beyond his books.

When he had given me my instructions for the evening, he had discussed other expectations. "My wife may ultimately insist that I undergo the trial myself," he said. "Some spurious reasoning—some insistence and delay. If so, I am prepared to meet her own challenge. At my signal, you will deliver the specimen jar to me, and . . ."

Calculating, as I said. Conniving always.

"Whatever happens," he had warned me, "you maintain your station unless I explicitly order otherwise, do you understand?"

I had given my bow. I had needed no reminding.

"Ah," the master said to my mistress now. "I see," he said. "Millicent . . ." And then a shrug. "As you wish."

At his fresh beckon, I picked up the jar—three beans remaining inside, each smaller than the one at my mistress's setting—and delivered it to him. He took the jar from me, and with quick sleight of hand and his same deliberate nonchalance, he joggled the smallest of the beans free.

Balancing it carefully between forefinger and thumb, he displayed it to my mistress.

"I have nothing to hide," he said. "Nothing to fear." He rolled the bean between his fingers with a certain relish. "But the first bite for the lady, yes?"

The phrase stung, I could feel it myself, and not simply as the next move in the game. His words offered a deliberate echo—a mockery—of a moment from early in their relationship: the master feeding a strawberry to a woman who had little room to say no.

In years past, she had delivered the produce—a girl, then a girl grown to a woman, and then a woman invited inside. A cup of tea, a bite of pastry, a bowl of strawberries.

One afternoon, he'd plucked the largest one from a bowl, dabbed it in Devonshire cream, raised it to her lips. She'd waved him off briefly, but he'd nudged it toward her mouth—"first bite for the lady"—with such insistence and such emphasis on the word *lady* that she relented.

The cream smeared her lips, and as she bit into the strawberry, its juices ran down the side of her chin.

"Messy, messy," he'd chided, laughing, and then leaned in further to clean her face, smearing his handkerchief red.

On a morning later, long since married by this point, sitting alone at the breakfast table after the master had gone on with his day, my mistress gestured toward an untouched bowl of strawberries.

"Do you enjoy these?" she asked me.

"Ma'am?" I replied. I had been discreetly examining a silver chalice, pondering whether it needed a bit of polish.

"Strawberries," she said. "The taste of them." Her expression revealed hints of vexation. "The texture."

"Is the lady displeased?" I asked. It was the beginning of the berry season. There was a bit of whiteness near the stem. Perhaps they were insufficiently ripe?

My mistress knitted her brows, tilted her head. "When I was younger, very young, before I moved here, my sister and I would spend whole days exploring. There were woods behind our home, a small lake tucked within. Our world was small, I realize now, only another tangled corner of countryside, but it seemed much wider to us, a sense of wonder at every turn, even the spots we'd already tromped through a hundred times or more. And along one of those turns was a patch of wild strawberries—always such a burst of joy to find them suddenly plump on their runners. Our fingers couldn't work quickly enough to pluck them up to our lips and . . ."

Her eyes remained fixed on the bowl, but her attention seemed somewhere far beyond it. The strawberries in front of her, I realized, had gone untouched, not a single one eaten.

"There came a time when I wanted more," my mistress said, her voice soft, words I was unclear if she meant me to hear. "There are many things I had not expected to miss."

Her life would surely be a cause of envy for many. Light supervision of the household I and another servant kept for them. A bit of correspondence and sociability. And if she had borne the master children . . .

Often she seemed simply to drift from room to room, bedroom, dining room, parlor, the master's library, some time at the piano, at her writing desk, wandering outdoors.

After a moment, she returned to herself. "I find myself not caring for strawberries anymore," she said. "And these will likely go to waste. I wondered if you might like one for yourself."

She lifted a berry from the bowl as she spoke, held its stem delicately between her lean fingers, proffered it my way.

A servant should not speak unless spoken to.

A servant should not have an opinion.

A servant should not—

Despite the rules, despite myself, I accepted the strawberry from her hand. Our fingers grazed lightly against one another. My forearm trembled as I lifted it to my own lips.

Though she may not have cared for the fruit any longer herself, my mistress seemed to take some small pleasure in my having one, her face brightening as I chewed—or at least I believed so in the glimpses I dared.

There was likely more to say, but such conversations were not appropriately to be shared.

"First bite for the lady, yes?"

Had the gloom deepened by some significant degree? The clouds thickened beyond the dining room windows? The candles faltered there atop the table?

The master was stuck in a rigid tableau—his bottom settled comfortably on that cushion, his fingers holding his tiny bean aloft, his steely stare still leveling itself along the length of the table.

There was motion, however, at my mistress's end of the room. She lifted her hand from her lap, rested her fingers once more on the edge of the dish, twisted it again lightly in place.

Murder afoot, I wanted to say. *Every choice matters.*

Having the sole knowledge of what was planned felt like the awfullest loneliness.

I should have cautioned my mistress, should have dared to step out of my role—I recognized this, I chided myself, too late. But it was required that I keep my appointed spot—that I maintain my self-constraint.

I did break from protocol, though, but only for a moment—and this in response to my mistress's own needs, which I could well argue was part of my charge.

As her fingers moved from the edge of the plate to the bean at its center, she glanced my way, and for once, I kept my own gaze steady, hoping the master would not notice.

Affection in the smile she gave me, perhaps a warm good-bye if needed—was that intended? This time I did not turn away. Instead, I risked the slightest nod and gave a heavy swallow of my own and hoped she understood.

My mistress plucked the bean from its bowl. Whatever hesitations she may have had before, she showed nothing but bravery now as she placed the *esere* in her mouth and swallowed it whole. Her expression was resolute, as if not only accepting what might come next but eager for it.

I, at last, felt some relief.

Perhaps she had indeed *known*.

My gaze shifted toward the master. The corners of his mouth had sharpened into a fouler sneer, and his eyes had narrowed further, thin slits now—his stare unblinking, relentless, sudden anger behind them.

Time crept forward, perhaps several minutes, all in silence. I did not look toward the clock in the corner, so intent was my own attention on both the master and my mistress, my gaze flicking back and forth between them, measuring the changes in their demeanor. With each second that passed, my mistress's spirits seemed to lighten and my master's grow heavier by the pound.

"Has my innocence been established to your satisfaction?" she asked.

"Time will tell," he said. "The truth will out."

"And perhaps next the truth of your own circumstances?"

"As I said, I have nothing to hide."

"Then neither anything to fear."

Where my mistress had set aside her hesitations for a sudden boldness, the master had become more cautious—moving his hand forward and back in the air, still rolling the bean between his fingers. If he'd hoped the one she ate would do its work and save him from his own next step, he'd been cheated.

It would have been no surprise if, at any moment, he had hurled the bean down the table, stood up and thrown his chair behind him, stalked out of the room. Pride must have held his hand.

"But perhaps," my mistress said, "perhaps there *is* something to fear?"

Even from my position against the wall, I could feel the master's sudden heat—humiliation and rage and the quick fever of his determination.

"I'm afraid of *nothing*," he said, and he popped the bean into his mouth—swallowing it whole as well, an indignant gulp. He grasped his wineglass and emptied it to the final drop. His stare now was openly malevolent.

He wiped his lips with the back of his sleeve. "You *knew* to swallow it whole," he said. "Where did you learn that?"

The rosiness of my mistress's cheeks was no blush, but a flush of pride.

"Isn't it a wife's duty to share her husband's interests? And don't I have time of a day to read?" She gestured toward the half-open door to the library. "We are the weaker sex, surely, but the opportunity to—"

"*You've* been in my library?" His sputtering now was real, his lips tangled. "Reading *science*?"

"Should I have confined myself to novels?" The mistress rolled her eyes. "Oh, you are not only old-fashioned, you are almost determinedly antiquated, a primitive yourself."

"Millicent doesn't think so." His hands fumbled toward his wineglass. "She believes that—"

"She has hardly given you a second thought," my mistress said. "Can you not recognize your own blindness, your own hypocrisy? Can you not see that I was only trying to—"

But whatever my mistress was trying to do, she never completed the thought.

As she had been speaking, the smacking of the master's lips had grown more pronounced—not in his usual manner while eating nor with some particular attempt to savor the wine he'd drunk. Instead, there evolved a slow pressing and then gaping and then puckering, as if he were searching for something along the tenderest parts of his lips—surprise and curiosity and confusion no longer pantomime but evidence of some desperation.

"What . . ." he spat. "What have you . . . ?"

Was it my mistress's innate kindness and generosity which pulled her from her chair? Would it have been too much against her good nature *not* to be drawn forward toward the man who had for so long mistreated her, who had in fact challenged her life this very evening? Could she ever have failed to lend a helping hand his way?

As she rose, she looked my way too, imploring. I was destined to help, wasn't I? It was my duty, correct?

But I had my orders: maintain my station unless the master explicitly ordered me otherwise.

Whatever her surprise at the master's sudden distress, perhaps my inaction puzzled her more. Her gaze darted between the two of us as she came around the table, but rather than directing herself toward the master, gasping and writhing, she ultimately came to stand beside me.

"What has happened?" my mistress said. "What *is* happening?"

"You—" I began softly, my hands behind my back.

But had I misstepped? Had I misunderstood?

The time has passed to reconsider.

"You," I told her, "are not the only one to have been reading from the master's books."

"All those times when you're . . . cleaning his library?"

"Straightening and dusting, yes," I said. "And enlightening myself."

"About the *esere* bean?"

"In many directions."

The master's fingers dug into the burgundy velvet of his seat, and the grip of his other hand had tightened on one of the lions' heads. His arm trembled, his fingers curled inside its open jaw, his skin tore against their wooden teeth. His own mouth was agape, and his tongue flicked in and out, a thirst seeking to be slaked.

He stared at us—pleading, accusation, likely both. But the words his mouth searched out, he could no longer find.

Neither of us stepped forward, myself still duty-bound. My mistress's reasons remained her own. She took my hand for support.

"Should we?" she asked. "Could we?"

I shook my head. It was, indeed, too late.

"Aconite," I told her. "*Aconitum Napellus,* to use the Latin designation. From the family *Ranunculaceae,* which also includes—perhaps surprisingly—the buttercup. Stories of aconite's potency date back to Greek mythology, the spit of Cerberus flung wildly from its three heads as Hercules dragged the beast from Hades—mythology on the top shelf of the corner cabinet, as you may know. *Napellus* is from the Latin for a tuber, perhaps literally a little turnip, the word maintaining its focus on the root of the plant where the poisons are held most dear. But the entirety of the plant can prove dangerous. Even touching the petals without gloves or other protection will bring a tingling to your bare fingers and worse to a cut on your skin, and the smallest ingestion of the root can prove fatal. Unfortunately, it is far too easy for the root itself to be confused with horseradish, as a story from up North proved only a few decades ago, an unfortunate cook who mistakenly grated it to help flavor a roast and killed the dinner party. This must have been what happened tonight, I would suggest, perhaps something with the root vegetables. The cook will feel some guilt, I'm sure, but no one could blame her. And if such a small misstep can be so devastating, one could only imagine the toxicity if someone had tried to use the plant for some purposeful contamination, perhaps the surface of a bean, for example—even the smallest bean, even the one that someone might choose if he felt a larger bean might pose some more substantial threat. And surprising, too, how common aconite is, how widely it can be found throughout the countryside, the loamiest of our soils so fertile for its growth, perhaps a plant you saw yourself in your own childhood, those wanderings you've told me about, those happier days. Monkshood we've called it, because of the shape of its flower, or wolfsbane as well, a direct translation of an even earlier word, referring to the use of the poison on arrows to kill wolves. The Greek *lycotonum*, I mean. And another name is Venus' chariot, which—"

Or that was what I might have said if my mistress had not shushed me after my initial sentence—first with her fingers, then with a "Hush," and then with a question. "You read Latin?"

"And have learned some Greek, but only rudimentarily."

. . . which finally gave us a topic for our own conversation.

The master's lips were, by this point, gratefully quiet, allowing us finally to speak in peace.

Knox Vomica
By Peter Lovesey

Want to write a fiendish mystery?
You'd better know this piece of history.
When the Roaring Twenties ended
Unbridled plotting was suspended.
Authors who aspired to fox
Obeyed Monsignor Ronald Knox.
His Ten Commandments of Detection
Controlled the use of misdirection:

Give the killer an early mention.
Play fair and honor this convention.

The supernatural has no place
In a true detective case.

You had better not presume
To introduce a secret room.

Do not place the least reliance
On poisoning unknown to science.

Every writer must eschew
Chinamen like Fu Manchu.

Mark one other prohibition:
Do not rely on intuition.

It is the rule in every thriller,
The sleuth must never be the killer.

Unmentioned clues are not fair play.
Get them on the page, okay?

If you employ a Watson, please,
Tell everything he knows and sees.

You must avoid the sin of sins:
An alibi involving twins.

* * *

And now with something of a splash
We dive into a verse form perfected by the inimitable Ogden Nash
And relate a story that will have Knox spinning in his grave and
crying, "Cheat!"
For every one of his ten rules was broken at the Mystery
Characters' Retreat,
Where brilliant amateurs, police, and private eyes
Gathered to chill out and socialize.

* * *

It was a Sunday evening, nine-thirty on the clock,
When Lord Peter Wimsey chaired a meeting and caused a seismic
shock.
"I dare say you are wondering why I called you to the library.
We're all trapped in Cliché Manor, the snow lies deep, our phones
are down, and there's no way out, not even bribery.
But that's not all: the evidence suggests
Some antisocial person has been murdering the guests.
Call it homicide or sacrificing,
Face it, friends, the body count is much too high —and rising,
And no one has got near to unraveling the truth,
Which is deplorable considering each of you has the reputation of
being a fictional super-sleuth.
While this murderer roams free,
Where did I find Dave Robicheaux, Jack Reacher, Albert Campion,
and Travis McGee?
In the games room playing pool.
While Nero Wolfe, Mike Hammer, Harry Bosch, and Jessica Fletcher
got up a poker school.
I was told (Dear Lord, I hope this isn't true),
They were all cleaned out by little Nancy Drew.
Meanwhile those peculiar noises from the cellar
Were found to have been made by Ms. V. I. Warshawski — in the
arms of Detective Steve Carella.
You may laugh, but I regard it as a matter of regret
That while a serial killer is on the loose, Sam Spade, Easy Rawlins,

Matthew Scudder, and the Continental Op are stretched out on the
Afghan carpet passing round a strange-smelling cigarette.
In short, it's time for action, we can't ignore this anymore.
Brace up, you feckless characters. Where's your esprit de corps?
Get this into your woolly heads: nothing is fine and dandy.
A killer is among us and here's his modus operandi:
Each victim is disposed of behind his own locked bedroom door
Leaving body parts and bloodstains spread across the floor.
The perpetrator has a trademark of a most unusual style,
The victims' clothes are found next morning in a neatly folded pile.
Last night we lost Inspectors Barnaby and Banks,
Which destroys Miss Marple's theory that this monster is picking
  out the Yanks.
We Brits are just as much at risk as anybody here.
And I'm the son of the Duke of Denver, Old Etonian, graduate of
Balliol, and hereditary peer."
Lord Peter's rousing oratory did not go unrewarded.
They sprang up from their armchairs and heartily applauded.
"The game's afoot!" cried Sherlock Holmes and Watson crowed,
  "Bravo!"
"Poirot is with you all the way," affirmed Hercule Poirot,
"And incidentally, *mes amis*, did anyone observe a trail of footprints
  in the snow?"
"I saw no footprints," Holmes replied. "Is this some cryptic joke?"
"I saw none either," Poirot said. "That is why I spoke."
"Oh dear," remarked Miss Marple. "I hate to make a fuss,
But there's only one deduction: the killer must be one of us."
All present eyed each other, suspicious to a man,
For one of Knox's golden rules had just gone down the pan.
It is the rule in every thriller
The sleuth must never be the killer.
The characters were dumbstruck, but Lord Peter broke the spell
With a bold suggestion that went down rather well.
"We can alibi each other and clear our names outright.
Anyone who shared a room can vouch for someone else last night.
I'm married now to Harriet Vane, as most of you will know.
We got to bed quite early, some time before the snow.
Moreover, I can tell you — if it isn't indiscreet —
Tommy and Tuppence Beresford pre-booked the honeymoon suite."
Ellery Queen announced to all he was in a family bubble
With Inspector Queen, his father. They occupied a double.

"And I was with my brother, Joe," a youth called Frank declared.
"We are the famous Hardy Boys and we have always shared."
Successively more sleuths spoke up to earn themselves some cover.
No one was shy. There was no shame admitting to a lover,
For almost all detectives indulge in one-night stands.
Sherlock Holmes and Irene Adler were quick to raise their hands.
Van der Valk and Maisie Dobbs admitted they were sharing.
Gervase Fen and Hetty Wainthropp, a most unlikely pairing.
Rebus and Meg Langslow had lingered all night in the bar
With Miss Smilla and Kurt Wallander, from Scandinavian noir.
Inspector Montalbano had entertained Cordelia Gray.
Aimée Leduc volunteered that she was dating Jules Maigret.
Lieutenant Kojak and Miss Silver had started an affair.
Father Brown and Brother Cadfael claimed they spent the night in
  prayer.
Lindsay Gordon and Kate Delafield were a striking Lesbian match.
The elegant Miss Fisher was Lew Archer's latest catch.
Inspectors Morse and Wexford said that life could get no better
Than making up a threesome with Dr. Kay Scarpetta.
(If you think this conduct somewhat infra dig,
You ought to see what happens at a science fiction gig.)
I'd have mentioned Precious Ramotswe, but she's difficult to rhyme.
"No one shared my bed," somebody said. "Does that constitute a
  crime?"
All eyes turned to focus on cheerful Charlie Chan
And another of the rules went down: he was a Chinaman.
Every writer must eschew
Chinamen like Fu Manchu.
"Discrimination stinks like hell,"
Muttered Doctor Gideon Fell.
But Charlie wasn't done: "I share my room with next of kin.
Jackie Chan, top kung fu man, lookalike and twin."
"That makes it worse," Lord Peter said. "The rule is crystal clear:
Twins identical or not are strictly banned from here.
You must avoid the sin of sins,
An alibi involving twins."
"Come, come," Fell said, "That's just a rule.
Let's think this through and keep our cool.
Getting back to the murders, I'm
Of the opinion this is a locked-room crime.
The corridors of Cliché Manor are a virtual catacomb

Ideal for an assassin working from a hidden room.
After dark he makes his entrance through a secret panel,
Silences his victims with chloroform-soaked flannel,
Slaughters them and exits through his private passageway,
Cleans up, and joins the rest of us for another normal day."
"That's not permitted either," Lord Peter chided Fell.
"Knox hated hidden passages and secret rooms as well.
You had better not presume
To introduce a secret room."
Then Flavia de Luce, the pre-teen detective, said,
"I pass my time productively communicating with the dead
By various methods scientific,
Chemistry, to be specific.
The victims may have things to say —"
"No, no," Lord Peter butted in, "that's not the way.
My child, the rules prohibit it.
Monsignor Knox would have a fit.
The supernatural has no place
In a true detective case."
From underneath a cloud of smoke,
The laid-back Philip Marlowe spoke:
"You guys need a problem solver?
I pack a point-three-eight revolver."
"Ahem," said Father Brown, "I have this feeling in my gut —"
"Intuition," Wimsey said. "Another rule goes phut.
Mark one other prohibition:
Do not rely on intuition."
Everyone inside the room was feeling the suspense,
Not helped because Lord Peter was getting far too tense.
"I should have raised this earlier," Dr. Watson said,
"I witnessed something fishy I've been keeping in my head."
"Then keep it there," Lord Peter snapped. "Stop taking us for fools.
By holding back the evidence, you've broken two more rules.
Unmentioned clues are not fair play.
Get them on the page, okay?
If you employ a Watson, please
Tell everything he knows and sees."

The rules were sinking through the sand,
When Dr. Thorndyke raised his hand.
"Fellow sleuths, with your consent
I plan a small experiment,

Researching what the victims ate
With the balsamic vinaigrette.
A toxic extra to the dinner,
Unseen in the salad spinner,
Bits of furry caterpillar,
Which I suspect may be the killer."
Lord Peter said, "This doesn't wash.
I never heard such utter tosh.
It plainly doesn't fit the facts
Of butchered bodies, ghastly acts.
Your theory isn't fit for sharing.
Your caterpillar is a huge red herring."
Dr. Thorndyke simply grinned.
"In your eyes I may have sinned.
I won't be making an apology
For something new to toxicology."
Lord Peter sighed and shook his head.
"That's another rule stone dead.
Do not place the least reliance
On poisoning unknown to science."
"Then what is left?" enquired Miss Pink.
"We've broken every rule, I think."
"Not so," remarked Jemima Shore.
"We've broken nine. There is one more."
"So flipping right!" Lord Peter cursed.
"In Knox's list, this one came first:
Give the killer an early mention.
Play fair and honor this convention.
We're far too smart to upset that,
Pulling a rabbit from a hat.
The puzzle is not worth a jot
Without the perp within the plot."

* * *

What happened next was truly strange.
Lord Peter underwent a change.
He seemed uncertain what to say.
His confidence had drained away.
He shook his head and gave a frown.
"I really hate to let you down,
But after questioning every guest —
All innocent: not one confessed —

The killer wins. He is not caught.
My finest efforts came to naught."
A tear rolled down Lord Peter's cheek.
He looked and sounded awfully bleak.
* * *

Then in the Dunkirk of defeat,
Agatha Raisin was sent a tweet,
A masterstroke from Lincoln Rhyme,
The quadriplegic who dissects crime.
"I hesitate to muddy the waters,
But have you explored the servants' quarters?"
Lord Peter gulped and looked askance.
"I'd rather go without my pants
Than mingle with the hoi polloi,
The chambermaids, the stableboy.
One hesitates to show one's face
In such an unfamiliar place."
He heaved the heaviest of sighs.
"Would someone care to deputize?"
* * *

So Father Brown took on the chore
Below stairs through the green baize door,
There to rub shoulders with the staff,
Slumming on everyone's behalf.
* * *

The little priest was back "toot-sweet",
Complexion whiter than a sheet.
"Lord Peter, I regret to say,
Someone has *eaten* your valet."
"Bunter?" Lord Peter gasped in shock,
"My batman, boon companion, rock?"
With that, he swooned and left the story,
So missed his chance to claim the glory.
He'd held the floor an hour, all told,
And now the floor held him, out cold.
* * *

So who would step up to the plate?
In truth there wasn't time to wait.
The die was cast, the chips were down.
The day was saved by Father Brown.
"I've worked it out. It's all in place.

I've cracked the Cliché Manor case.
And so to me the duty falls
To toll the bell for Knox's rules.
A culprit you've not met till now
Will step onstage and take a bow.
This is the ultimate outrage —
The first rule broken on the final page.
Give the killer an early mention.
Play fair and honor this convention.
We faced uncomfortable truths.
Folded clothes and eaten sleuths,
Proof of cannibalistic acts —
These were the disturbing facts.
Locked rooms gave no security
When someone had a master key.
The solution isn't subtle. How I wish it could be subtler.
It's obvious whodunit . . . Hannibal— the butler."

* * *

(With apologies to Margery Allingham, Donna Andrews, M. C. Beaton, Earl Derr Biggers, Cara Black, Lawrence Block, Alan Bradley, James Lee Burke, Andrea Camilleri, John Dickson Carr, Jackie Chan, Raymond Chandler, G. K. Chesterton, Lee Child, Agatha Christie, Michael Connelly, David Cook, Patricia Cornwell, Edmund Crispin, Jeffery Deaver, Colin Dexter, Franklin W. Dixon, Arthur Conan Doyle, Katherine V. Forrest, Antonia Fraser, Nicolas Freeling, R. Austin Freeman, Caroline Graham, Kerry Greenwood, Dashiell Hammett, Thomas Harris, Peter Høeg, P. D. James, Ronald Knox, John D. MacDonald, Ross Macdonald, Henning Mankell, Abby Mann, Ed McBain, Val McDermid, Gwen Moffat, Walter Mosley, Ogden Nash, Sara Paretsky, Ellis Peters, Ellery Queen, Selwyn Raab, Ian Rankin, Ruth Rendell, Peter Robinson, Sax Rohmer, Dorothy L. Sayers, Georges Simenon, Mickey Spillane, Rex Stout, Patricia Wentworth, and Jacqueline Winspear)

Contributors

Jeffrey Marks has been nominated for an Edgar (Mystery Writers of America), three Agathas (Malice Domestic), two Macavity awards (MRI), three Anthony awards (Bouchercon), and a Maxwell award (DWAA). He won the Anthony for his biography of Anthony Boucher. His short works have appeared in anthologies and *AHMM*. In his "spare time" he is the editor/publisher for Crippen & Landru. Marks writes from his home in Cincinnati, which he shares with his husband and three dogs.

Donna Andrews was born in Yorktown, Virginia and now lives in Reston, Virginia. *Birder, She Wrote* (August 2023) and *Let It Crow! Let It Crow! Let It Crow!* (October 2023) are the 33rd and 34th books in her Agatha-, Anthony-, and Lefty-winning Meg Langslow series. She is also the co-editor, with Barb Goffman and Marcia Talley, of ten—soon to be eleven—short story anthologies. She is a longtime member of MWA and Sisters in Crime and currently serves as MWA's Executive Vice President. Website: http://donnaandrews.com

Frankie Y. Bailey is a criminal justice professor and the author of books and short stories featuring crime historian Lizzie Stuart, Albany police detective Hannah McCabe, and 1940s former Army nurse Jo Radcliffe. Frankie is currently working on nonfiction books about gangster movies and about dress, appearance, and criminal justice. She is also working on the sixth Lizzie Stuart book and a historical thriller.

Nikki Dolson is the author of the novel *All Things Violent* and the story collection Love and Other Criminal Behavior. Her stories have appeared or are forthcoming in *Southwest Review, Best American Mystery and Suspense, Vautrin, TriQuarterly, Tough,* and other publications.

Martin Edwards has received several lifetime awards for his fiction and nonfiction, including the CWA Diamond Dagger for the sustained excellence of his writing and the Edward D. Hoch Memorial Golden Derringer for his short fiction. He has published twenty-two novels, including the Lake District Mysteries and Rachel Savernake series, and has won two Edgar awards. He has been President of the Detection Club since 2015.

Greg Herren is an award-winning author and editor from New Orleans. His next two novels, *Mississippi River Mischief* and *Death Drop* will be released in Fall 2023. He has published over forty novels and over fifty short stories, and has edited over twenty anthologies. He lives in New Orleans with his partner of twenty-eight years.

Naomi Hirahara is an Edgar Award–winning author of multiple traditional mystery series and noir short stories. Her final Mas Arai novel, *Hiroshima Boy*, was nominated for two awards in Japan. Her first historical mystery, *Clark and Division*, follows a Japanese American family's move to Chicago in 1944 after being released from Manzanar. Its follow-up, *Evergreen*, based in 1946 Los Angeles, was published in August 2023. A former journalist with the Rafu Shimpo newspaper, Naomi has written numerous nonfiction history books and curated exhibitions.

Toni L.P. Kelner, who also writes as Leigh Perry, recently celebrated her thirtieth anniversary as a mystery writer. She's published seventeen novels and one collection, and has co-edited seven anthologies. She won the Agatha Award for Best Short Story, and her short fiction has been nominated for the Anthony, the Macavity, and the Derringer. Reading stories on Reddit is one of her favorite ways to procrastinate, but darned if it didn't inspire this short story.

Richie Narvaez is the Agatha- and Anthony–winning author of the thriller *Hipster Death Rattle* and the YA whodunnit *Holly Hernandez and the Death of Disco*, as well as the collections *Roachkiller and Other Stories* and *Noiryorican*.

Gigi Pandian is a *USA Today* bestselling and multi-award-winning mystery author and locked-room-mystery enthusiast. The child of cultural anthropologists from New Mexico and the southern tip of India, she spent her childhood being dragged around the world on their research trips, which inspired her fiction. She's been awarded Agatha, Anthony, Lefty, and Derringer awards, and been a finalist for the Edgar. Gigi writes the Accidental Alchemist mysteries, Jaya Jones Treasure Hunt mysteries, and Secret Staircase mysteries. She lives in Northern California with her husband and a gargoyle who watches over their backyard vegetable garden. Learn more at www.gigipandian.com

SJ Rozan's twenty novels and eighty-plus short stories have won multiple awards, including the Edgar, Shamus, Anthony, Nero, Macavity, and the Japanese Maltese Falcon. She's been honored with Life Achievement awards from both the Private Eye Writers of America and the Short Mystery Fiction Society. Many of her stories have appeared in various "Best Of" collections, and she's edited three anthologies. She lives in New York City. Website: www.sjrozan.net

Daniel Stashower is a *New York Times* bestselling author and a winner of the Edgar, Anthony, and Agatha awards. His most recent book is *American Demon: Eliot Ness and the Hunt for America's Jack the Ripper*. His previous books include *The Hour of Peril*, *The Beautiful Cigar Girl*, and *Teller of Tales: The Life of Arthur Conan Doyle*.

Marcia Talley is the Agatha– and Anthony–Award-winning author of *Disco Dead* and eighteen previous novels featuring Maryland sleuth Hannah Ives. She is editor/author of two collaborative serial novels, *Naked Came the Phoenix* and *I'd Kill for That*. Her short stories appear in more than a dozen collections. Marcia is president of the Mid-Atlantic chapter of MWA and national past-president of Sisters in Crime. She divides her time between Annapolis, Maryland and a quaint, Loyalist-style cottage on Elbow Cay in the Bahamas, not far from the imaginary island where this story takes place.

Art Taylor is the Edgar Award–winning author of two collections: *The Adventure of the Castle Thief and Other Expeditions and Indiscretions* and *The Boy Detective & the Summer of '74 and Other Tales of Suspense*, both published by Crippen & Landru. His debut book, *On the Road with Del & Louise: A Novel in Stories*, won the Agatha Award for Best First Novel, and his short fiction has also won the Agatha, Anthony, Derringer, and Macavity Awards. He is an associate professor of English and creative writing at George Mason University. Website: www.arttaylorwriter.com.

Peter Lovesey is the author of more than forty mystery novels and six collections of short stories. He started in 1970 with the Sergeant Cribb series, which was later televised. More recently he wrote a series featuring Peter Diamond, a detective based in Bath, England. He has won many international awards. In 2000 he received the Diamond Dagger of the Crime Writers Association and in 2018 he was honored as Grand Master of the MWA..

School of Hard Knox

SCHOOL OF HARD *Knox* is printed on 60-pound paper, and is designed by Jeffrey Marks using InDesign. The type is Garamond, a group of fonts named for French engraver Claude Garamon. The cover is by Ezra Cumbo. The first edition was published in a perfect-bound softcover edition and a clothbound edition accompanied by a separate pamphlet of Ronald A. Knox's "The Adventure of the First Class Carriage." *School of Hard Knox* was printed by Southern Ohio Printers and bound by Cincinnati Bindery. The book was published in September 2023 by Crippen & Landru Publishers.

Crippen & Landru, Publishers

P. O. Box 532057

Cincinnati, OH 45253

Web: www.Crippenlandru.com

E-mail: orders@crippenlandru.com

Since 1994, Crippen & Landru has published more than 100 first editions of short-story collections by important detective and mystery writers.

This is the best edited, most attractively packaged line of mystery books introduced in this decade. The books are equally valuable to collectors and readers. [Mystery Scene Magazine]

The specialty publisher with the most star-studded list is Crippen & Landru, which has produced short story collections by some of the biggest names in contemporary crime fiction. [Ellery Queen's Mystery Magazine]

God bless Crippen & Landru. [The Strand Magazine]

A monument in the making is appearing year by year from Crippen & Landru, a small press devoted exclusively to publishing the criminous short story. [Alfred Hitchcock's Mystery Magazine]

Previous
Crippen & Landru
Publications

Challenge the Impossible: The Impossible Files of Dr. Sam Hawthorne by Edward D. Hoch. Full cloth in dust jacket, signed and numbered by Josh Pachter, $45.00. Trade softcover, $19.00.

Nothing Is Impossible: Further Problems of Dr. Sam Hawthorne by Edward D. Hoch. Full cloth in dust jacket, signed and numbered by the publisher, $45.00. Trade softcover, $19.00.

Swords, Sandals And Sirens by Marilyn Todd.

Murder, conmen, elephants. Who knew ancient times could be such fun? Many of the stories feature Claudia Seferius, the super-bitch heroine of Marilyn Todd's critically acclaimed mystery series set in ancient Rome. Others feature Cleopatra, the Olympian gods, and high priestess Ilion blackmailed to work with Sparta's feared secret police. Full cloth in dust jacket, signed and numbered by the author, $45.00. Trade softcover, $19.00.

All But Impossible: The Impossible Files of Dr. Sam Hawthorne by Edward D. Hoch. Full cloth in dust jacket, signed and numbered by the publisher, $45.00. Trade softcover, $19.00.

Sequel to Murder by Anthony Gilbert, edited by John Cooper. Full cloth in dust jacket, $29.00. Trade softcover, $19.00.

Hildegarde Withers: Final Riddles? by Stuart Palmer with an introduction by Steven Saylor. Full cloth in dust jacket, $29.00. Trade softcover, $19.00

Shooting Script by William Link and Richard Levinson, edited by Joseph Goodrich. Full cloth in dust jacket, signed and numbered by the families, $47.00. Trade softcover, $22.00.

The Man Who Solved Mysteries by William Brittain with an introduction by Josh Pachter. Full cloth in dust jacket, $29.00. Trade softcover, $19.00

Constant Hearses and Other Revolutionary Mysteries by Edward D. Hoch. Full cloth in dust jacket, signed and numbered by Brian Skupin, $45.00. Trade softcover, $19.00.

Subscriptions

Subscribers agree to purchase each forthcoming publication, either the Regular Series or the Lost Classics or (preferably) both. Collectors can thereby guarantee receiving limited editions, and readers won't miss any favorite stories.

Subscribers receive a discount of 20% off the list price (and the same discount on our backlist) and a specially commissioned short story by a major writer in a deluxe edition as a gift at the end of the year.

The point for us is that, since customers don't pick and choose which books they want, we have a guaranteed sale even before the book is published, and that allows us to be more imaginative in choosing short story collections to issue.

That's worth the 20% discount for us. Sign up now and start saving. Email us at orders@crippenlandru.com or visit our website at www.crippenlandru.com on our subscription page.

Printed in the USA
CPSIA information can be obtained
at www.ICGtesting.com
LVHW041511271023
762201LV00013B/1755